She was the most beautiful woman he had ever met

Blond and tanned, slim and coy. Her laugh had been special, her touch divine.

Though he'd fought his attraction to her, he couldn't resist the wide innocence in her eyes, the genuine smile that curved her lips, her ingenious wit. His hands tightened around his glass as he remembered the scent of her perfume, the feel of her skin rubbing against his, the wonder of looking down into her eyes as he'd made love to her.

And it had all changed the night a maniac had held a knife to her beautiful throat.

Now Kaylie was beautiful but mature, her humor sharper, her sarcasm biting. Yet he still wanted her—more than a man with any sense should want a woman.

And her life was being threatened once again.

FAMILY

Lisa JACKSON

Obsession

MARRIED FOR A MINUTE

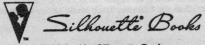

Silhouette Books

Published by Silhouette Books
America's Publisher of Contemporary Romance

SILHOUETTE BOOKS
300 East 42nd St.,
New York, N. Y. 10017

ISBN 0-373-82157-3

OBSESSION

Copyright © 1991 by Lisa Jackson

This edition published by arrangement with Harlequin Books S.A.

® and TM are trademarks of Harlequin Books S.A., used under license. Trademarks indicated with ® are registered in the United States Patent and Trademark Office, the Canadian Trade Marks Office and in other countries.

Look us up on-line at: http://www.romance.net

Printed in U.S.A.

Dear Reader,

As those of you who have read my books know, family is a very important part of my life. I was ecstatic to be a part of the FAMILY series for Silhouette, and I think *Obsession* is a perfect choice to be part of this series.

Obsession is a book about first love, innocent love, independence and reunion. It's about two people, Kaylie Melville and Zane Flannery, once married, now divorced, but who love passionately and forever. Zane, once Kaylie's bodyguard and husband, loved her fiercely enough to let her go when his love was too smothering for his younger, famous wife. He loved her enough to let her grow and become her own woman.

Now, years later, she's become a confident, independent woman whose life is threatened by the same man who nearly killed her years ago. Zane, still in love with his beautiful ex-wife, is still concerned for her safety. At the onset of a threat to Kaylie, Zane forces himself back into her life. It's one thing to let her grow into her own woman, quite another to sit back and watch while she puts herself in jeopardy. A man of action, Zane throws himself, body and soul, into protecting her.

At first Kaylie resents his intrusion into her life. She can handle herself. But as the story unfolds and Zane proves his newfound respect for her, she realizes her heart has never forgotten him, and begins to fall in love with him all over again. Her feelings have matured, and she realizes that he is and was her family—her life. She can be her own woman while loving him.

Join Zane and Kaylie in a celebration of rediscovered love, reawakened passion and a reunion of the heart in this love story. It's about love and self-awareness, passion and confidence, danger and reunion.

Enjoy!

Lisa Jackson

Please address questions and book requests to:
Silhouette Reader Service
U.S.: 3010 Walden Ave., P.O. Box 1325, Buffalo, NY 14269
Canadian: P.O. Box 609, Fort Erie, Ont. L2A 5X3

Prologue

Whispering Hills Hospital

The patient rocked slowly back and forth in his chair. His eyes, deep-set and pale blue, stared at the television screen, and though he didn't speak, his lips moved, as if he were trying to say something to the woman on the small color screen, the cohost of *West Coast Morning*.

Kaylie, her name was. He had a picture of her. The one they hadn't found. The one the orderlies had overlooked. It was old and faded, the slickness nearly worn off, but every night he stared at that picture and pretended she was there, with him, in his hospital bed.

She was so beautiful. Her long blond hair shimmered in soft curls around her face, and her eyes were green-blue—like the ocean. He'd seen her once, touched her, felt her quiver against him.

He sucked in his breath at the familiar thought. He could almost smell her perfume.

"Hey! Lee, ol' buddy. How about some sound?" The orderly, the tall lanky one called Rick, walked to the television and fiddled with the controls. The volume roared, and the singsong jingle for cereal blared in a deafening roar to the patient's ears.

"Noooo!" the patient cried, clapping his hands to the sides of his head, trying to block out the sound. "No, no, no!"

"Okay, okay. Hey, man, don't get upset." Rick held his palms outward before quickly turning down the volume. "Hey, Lee, ya gotta learn to chill out a little. Relax."

"No noise!" the patient said with an effort, and Rick sighed loudly as he stripped the bed of soiled sheets.

"Yeah, I know, no noise. Just like every day at this time. I don't get it, you know. All day long you're fine, until the morning shows come on. Maybe you should watch something else—"

But the patient didn't hear. The program had resumed, and Kaylie—his Kaylie—was staring into the camera again, smiling. For him. He felt suddenly near tears as her green eyes locked with his and her perfect lips moved in silent words of love. It won't be long, he thought, his own lips twitching. Reaching deep into his pocket, he rubbed the worn picture between his thumb and forefinger.

Just wait for me. I'll come to you. Soon.

Chapter One

"Who is this?" Zane Flannery demanded, his fingers clutching the phone's receiver in a death grip.

"Ted." The voice was barely audible; rough as a shark's skin. Zane couldn't identify the caller as a man or woman.

"Okay, Ted. So what is it?" Zane's mouth had turned to cotton, and the numbing fear that had gripped him ever since "Ted's" call the day before gnawed at his guts.

"It's Kaylie. She's not safe," the voice grated out.

Kaylie. Oh, God. A knot of painful memories twisted his stomach. "Why not?"

"I told you. Lee Johnston's about to be released."

Zane managed to keep his voice steady. "I went to the hospital. No one there is saying anything about letting him out." In fact, no one had said much of anything. Dr. Anthony Henshaw, Johnston's doctor, had been particularly tight-lipped about his patient. Phrases like patient confidentiality and maintaining patient equilibrium, had kept spouting from the doctor's mouth. He'd even had the gall to tell Zane point-blank that Zane wasn't Kaylie's husband any longer. That Zane had no *right* to be involved. Just because Zane was owner of the largest security firm on the West Coast didn't give him the authority to turn the hospital upside down or "persecute" one of his patients. Zane liked that. "Persecute." After what Johnston had attempted to do to Kaylie.

The man had nearly killed Kaylie, and now Zane was accused of "persecuting" the maniac. Figures.

In the well-modulated voice of one who weighs everything before he speaks, Henshaw had informed Zane that Johnston was still locked away and that Zane had nothing to worry about. As a patient of Whispering Hills hospital, Johnston was being observed constantly and there was nothing to fear. Though Lee was a model patient, Dr. Henshaw didn't *expect* Johnston to be released in the very near future. He *assumed* Johnston would remain a patient for "the time being."

Not good enough for Zane. He didn't work well with words like expect or assume.

Pacing between his desk and window, stretching the phone cord taut, Zane felt as helpless as he had seven years ago when Lee Johnston had nearly taken Kaylie's life.

"Why should I believe you?" Zane asked the caller, and there was a long silence. Ted was taking his time.

Zane waited him out.

"Because I care," the raspy voice stated. The phone went dead.

"Son of a bitch!" Zane slammed down the receiver and rewound the tape he'd made of the call.

Startled, the dog lying beneath Zane's desk barked, baring his teeth, dark eyes blinking open. Hairs bristled on the back of the brindled shepherd's neck.

"Relax, Franklin," Zane ordered, though his own skin prickled with dread and cold sweat collected on his forehead, underarms and hands. "Son of a damned—"

The door to his office burst open, and Brad Hastings, his second in command, strode in. A newspaper was tucked under his arm. "I called the police," he said, obviously aggravated. His dark eyes were barely slits, his nostrils flared. Not more than five-eight, but all muscle, Brad had once been a welterweight boxer and had been with Flannery Security since day one. Hastings was a force to be reckoned with. "There's nothing new on Johnston. He's locked up all right, just like Henshaw told you. As for the doctor, he seems to be on the level. He's been Johnston's shrink for five years."

And in those five years, Henshaw hadn't told Zane anything about his patient. Zane had checked in every six months or so and been told curtly that Mr. Johnston was still a patient and not much more.

When Dr. Loyola had been at Whispering Hills, things had been different. Loyola had been the admitting doctor. *He* understood the terror his patient inspired and *he'd* kept Zane informed of Johnston's progress or lack thereof. But Loyola was long gone, and no one now employed at the hospital considered Johnston a threat.

Except "Ted." Whoever the hell he was. Zane tried to concentrate. "What about this Ted character?" Zane played back the tape, making a second copy as he did, and as Hastings listened, Zane tried to envision the man who was giving him the warning.

The tape ended. Zane rewound it again and took the copy from the recorder.

Hastings scratched the back of his balding head. "No Ted at Whispering Hills. No Ted listed as a friend or family member of Johnston."

"You checked all the workers at the hospital? Cafeteria employees, nurses, orderlies, janitors, gardeners?"

"No one with the name Theodore or Ted. The last guy to work there named Ted left two and a half years ago. He lives in Mississippi now, doesn't know a thing about what's happening at Whispering Hills these days. I talked to him myself."

Zane felt helpless, like a man struggling to desperately cling to a rope that was fraying bit by bit.

"What about a woman? Teddie, maybe," he said thoughtfully, "or Theresa, Thea, something like that?"

"You think that—" Hastings motioned skeptically toward the tape "—is a woman?"

"I couldn't tell, but I thought whoever called was disguising his or her voice…" He felt another wave of bone-chilling fear. What if the caller were Johnston himself? What if he'd had access to a phone and Bay Area phone book? What if that madman was calling Kaylie at the station?

Zane grabbed the phone again, punched out the number of the television station where she worked and drummed his fingers impatiently as the receptionist answered, then told him that Kaylie had left for the day.

Cursing under his breath, he hung up and dialed her apartment. A recorder answered. He didn't bother to leave another message, but slammed the receiver down in frustration. *Get a grip, Flannery,* he ordered himself, but couldn't quell the fright.

Why hadn't Kaylie returned his calls? he wondered, panicking. Maybe it was already too late!

"Look, she's all right," Hastings said, as if reading his boss's thoughts. "Otherwise you would've heard. Besides, she was on the show this morning, and you know for a fact that Johnston's still at the hospital."

"For now."

Glancing surreptitiously at Zane, Hastings snorted. "I hate to bring up more bad news, but have you seen this?" He slapped the newspaper onto Zane's desk. The paper opened, and Zane realized that he was staring at page four of *The Insider,* a tabloid known for its gossip-riddled press. A grainy picture of Kaylie and the cohost of *West Coast Morning,* Alan Bently, stared up at him. They were seated at a table, laughing and talking, and Alan's arm was slung over Kaylie's shoulders. The bold headlines read: Wedding Bells For San Francisco's Number One Couple? And in smaller type: Is Kaylie Still His Number One OBSESSION?

"How can they print this stuff?" Zane growled, more irritated by the story than he had any right to be. Half of anything *The Insider* printed was purely sensationalism—nothing more than rumors. Yet Zane was infuriated by the picture of Alan and Kaylie together, and he was sickened at the hint of their marriage. It had to be a rumor just to boost ratings. He was certain Kaylie would never fall for a clown like Bently.

Worst of all was the reference to Kaylie's last movie, *Obsession*, a film that was, in Zane's estimation, the beginning of the end of his short-lived but passionate marriage to Kaylie.

Tossing the paper into the trash, Zane didn't comment, he just strode across the room and opened his closet door. He yanked his beat-up leather jacket from a hanger, and while shoving the copy of the anonymous caller's warning into the pocket of his jacket, he pushed aside any lingering jealousy he felt for Alan Bently. Zane didn't have time for emotion, especially not petty envy. Not until Kaylie was safe. A plan had been forming in his mind ever since the first chilling call from "Ted." It was time to put it into action.

Kaylie wouldn't like it. Hell, she'd fight him every step of the way. But that was just too damned bad. This time she was going to do things his way. He explained his plan to Hastings, instructed his right-hand man to take care of business and put Kaylie Melville's safety at the top of the list. "And give a copy of the tape to the police!"

Satisfied that Hastings could handle the business, he said, "I want every available man on the case. I don't give a damn about the costs. Just find out who this Ted is and what his connection is to Kaylie. And start tracing calls—calls that come in here, or to her house, or to the station where she works. I want to know where this nut case is!"

"Is that all?" Hastings mocked.

"It's all that matters," Zane muttered, shoving his fists into the pockets of his jacket. He whistled to the dog, and the sleek shepherd lifted one ear, then rose and padded after him.

Kaylie would kill him if she realized what he had planned but he didn't care. He couldn't. Her life was more important than her damned pride.

Outside, the morning air was warm. Only a few clouds were scattered over the San Francisco sky. Zane unlocked the door of his Jeep, and the dog hopped into the back. He had one more phone call to make, he thought, pulling into the clog of traffic.

He made the call from his cellular phone.

Once his plan was set, he went about finding his headstrong ex-wife.

Hours later, Zane had tracked her down. She hadn't been at her apartment, nor had she gone back to the station, so he guessed she'd decided to spend the evening alone, at the house they'd shared in Carmel.

He parked in the familiar driveway and second-guessed himself. His plan was foolproof, but she would be furious. And she might end up hating him for the rest of her life.

But then, she didn't much like him now. She'd made it all too clear that she didn't want him in her life when she'd scribbled her signature across the divorce papers seven years before.

So why couldn't he forget her? Leave her alone? Let her fend for herself as she claimed she wanted to do?

Because she was in his blood. Always had been. Always would be. His personal curse. And he was scared.

He let the dog out of the Jeep, and the shepherd began investigating the small yard, scaring a gray tabby cat and sniffing at the shrubs.

"Stay, Franklin," Zane commanded when the dog attempted to wander too far.

Pressing on the doorbell, he waited, shifting from one foot to the other. The house was silent. No footsteps padded to the door. Leaning on the bell again, he heard the peal of chimes within. Still no response.

Don't panic, he told himself, unnerved that he couldn't find her. Reaching into his pocket, he withdrew a set of keys he hadn't used in years and slid a key into the lock.

The lock clicked. The dead bolt slid easily.

So she hadn't bothered to change the locks. *Not smart, Kaylie.*

With a grimace, Zane pocketed his key and shoved on the familiar front door. It swung open without the slightest resistance, and he stood staring at the interior of the house that had once been his.

Swearing under his breath, he ignored the haunting memories—memories of Kaylie. Always Kaylie. God, how could one woman be imbedded so deeply in a man?

With another reminder to Franklin to stay, he closed the door behind him. Tossing his battle-worn leather jacket over the back of the couch, he surveyed the living room. Nothing much had changed. Except of course that he didn't live here, and he hadn't for a long, long time.

The same mauve carpet stretched through the house. The windows were spotless, the view of Carmel Bay as calming as he had always found it. And the furniture hadn't been moved or added to. Familiar pieces covered in white and gray were grouped around glass-topped tables. Even the artwork, framed watercolors of dolphins, sailing ships and sea gulls, provided the same splashes of blue, magenta and yellow as they had when he and Kaylie had shared this seaside cottage.

But all of the memorabilia from their marriage—the pictures, tokens and mementos of their short life together—were gone. Well, most of them, he thought as he spied a single snapshot still sitting on the mantel.

The picture was of Kaylie and him, arms linked, standing ankle-deep in white, hot sand on their honeymoon in Mazatlán. He picked up the snapshot and scowled at the heady memories of hot sun, cold wine and Kaylie's supple body yielding to his. The scent of the ocean and perfume mingled with the perfume of tropical flowers and a vision of a vast Mexican sky.

Dropping the photograph as if it suddenly seared his fingers, he snorted in disgust. No time to think about the past. It was over and done. Already, just being near Kaylie was making him crazy. Well, he'd better get used to it.

He crossed the room. Freshly cut flowers scented the air and reminded him of Kaylie. Always Kaylie. Despite the divorce and the past seven painful years alone, he'd never truly forgotten her, never been able to go to bed at night without feeling a hot pang of regret that she wasn't beside him, that he wasn't in her life any longer.

Shoving the sleeves of his pullover up his forearms, he

walked to the recessed bar near a broad bank of windows. He
leaned on one knee, dug through the cabinet and smiled faintly
when he found his favorite brand of Scotch, the bottle dusty
from neglect, the seal still unbroken. With a flick of his wrist
he opened the bottle, just as, by confronting her, he was re-
opening all the old hurt and pain, the anger and fury, and the
passion.... As damning as it was exciting. Closing his eyes,
he reined in his runaway emotions—emotions over which he
usually had tight control. Except where Kaylie was concerned.

"Fool." Straightening, he poured himself a stiff shot.
"Here's to old times," he muttered, then tossed back most of
the drink, the warm, aged liquor hitting the back of his throat
in a fiery splash.

Home at last, he thought ironically, topping off his glass
again as he sauntered to the French doors.

Through the paned glass, he stared down the cliff to the
beach below. Relief, in a wave, washed over him. There she
was—safe! With no madman stalking her. She walked from
the surf, wringing saltwater from her long, sun-streaked hair
as if she hadn't a care in the world. If she only knew.

Wearing only a white one-piece swimming suit that molded
to her body, sculpting her breasts and exposing the tanned
length of her slim legs, she tossed her thick, curly mane over
her shoulders.

His gut tightened as he watched her bend over and scoop
up a towel from the white sand. The next couple of weeks
were going to be hell.

Kaylie shook the sand from her towel, then looped the terry
cloth around her neck. The last few rays of sun dried the water
on her back and warmed her shoulders as she slipped into her
thongs and cast one last longing glance at the sea. Sailboats
skimmed the horizon, dark silhouettes against a blaze of magenta and gold. Gulls wheeled high overhead, filling the air
with their lonely cries.

The beach was nearly deserted as she climbed up the weathered staircase to the house. Leaving her thongs on the deck,
she pushed open the back door, then tossed her towel into the

hamper in the laundry room. Maybe she'd pour herself a glass of wine. Pulling down the strap of her bathing suit, she headed for the bedroom. First a long, hot shower and then—

"How're you, Kaylie?" a familiar voice drawled.

Kaylie gasped, stopping dead in her tracks. The hairs on the back of her neck rose, and she spun around quickly, drops from her hair spraying against the wall. *Zane? Here? Now? Why?*

Draped over the couch, long jean-clad legs stretched out in front of him, he looked as damnably masculine as he ever had. His ankles were crossed, his expression bland, except for the lifting of one dark brow. However, she knew him too well and expected his pose of studied relaxation was all for show.

His steely gray gaze touched hers, and his lips quirked. For a few seconds she remembered how much she had loved him, how much she had wanted to spend the rest of her life with him. With an effort, she closed her mind to such traitorous thoughts. Her throat worked, and slowly she became conscious that one strap of her swimsuit dangled over her forearm, leaving the swell of her breast exposed.

"W-what the devil are you doing here—trying to scare me to death?" she finally sputtered, adjusting the strap back over her shoulder. But before he could respond, she changed her mind and shook her head. She wasn't up to talking to Zane— not now, probably not ever. "No, wait, don't answer that, I don't think I want to know."

He didn't budge, damn him, just lounged there, on *her* couch, drinking *her* Scotch, stretched out and making himself comfortable. His nerve was unbelievable, and yet there was something about him, something restless and dangerous that still touched a forbidden part of her heart. And she knew he wouldn't have shown up without a reason.

His scuffed running shoes dropped to the floor. "You didn't call me back."

She felt a jab of guilt. She'd gotten his messages, but hadn't worked up the courage to talk to him. "And that's why you're here?"

"I was worried about you."

"Oh, please, don't start with this," she said, reminded of the reasons she'd divorced him, his all-consuming need to protect her. "You don't have to worry about me or even be concerned that—"

"Lee Johnston's going to be released."

The words were like frigid water poured over her, stopping her cold. Zane's feigned casualness disappeared.

"He's *what?*" she whispered. In her mind's eye, she pictured Lee Johnston, a short, burly man with flaming red hair and lifeless blue eyes. And she remembered the knife—oh, God, the long-bladed knife that he'd pressed to her throat.

"Y-you're sure about this?" Oh, Lord, how could she keep her voice from quavering? The look on his face convinced her that he believed she was in grave danger, and yet she didn't want to believe it. Not entirely. There were too many dimensions to Zane to take anything he said at face value. Although she'd never known him to lie.

He hesitated, rubbing the back of his neck thoughtfully. "Someone called me."

"Who?"

"I don't know. Someone who called himself 'Ted.'"

"Ted? Ted who?" she asked.

"I wish I knew. I thought maybe you could help me figure it out," he admitted, launching into his short tale and starting with the first nerve-jangling call from "Ted," and ending with his gut feeling that Dr. Henshaw was holding out on him. "Do you have a recorder—a tape player?"

She nodded mutely, then retrieved the portable player from her bedroom. Zane picked up his jacket and took out a small tape, which he snapped into the machine. A few seconds later, "Ted's" warning echoed through the room.

"Oh, my God," Kaylie whispered, her hand to her mouth. She listened to the tape twice, her insides wrenching as the warning was repeated. Zane, though he attempted to appear calm, was coiled tightly, his features tense, his eyes flicking from her to the corners of the room, as if he half expected someone to jump out and attack her.

Why now? she wondered frantically. *Why ever?*

She bit her lower lip, then thinking it a sign of weakness, stopped just as the tape clicked off. "Why did this 'Ted' guy call you? Why not me?"

"Beats me," Zane admitted, sipping amber liquor from a short glass, his jaw sliding pensively to the side. "None of this is official. At least not yet." Zane's features were hard, and a quiet fury burned in his eyes. "So far we've only got this guy's—whoever he is—word for it. I talked with Johnston's psychiatrist and I didn't like what he said."

"But he didn't say Johnston would be released." She turned pleading eyes up at him.

"No, but I've got a gut feeling on this one. Henshaw was being too careful. My bet is that the man's going to walk, Kaylie. Whoever called me had a reason."

"Oh, God." Her whole body shook. Stark moments of terror returned—memories of a deranged man who'd sworn he'd kill for her. "They can't let him go. He's sick! Beyond sick!"

Zane lifted a shoulder. "He's been locked up a long time. Model patient. It wouldn't surprise me if the courts decide he got better."

Her world spun back to that horrible night when Johnston had threatened her, waved a knife in front of her eyes, his other arm hard against her stomach as he'd dragged her from the theater. He'd sworn then that he would kill for her and he wanted her to witness the sacrifice....

In her mind's eye, she could still see his crazed smile, feel him tremble excitedly against her, smell the scent of his stale breath.

She sagged against the wall and felt the rough texture of plaster against her bare back. *Think, Kaylie,* she told herself, refusing to appear weak. Swallowing back her fear, she straightened and squared her shoulders. She couldn't fall apart—she wouldn't! Forcing her gaze to Zane's, she silently prayed she didn't betray any of the panic surging through her veins. "I think I'd better talk to Henshaw myself."

"Be my guest."

On weak legs she walked into the kitchen, looked up the number of the mental hospital, and dialed with shaky fingers.

A receptionist answered on the fourth ring. "Whispering Hills."

"Yes, oh, I'd like to talk to Dr. Henshaw, please. This is Kaylie Melville—I, um, I know one of his patients."

"Oh, Miss Melville! Of course. I see you on television every morning," the voice exclaimed excitedly. "But I'm sorry, Dr. Henshaw isn't in right now."

"Then maybe I could speak to someone else." Kaylie tried to explain her predicament, but she couldn't get past square one with the cheery voice on the other end of the line. No other doctor would talk to her, nor a nurse for that matter. On impulse she asked to talk to Ted and was informed that no one named Ted was employed by the hospital. Before the receptionist could hang up, Kaylie asked, "Please, just tell me, is Mr. Lee Johnston still a patient there?"

"Yes, he is," she said, whispering a little. "But I really can't tell you anything else. I'm sorry, but we have rules about discussing patients, you know. If you'll leave your number, I'll ask Dr. Henshaw to call you."

"Thanks," Kaylie whispered, replacing the receiver. She poured herself a glass of water and tried to quiet the raging fear. *Think, Kaylie, think! Don't fall apart!* She drank the water, then made fists of her hands, willing herself to be calm.

When she walked back into the living room, Zane still sat on the couch, his elbows propped on his knees, his silvery eyes dark with concern. A part of her loved him for the fact that he cared, another part despised him for shoving his way back into her life when she'd just about convinced herself that she was over him.

"Well?"

"I didn't get very far. Henshaw's out. He'll call back."

The furrow in Zane's brow deepened.

Kaylie, trying to take control of the situation, said, "I'll— I'll talk to my lawyer."

"I already did."

"You *what?*" she demanded, surprised that Zane would call *her* attorney, the very man who had drawn up the papers for their divorce.

"I called Blake. His hands are tied."

She was already ahead of him. "Then I'll talk to Detective Montello. He was the arresting officer. Surely he'd..." Her voice faded as she saw him shake his head, his dark hair rubbing across the back of his collar. "Unless you've already called him, too."

"Montello's not with the force any longer. The guy who took his place says he'll look into it."

"But you don't believe him," she said, guessing, her heart beginning to pound at the thought of Lee Johnston on the loose. Icy sweat collected between her shoulder blades.

"I just don't want to take any chances."

For the first time, she thought about him being in the house—waiting for her when she finished her swim. "Wait a minute, how did you get in here?"

Zane glanced away, avoiding her eyes. "I still have my keys."

"You *what?*" she demanded, astounded at his audacity. He hadn't seemed to age in the past seven years. His hair was still a rich, coffee brown, his features rough hewn and handsome. His eyes, erotic gray, were set deep behind thick black brows and long, spiky lashes. "But you gave them to me," she said.

He offered her that same, off-center smile she'd found so disconcerting and sexy in the past. "I had an extra set."

"And you kept them. So that seven years later you could break and enter? Of all the low, despicable... You have no right, *no right* to barge in here and make yourself at home—"

"I still care about you, Kaylie."

All further protests died on her lips. Emotions, long buried, enveloped her, blinded her. Love and hate, anger and fear, joy and sorrow all tore at her as she remembered how much he had meant to her. Her breath was suddenly trapped tight in her lungs, and she had to swallow before she could speak. She shook her head. "Don't, okay? Just...don't." She willfully controlled the traitorous part of her that wanted to trust him, to believe him, to love him again. Instead she concentrated on the truth. She couldn't allow herself to feel anything for him.

What they'd shared was long over. And their marriage hadn't been a partnership. It had been a prison—a beautiful but painful fortress where their fragile love hadn't had a ghost of a chance.

"Look, Kaylie, I just thought you should know that Johnston's about to become a free man—''

"Oh, Lord." Her knees went weak again, and her insides turned cold.

Zane sighed, offering her a tender look that once would have soothed her. But he didn't cross the room, didn't hold her as he once would have. Instead he rubbed impatiently at the back of his neck and glanced at a picture on the mantel—the small snapshot of their honeymoon. "Johnston was obsessed with you before, and I doubt that's changed."

"I haven't heard from him in a long while."

"No letters?"

She shook her head, trying to convince herself that Lee Johnston had forgotten her. After all, it had been years since that terrifying encounter, and the man had been in a mental hospital, receiving treatment. Maybe he'd changed....

"Don't even think it," Zane warned, as if reading the expressions on her face. "He's a maniac. A psycho. He always will be."

Deep down, Kaylie knew Zane was right. But what could she do? Live her life in terrified paranoia that Lee Johnston might come after her again? No way. She glanced down and noticed that she was wearing only her bathing suit still. "Your information could be wrong," she said, walking to the laundry room, where she snagged her cover-up off a brass hook near the door. Standing half-naked in front of him only made the situation worse. She struggled into the peach-colored oversize top and pulled her hair through the neck hole only to find that Zane had followed her and was standing in the arch between the kitchen and laundry room, one shoulder propped against the wall. His gaze flicked down her body to her thighs, where the hem of her cover-up brushed against her bare skin.

"And the call?"

"A crank call."

"You really think so?" he asked.

"I—I don't know." Kaylie cleared her throat and tried to concentrate on the conversation. "But I think you overreacted by driving all the way down here—"

"I called, damn it," he snapped, his patience obviously in shreds as his eyes flashed back to hers. "But you didn't bother to call me back."

She felt another guilty pang, but ignored it. She'd considered returning his call and had even reached for the phone once or twice, but each time she'd stopped, unsure that she could deal with him and unwilling to complicate her life again.

"You didn't say anything about Johnston—"

"Of course not! I didn't want to freak you out with a message on your recorder."

"Well, you're doing a damn good job of it now," she snapped, her own composure hanging by a thread. Just seeing Zane again sent all her emotions reeling, and now this...this talk about Johnston. It was just too much. Her nerves were stretched to the breaking point.

Zane's voice was softer. "Look, Kaylie, I think you should take some precautions—go low profile."

"Low profile?" she repeated, trying to get a grip on herself as she walked past him into the kitchen. She couldn't let him see her falling apart; she'd fought hard for her independence and she had to prove to him—and to herself—that she was able to take care of herself. She picked up a small pitcher and began watering the small pots of African violets behind her sink. But as she moved the glass pitcher from one small blossom to the next, the stream of water spilled on the blue tiles. She mopped up the mess with a towel and felt Zane's eyes watching her, taking stock of her nervousness. "And what do you think I should do?" she asked, glancing over her shoulder.

His gaze, so rock steady it was maddening, met hers. "First of all, install new locks—a couple of dead bolts and a security system. State-of-the-art equipment."

"With lasers and sirens and a secret code?" she mocked, trying to break the tension.

"With motion detectors and alarms. But that won't be

enough. If Johnston's released, you'll need me, Kaylie. It's as simple as that.''

Desperate now, she tried to joke. "You? As what? My bodyguard again?'' She watched him flinch. "I don't think so—''

His hand shot out and he caught her wrist, spinning her around. She dropped her dish towel. "I'm serious, Kaylie,'' he assured her, his voice low, nearly threatening. "This is nothing to joke about!''

Was he out of his mind? The inside of her wrist felt hot, and she fought the urge to lick her lips.

"And I think it would be best if you took some time off—''

"Now, wait a minute, I can't leave the station high and dry!''

"Your career just about did you in before,'' he reminded her, then glanced down to where his fingers were wrapped around her arm. Slowly he withdrew his hand. "You need a less visible job.'' Then, as if realizing his request bordered on the ridiculous, he wiped his palms on his jeans and added, "Why don't you just ask for a leave of absence until this mess with Johnston is straightened out?''

"No way. I'm not going to live the rest of my life in high anxiety—especially over some stupid call.'' Though she was afraid, she couldn't give in to the fear that had numbed her after Johnston's last attack. And the man *was* still locked away.

Tossing her damp curls over her shoulder, she reached down and grabbed the towel from the floor. Her wrist, where Zane had held it so possessively only seconds before, still burned, but she ignored the sensation, refused to rub the sensitive spot where the pads of his fingers had left their impressions.

"Look, Kaylie,'' he said, his voice edged with exasperation. "I'm just trying to help you.''

"And I appreciate it,'' she replied, though they both knew she was lying, that the question of her independence had been a determining factor in their divorce. "I—I'll take care of myself, Zane. Thanks for the warning,'' she heard herself say, though a part of her screamed that she was crazy to let him go—that she needed him to keep her safe. She extended her hand, palm up. "Now, I think you have something of mine?" When he didn't move, she prodded him again. "The keys?"

Zane's eyes darkened to the shade of storm clouds.

Her heart began to pound. He wasn't giving up. She could see his determination in the set of his jaw.

"How about a deal?" he suggested, not moving.

"Believe me, I'm not in the mood."

"The keys for a date."

"For a *date?* Get real—"

"I am, Kaylie. You go out with me, just for old times' sake, and I'll turn the keys over to you."

"And in the meantime you won't make an extra set?"

"We'll go tonight. I won't have time to do anything so devious."

Kaylie wasn't so sure. And she was tempted, far more than she wanted to be. Standing so close to Zane, seeing the shading of his eyes, feeling the raw masculinity that was so uniquely his, she was lured into the prospect of spending some time with him again. There had been a time in her life when he'd been everything. From bodyguard to lover to husband. Her life with him had seemed so natural, so right...until the horrid night when their safe little world was thrown upside down. All because of Lee Johnston.

Kaylie had fallen in love with Zane, trusted him, relied upon him. Now her throat grew dry, and she shook all the happy memories aside. She couldn't trust herself when she thought of the first magic moments they'd shared—when their love had been new and fresh, before Zane had become so intolerably overprotective and domineering. No. Her dependence on him was long over. Now she was older, and wiser, and on to his tricks. She wouldn't repeat past mistakes. "I don't think a date would be such a good idea."

"Come on, Kaylie, what've you got to lose?" he asked, his voice low and disturbingly familiar.

Everything she thought, her palms beginning to sweat.

"You've got other plans tonight?" he asked.

"No—"

"No date with Alan?" he mocked, obviously referring to the ridiculous article in *The Insider*. Her producer had left a copy of the rag on her desk as a joke. She wasn't engaged to Alan and never would be, but no amount of denial to the press had seemed to change the public's view that she and Alan, who had once been costars of *Obsession* and were now cohosts of a popular morning show, were not lovers.

"No date with Alan," she said dryly.

"Then there's no reason not to spend a little time with me. Come on," he insisted, his smile irresistible.

"But—" *Why not? It's just a few hours,* a voice inside her head teased. *Wouldn't it be nice to rely on him just a little and find out what he really knows about Lee Johnston? What could it hurt?* She looked up at him and swallowed hard. There was a tiny part of her, a feminine part she tried to deny, that loved Zane's image of power and brooding masculinity, that being around him did make her feel warm inside. But being around Zane was unsafe—her emotions were still much too raw.

"Let's go. I know a great place in the mountains. You can tell me all about your career as a talk-show hostess and maybe you'll be able to convince me that you'll take all the precautions necessary to keep you safe from Johnston."

"Okay," she finally agreed, telling herself she *wasn't* excited about the prospect of spending time with him. "But I'll need time to change."

"I'll wait," he said amiably as he walked back to the bar. She watched him pour a drink, as she'd watched him a hundred times before. His shirt was a dark blue. His sleeves were pushed over his forearms to expose dark-skinned muscles that moved fluidly as he handled the bottle and glass. And his hands... She shouldn't even look at his long, sensual fingers and blunt-cut nails.

She swallowed hard against the memories—erotic memories that she'd hoped she'd forgotten. His gaze found hers in the mirror over the bar, and he smiled a little sexy smile. Her insides quivered.

Turning quickly, before she stared any longer, she headed for the bedroom and told herself that she was a fool, but now that she'd committed herself, somehow she'd get through the evening ahead.

Chapter Two

Zane tried to ignore the disturbing sensations—sensations that were way out of line. Kaylie was his ex-wife for crying out loud, and here he was, pouring himself another drink, feeling like a teenager in the throes of lust. Returning to this house—this cottage by the sea where he and Kaylie had spent hours making love—had probably been a mistake of colossal proportions, but he'd had no choice. Not if he wanted his plan to work. And he did. More than anything.

After the divorce he'd promised himself he'd give her room to grow. When he'd married her she'd been nineteen, and the most beautiful woman he'd ever met. Blond and tanned, slim and coy. Her laugh had been special, her touch divine.

Though he'd fought his attraction to her, he couldn't resist the wide innocence in her eyes, the genuine smile that curved her lips, her ingenious wit, though it was often used at his expense. His hands tightened around his glass as he remembered the scent of her perfume, the feel of her skin rubbing against his, the wonder of looking down into her eyes as he'd made love to her. And it had all changed the night a maniac had held a knife to her beautiful throat.

Now Kaylie was beautiful but mature, her humor sharper, her sarcasm biting. Yet he still wanted her—more than a man with any sense should want a woman.

And now her life was threatened.

Paralyzing fear gripped him. Living without her had been hell. He'd just have to convince her that they belonged together. Hearing the bedroom door open, he turned, and his throat went desert dry.

She was dressed in a white off-the-shoulder dress, her blond curls swept away from one side of her face, her eyes glinting with a gloriously seductive green light. "Okay, cowboy, this is your ride. Where're we going?"

The line was from one of her movies—she'd said it to him as well, late at night, when they had been alone in bed. Had she remembered? Undoubtedly. Zane's diaphragm pressed hard against his lungs. "It's a surprise."

She tilted her head at an angle. "Well, it had better be a short surprise. I have to get up at five tomorrow to tape the show."

"I'll have you back by ten," he lied, pretending ease as he snagged his scuffed jacket off the back of the couch and walked with her to the front door.

He reached for the knob, but she laid a hand across his. "This is all on the up and up, isn't it? One dinner and then you'll hand over the keys?"

His gut twisted. "That was the bargain."

"Then I'll trust you," she said, the corners of her beautiful mouth relaxing.

He felt a twinge of guilt at deceiving her, but shrugged it off as he opened the door and she swept outside ahead of him. He'd played by her rules long enough. Now it was time she played by his.

Kaylie was nervous as a cat when, as they walked outside, she discovered a large brown and black shepherd lying on the porch. "Who are *you?*"

"Man's best friend. Right, Franklin?" Zane said, whistling as he opened the back door of the Jeep and the dog leaped inside.

"You bring him on all your dates?" she teased.

He flicked her an interested glance. "My chaperon," he drawled. "Just to keep you in line."

"Me?" she replied, but grinned as she slid into the passenger side. Maybe this date wouldn't turn out to be the disaster she'd predicted.

Casting a glance in his direction as he climbed behind the wheel, she realized that he would never change. He'd always be strong, arrogant, determined, stubborn and self-righteous. But funny, she reminded herself. He had been blessed with a sense of humor.

Still, she was uneasy. She'd seen his mouth turn down when she'd quoted one of his favorite lines from an old movie. She'd done it on purpose, to check his reaction. He'd tried to hide his surprise, but she'd noticed the ghost of change in his eyes.

So why hadn't she refused to get into the Jeep with him?

Kaylie cast her eyes about, not wanting to confront her actions. A part of her was still intrigued with him. And she'd been lonely in the past seven years. She'd missed him far more than she'd ever admit. Yes, she couldn't handle the way he'd overreacted and tried to treat her like some fragile possession, but she'd missed his smile. She recalled it now with bittersweet poignancy, how that lazy slash of white would gleam against a darkened jaw as she'd awakened in his arms.

Her heart pounded at the memory, and she silently cursed herself for being a nostalgic idiot. So she missed his sexy looks, his playful grin, his presence in her house.

He headed east, leaving the sun to cast a few dying rays over the darkening waters of the Pacific. The sky had turned a dusky shade of lavender, reflected in the restless sea.

Zane drove without saying much, but she could sense him watching her, smell the clean earthy scent of his after-shave. She'd been crazy to agree to this, she decided. She was much too aware of him.

"Why did we leave the city?" she asked, to break the awkward silence stretching between them.

"Because I discovered a place you'll like."

"In Kansas?"

His sensual lips twitched. "Not quite."

"So let me get this straight. You thought, 'Gee, Lee Johnston's about to be released from the hospital—this would be a great time to break into Kaylie's house and take her to dinner in some restaurant in Timbuktu.'"

He grinned. "You're astounding, Kaylie. The way you read me like a book," he said sarcastically. "You know, that's exactly what I thought!"

She rolled her eyes and held her tongue for the rest of the journey.

Two hours later, Kaylie's stomach rumbled as she stepped out of his Jeep and eyed the restaurant he'd chosen. She'd expected him to take her to one of their old haunts along the waterfront in Carmel where they could eat seafood and laugh, drink a little wine and remember the good times—the few carefree times they'd shared as man and wife. When he'd mentioned the mountains, her interest had been piqued.

This place, this ivy-covered, two-storied house that looked as if it had been built before the turn of the century, wasn't like Zane at all. Mystified, she walked up the worn steps to a wide plank porch. A few rockers moved with the wind, and leaves in the surrounding maple and ash trees rustled as they turned with the breeze. *Quaint,* she thought. And so unlike Zane.

She eyed him from beneath her lashes, but his strong features seemed relaxed, his face handsome and rakish, one thatch of dark hair falling over his eyes. He shoved the wayward lock from his forehead, but it fell back again, making him look less than perfect and all the more wonderful.

Get a grip, she reminded herself as they walked into the old house and Zane tied Franklin to a tree near the entrance.

"You sure he won't scare the guests?" Kaylie asked.

"This ol' boy? No way," Zane said, rubbing the dog behind his ears.

Inside, a maître d' escorted them to a small table in what once had been the parlor.

Zane ordered wine for them both, then after a waiter had poured them each a glass of claret, Zane touched his glass to hers. "To old times," he said.

"And independence," she replied.

They dined on fresh oysters, grilled scallops, vegetables and crusty warm bread. Zane's features seemed sharper in the candlelight, his eyes a warmer shade of gray as he poured the last of the bottle into their glasses, then ordered another.

Conversation was difficult. Kaylie talked of work at the station; Zane listened, never contributing. As if in unspoken agreement, they didn't discuss Lee Johnston.

"So where'd you get the dog?" she asked as he topped off her glass. She was beginning to relax as the wine seeped into her blood.

"He used to work for the police."

"What happened—they fire him?"

"He retired."

Kaylie stifled a yawn and tried not to notice the play of candlelight in his hair. "And you ended up with him."

Zane shrugged. "We get along."

"Better than we did?" she asked, leaning back in her chair and sipping from her glass.

"Much."

"He must do just as you say."

Zane's teeth flashed in the soft light. "That's about the size of it."

Kaylie was caught up in the romantic mood of the old house with its wainscoted walls and flickering sconces. A fire glowed in the grate and no one else was seated in the small room, though there were four other tables near the windows.

"How'd you arrange this?" she asked, finishing her second—or was it her third?—glass of wine. Pinpoints of light reflected against the crystal.

"Arrange what?"

She motioned to the empty room. "The privacy."

"Oh, connections," he said offhandedly, and she was reminded again of how powerful he'd become as his security business had taken off and his clientele had expanded to the rich and famous. He'd opened an office that catered to Beverly Hills, another to Hollywood, as well as San Francisco, Portland, Seattle and on and on. In seven years his business had prospered, as if he'd thrown himself body and soul into the company after their divorce.

He refilled her glass. "I thought we should be alone."

"What? No bodyguards? No private investigators?" she teased, then regretted her sarcasm when his eyes darkened.

"I think we should declare a truce."

"Is that possible for divorced people?" she asked, and watched as he twisted his wineglass in his fingers.

"Mature divorced people."

"Oh, well, we're that, aren't we? And I guess you're bodyguard enough, right?" She sipped the wine and felt a languid sleepiness run through her blood. Maybe she should slow down on the claret. It was just that she was so nervous around him. Her muscles relaxed, and she slumped lower in her chair, eyeing him over the rim of her glass. He was so handsome, so erotically male, so…dangerous to be around.

The waiter cleared their plates and brought coffee. He offered dessert, but both Zane and Kaylie declined.

"Well," she said as Zane reached into his wallet for his credit card, "don't forget the keys."

"The what?"

"Your end of the bargain. The keys to my house."

"Oh, right." He dropped his credit card on the tray, then reached into his pocket and withdrew a key ring from which he extracted two keys. He slid them across the table. "There you go. Front door and garage."

She could hardly believe it as she plopped the keys into her wallet. "No strings attached?"

Something flickered in his eyes, but quickly disappeared. "No strings."

Kaylie felt a twinge of remorse for thinking so little of him. Why couldn't she open her heart and trust him—just a little?

Because she couldn't trust herself around him, she thought with realistic fatalism.

They walked outside and into a balmy night. The sky had darkened, and jewellike stars winked high over the mountains. Zane opened the Jeep door for Kaylie, and Franklin hopped onto the passenger seat, growling as Zane ordered him into the back.

"You're in his space," Zane explained. The dog jumped nimbly into the back seat, but his dark eyes followed Kaylie's every move as she climbed inside.

"I don't know if that's so safe."

"He's fine. He likes you."

"Oh, right."

Once back on the road, Zane switched on the radio, and the soft music, coupled with the drone of the engine and the security of being with Zane again made Kaylie feel a contentment she hadn't experienced in years.

Drowsy from the wine, she leaned her head against the window and glimpsed his profile through the sweep of her curling, dark lashes. His hair brushed his collar, his eyes squinted into the darkness as he drove, staring through the windshield.

The road serpentined through dark forests of pine. Every once in a while the trees receded enough to allow a low-hanging moon to splash a silvery glow over the mountainside.

Kaylie leaned back against the leather seat and closed her eyes. The notes of a familiar song, popular during the short span of their marriage, drifted through the speaker. She punched a button on the radio and classical music filled the interior of the Jeep. That was better. No memories here. She'd just let the music carry her away. Her muscles relaxed, and she sighed heavily, not intending to doze off.

But she did. On a cloud of wine and warmth she drifted out of consciousness.

Furtively, his palms sweating, Zane watched her from the corner of his eye. He noticed that her jaw and arms slackened and her breasts rose and fell in even, deep breaths.

Ten minutes passed. She didn't stir. *It's now or never,* he thought as he approached the intersection. Turning off the main road and heading into the mountains, he guided the car eastward.

There was a chance she'd end up hating him for his deception and high-handedness, but it was a chance he had to take. He frowned into the darkness, his eyes on the two-lane highway that cut through the dark stands of pine and redwood. *Don't wake up,* he thought as the seconds ticked by and the miles passed much too slowly.

It took nearly an hour to reach the old logging road, but he slowed, rounded a sharp corner and shifted down. From here on in, the lane—barely more than two dirt ruts with a spray of gravel—was rough. It angled up the mountain in sharp switchbacks.

He drove slowly, but not slowly enough. Before he'd gone two miles, Kaylie stirred.

The Jeep hit a rock and shimmied and she started. Stretching and swallowing back a yawn, she blinked, her brows knit in concentration. "Where are we?"

"Not in Carmel yet."

"I guess not," she said, rotating the crick out of her shoulders and neck as her eyes adjusted to the darkness. "What is this—a park?"

"Nope."

"Zane?"

He heard her turn toward him. The air was suddenly charged. For a few seconds all he heard was the thrum of the engine and the strains of some familiar concerto on the radio.

Finally she whispered, "We're not going back to Carmel, are we?"

No reason to lie any longer. "No."

"No?"

When he didn't answer, pure anger sparkled in her eyes. "I knew it! I knew it!" she shouted. "I should have never trusted you!" She flopped back in the seat. "Kaylie, you idiot!" she ranted, outraged. "After all he's done to you, you trust him!"

Zane's heart twisted.

She skewered him with a furious glare. "Okay, Zane, just where are you taking me?"

"To my weekend place."

"In the boonies?"

"Right." He nodded crisply.

"But you don't have—"

"You don't know what I have now, do you?" he threw back at her. "In the past seven years I've acquired a few new things."

"A mountain cabin? It's hardly your style."

"Maybe you don't know what my style is anymore."

"Then I guess I'll find out, won't I? I can hardly wait," she muttered, her eyes thinning in fury. She tossed her hair over her shoulder and waited, then quietly, her voice trembling with rage, she asked, "Why?"

"Because you won't listen to reason."

"I don't understand."

"We're talking about your life, damn it. And you were going to go on as if nothing had happened, as if this—" he reached into his pocket and extracted the tape "—doesn't exist! Well, it does, damn it, and until I find out if there's any reason to believe 'Ted,' I'm going to make sure you're safe."

"You're what? How?" she asked, though she was beginning to understand. "I think you'd better stop this rig and turn it around, right now," she ground out.

"No way."

"I'm warning you, if you don't take me home, I'll file charges against you for kidnapping!"

"Go right ahead," he said with maddening calm. He cranked on the wheel to round another corner.

"You can't do this!" she cried. What was he thinking?

"I'm doing it, aren't I?"

"I mean it, Zane," she said, her voice low and threatening. "Take me back to Carmel right now, or I'll make your life miserable!"

"You already have," he said through tightly clenched teeth. "The day you walked out on me."

"I didn't—"

"Like hell!" he roared, and from the back seat Franklin growled. Zane flicked her a menacing glance. "You didn't give me—us—a chance."

"We were married a year!" Even to her own ears, it sounded as brief as it had been.

"Not long enough!"

"This is madness!"

"Probably," he responded with deceptive calm, wheeling around a final corner. The Jeep lurched to a stop in the middle of a clearing. "But, damn it, this time I'm not taking any chances with your life!"

Kaylie stared out the window at the massive log cabin. Even in the darkness, she could see that the house was huge, with a sloping roof, dormers and large windows reflecting the twin beams of the headlights. "Where are we?" she demanded.

"Heaven," he replied.

She didn't believe him. Her heart squeezed at the thought of being alone with him. How would she ever control the emotions that tore through her soul?

Oh, no, Kaylie thought, this giant log house wasn't heaven. To her, it looked like pure hell!

Chapter Three

"This will never work," Kaylie predicted as Zane cut the engine.

"It already has." He walked out to the back of the vehicle, opened the hatchback, unrolled a trap and yanked out two suitcases. Franklin scrambled over the back seat and bounded onto the gravel road.

Thunderstruck, Kaylie didn't move. *His suitcases,* for crying out loud! Her heart dropped to her knees. Zane had planned this kidnapping before they left Carmel. And she'd been played for a fool!

"Let's go inside," he said.

"You're not serious. This is a colossal joke, right?" But she knew from the rigid thrust of his chin that he wasn't joking.

To his credit, he did seem concerned. The lines around the edges of his mouth were harsh, and he actually looked disconcerted by her outrage. "Look," he finally said, glaring down at her. "Are you planning to stay out here and freeze?"

"No, I'm going to wait for common sense to strike you so that you'll drive me back home!"

"It's gonna be a long wait."

That did it. She hopped out of the Jeep. Her sandaled feet crunched in gravel as she marched up to him. "This is crazy, Zane, just plain crazy."

"Maybe." He strode up the plank steps, fumbled with a key in the dark and shoved hard on a heavy oak door.

"If you think I'm going in there with you, you've got another think coming!"

He ignored her outburst. A few seconds later, the house lights blazed cozily from paned windows. "Come on, Kaylie," he called from deep in the interior. "You're here now. You may as well make the best of it."

But she wasn't done fighting yet. Crossing her arms over her chest, she waited. She'd be damned if she'd walk into this...this prison for God's sake! She had no intention—

He clicked on the porch lights and stood on the threshold of the log house. Kaylie didn't budge. As if rooted to the gravel drive, she tried to ignore the fact that he nearly filled the doorway, his shoulders almost touching each side of the doorjamb. And she refused to be swayed by the handsome sight of his long, lean frame, thrown in relief by the interior light behind him. She was just too damned mad.

"It's gonna get cold out here."

"I'm not going inside."

"Oh, yes, you are."

"No way, Flannery," she argued, her head pounding from too much wine, her pride deflated. "What's going to happen is that you're going back into the house for your keys, then you're going to climb back into this damned Jeep and take me home. Maybe I'll forget about pressing charges for breaking and entering and kidnapping and you'll be a free man!"

He shook his head and rolled his eyes to the night-darkened heavens. "Don't you know you can't bully me, Kaylie?"

"And here I thought you were the one doing the bullying!" she snapped back. It didn't matter what his reasons for bringing her here were. Whether Lee Johnston was in the hospital

or on the loose, Zane had no right, *no right,* to force his will
on her. The fact that he'd purposely planned to shanghai her
was more than she could take.

Slowly, his face knotted in frustration, he started back down
the steps. His eyes were trained on her face. ''Come on, Kaylie.''

''Out of the question.''

''Look, you're getting into that house if I have to carry you
in there myself!''

''No way.'' Her throat went dry as he advanced on her. She
had the urge to run as fast as her legs would carry her, but
she didn't want to give him the satisfaction of seeing her flee.
No, by God, she'd stand up to him. And hold her ground she
did, not moving an inch when he strode up so close that his
shoes nudged the toes of her sandals.

''We can do this the hard way, or you can make it easy.''

''Take me home, Zane,'' she said more softly. In the shadows she thought she saw him hesitate, and that flicker of doubt
gave her hope. Maybe he'd change his mind. She touched his
arm and watched his jaw clench. ''This is insane. We both
know it. Johnston's still under lock and key and I've got to
get back. Come on, Zane, this…this…stunt of yours is just
no good and I'm—I'm not moving until you assure me we're
going back to Carmel!''

''Have it your way,'' he said softly. His hands circled her
waist. ''But don't say I didn't warn you.''

''No, Zane, don't—'' she cried, mortified, as he lifted her
easily and her feet left the ground.

''I didn't bring you up here so that you could kill yourself
by catching pneumonia.'' He swung her over his shoulder and
hauled her, as a fireman would, toward the house. Her hair
fell over her face. All the blood rushed to her pounding head.

''Zane, this is ridiculous!'' she cried, clinging to his
sweater, feeling his muscles ripple beneath the knit. ''Let me
down, damn you. Stop! Zane, please!''

Up the porch stairs and into the house. He kicked the door
shut behind him and set her, sputtering and furious, on the

floor. ''You bastard!'' she barked, throwing her hair out of her eyes and tugging at her dress.

''Kaylie—''

''This is America, Zane. You can't take the law into your own hands!''

He winced a little at that, and storm clouds gathered in his eyes.

''Just because you're a private detective you don't have the right to go around...around...abducting helpless women!''

''Helpless? You?'' he flung back at her, shaking his head as he strode through a pitch-ceilinged living room and beyond. ''I'm the one taking my life in my hands by bringing you here!''

''Damn right,'' she agreed, right on his heels. ''All I'll give you is grief.''

''Amen.'' He flipped on the wall switch and walked briskly into the kitchen.

''So you may as well give me the keys—''

''Forget it!'' He turned and clamped big, angry hands over her bare shoulders. ''Now, listen, Kaylie, this is the way it is. I know what I've done by bringing you here. I don't need a lecture on kidnapping, abduction, the rights of the American people or women's lib! All I'm trying to do is make sure that you're safe.''

''Spare me—''

''I have. For seven years.'' His fingers tightened over her shoulders and his eyes searched her face. She felt his anger, but in his eyes she saw deeper emotions brewing. ''Just try to understand,'' he said quietly. ''You've got this job where every morning anyone west of the Rockies can switch on his television and see you and Alan Bently on the tube.''

''So?''

''So what's to prevent your personal nut case, Lee Johnston, from trying to do another number on you?''

''The law! The courts! Henshaw.''

Zane snorted, then shoved a hand through his hair in frustration. ''I deal with the law and the courts every day. Things don't always turn out like they're supposed to. As for Henshaw and Whispering Hills, I've got my doubts about that setup, too.''

"Johnston's been there seven years.''

"Then he's probably due for reevaluation,'' Zane said. "We'll know in a few days.''

"A few days?'' she echoed. He expected her to stay up here that long?

"That's how long it will take to check out the rumor. Maybe this Ted guy knows what he's talking about. Then again, maybe he doesn't. Believe it or not, I didn't bring you up here just to get you angry. I'm scared, damn it. Scared for you. When I think of what Johnston could have done to you— what he's still capable of...'' Zane shuddered. Rubbing his arms, he strode to the window and, leaning his palms on the counter, stared through the glass to the black night beyond.

Kaylie's heart softened a little. Though she was furious with him for abducting her, she couldn't help but feel a kindness toward him, a thawing of that cold part of her heart where she'd kept her memories of their short marriage. She had loved him with all of her young, naive heart, and no other man had ever taken his place. No man could. But she forced all those long-buried thoughts of love aside.

"You have no right to do this,'' she said quietly.

"I have every right.''

"Why?''

"Because I care, damn it.'' He whirled on her, and his gaze, flinty gray, drilled deep into hers. "I care more about you than anyone else on this planet—even more than your precious Alan Bently. If you haven't figured it out yet, that man's a leech. He only cares about you because he thinks a public romance with you will further his career.''

"Oh, save me—''

"It's true.''

"How do you know? Have you ever talked to Alan?''

He snorted derisively. "Of course not.''

"Well, if you had, you might have found out that I've never been involved with him.''

"That's not what the tabloids say.''

"*You* read the tabloids?" she repeated, amused.

"No, but where there's smoke, there's fire."

"And you care?"

His lips twisted downward. "I told you—I care about you. As for Bently, the man's the worst kind of opportunist. All those rumors that link you to Alan, I can just imagine what they do to the ratings."

"Wh-what?" she demanded, getting a glimmer of what he was alluding to.

"It's a ratings thing, isn't it? Your morning talk show is pitted against a couple of other shows, isn't it? I'll bet your network thought it would boost viewership if you and Alan got married."

"That's absurd!" she gasped.

"Is it?" He opened a cupboard and found a brand-new bottle of Scotch. With a hard twist of his wrist, he snapped open the cap, breaking the label, and after locating a small glass, poured himself a stiff shot.

He took a slow swallow, and her gaze traveled from his firm chin to the silky way his Adam's apple moved in his neck. God, he could reach her as no other man could. There was an irresistible male force surrounding him, and she was oh, so susceptible. She dragged her gaze away.

"I know you never believed it, Kaylie, but I loved you. More than any man should love a woman. I was the one who was obsessed."

"And now?" she asked, her voice trembling. They were wading in hazardous water. "Did you bring me up here because of Johnston? Or was there another reason?"

His gaze locked with hers for a second. Then he tossed back his drink. "And now I'm protecting you. Period. If you think this is some kind of exotic seduction, guess again. I don't have to go to so much trouble."

"I'd hope not," she said evenly, though emotions were tearing through her, "because if you did, you would've lived a very celibate life in the past seven years!"

"Maybe I have," he said, but he had to have been joking. Dear Lord, when she thought of his passion, his wild lovemaking, his wanton sense of adventure in the bedroom, delicious chills still skittered down her spine. No, Zane Flannery might have gone seven days without a woman, possibly even a month or two, but seven years—never! His sexual appetite was too primal, too instinctive. She studied the rock-hard jut of his chin, the angle of his cheeks, the authority in the curve of his thin lips.

He eyed her just as speculatively. "And what about you, Kaylie?" he asked suddenly, his eyes darkening to the color of a winter storm. "What about your sex life?"

She hadn't blushed in years, but now a red heat stole steadily up her neck and face, stinging her cheeks. "I don't think we should be discussing this!"

"It's just one question. A pretty straightforward question."

She swallowed back the urge to lie and tell him that she'd had a dozen or so lovers. "My work keeps me pretty busy," she hedged. "I haven't had time for too many relationships."

"Neither have I," he replied, his gaze finding hers. The silent seconds stretched between them. Kaylie heard only the rapid cadence of her heartbeat, the air whispering through his lungs. "I wasn't lying when I said I loved you, Kaylie," he added, staring into the amber depths of his glass. "You can deny it all you want, you can even pretend that you didn't love me, but there it is. I handled it badly, I admit. But I just loved you too much." Drawing in a deep breath, he finished his drink, dropped his empty glass into the sink, then started out of the room. "Your bedroom is upstairs to the right. I'm next door. But don't worry about your virtue tonight. I'm just too damned tired from arguing with you to do anything about it."

Her throat closed in on itself as she watched him saunter out of the room, the dog at his heels. The faded fabric of Zane's jeans clung to his hips, and his buttocks moved fluidly, though his shoulders and back were ramrod stiff.

"Good night, Kaylie," he called over his shoulder as he mounted the stairs. "Turn out the lights when you go to bed."

"And what makes you think I'll stay here?" she replied,

following him to the stairs, but remaining at the bottom of the steps.

He paused at the landing, one hand resting on the banister. Turning, he towered over her, and again she noticed the torment in his eyes. "It's dark, and the nearest house is over ten miles away. The main road is even farther. Now, if you want to start making tracks through the wilderness, there's nothing I can do to stop you, but I will catch up to you."

"You have no right to do this! No right!" she screamed.

He suddenly looked tired. "That's a difference of opinion," he said, then mounted the rest of the steps, leaving her, fists clenched in fury, to stare after him. She felt a twinge of regret for the fleeting, giddy love they'd shared, but she shoved those old emotions into a shadowy corner of her heart. Loving Zane had been a mistake; marrying him had nearly stripped her of her own personality, and she wasn't about to fall into that trap again.

She glanced down at her hands and slowly uncoiled her fingers. Though she remembered her love with Zane as being unique, it was based on all the wrong emotions.

And now she was scared—frightened that the ominous warning on the tape was true. If only she could call someone—anyone—and find out the truth about Lee Johnston. Once she knew where she stood, she could face the rage of emotions Zane provoked in her.

Shivering, she walked outside and made her way to the Jeep. It was locked; the keys were not in the ignition and, of course, there was no mobile phone. Though she suspected he had a phone somewhere. But where? Miserably, she stared at the darkened dashboard. She didn't know the first thing about hot-wiring a Jeep—or any other car for that matter. Hot-wiring, as well as breaking into a car were among those valuable high school lessons she'd missed while growing up on a Hollywood back lot.

She kicked at the gravel in disgust and felt the breath of a mountain breeze touch her bare shoulders. Rubbing her arms, she stared dismally at the black woods looming all around her. If she left now, she wouldn't get far in sandals and a thin cotton dress. Nope. Zane had made sure escape was impossible. At least for tonight.

Turning on her heel, she started back up the steps. There had to be a way, she thought, refusing to give up. If she couldn't leave tonight, she'd find a way tomorrow.

Back in the house, she searched all the downstairs' rooms for a telephone, but though she found phone jacks, there wasn't one telephone in sight. She clenched her teeth in frustration. Damn the man. He'd made sure to thwart her. In the living room, hidden behind panels, she discovered a television, and she worried about her job. What would happen when she didn't show up tomorrow morning?

She turned on the power to the set but nothing happened. Then she noticed that the connecting cables swung free. Obviously the cable had been switched off.

She tried not to think of her position as cohostess of *West Coast Morning*. There was time enough to worry later. First she had to find a means of escape. And then, once back in the city, she'd check out Ted's warning personally, even drive to Whispering Hills to see Dr. Henshaw in person. With renewed purpose, she continued her quick search. In the pantry she found a flashlight and an old army jacket—not the most elegant or comfortable, but something to protect her from the elements, should she have to walk any distance. But taking off in the woods alone at night was too intimidating, even though it would serve Zane right to discover her gone come morning.

Leaving the jacket and flashlight untouched, she padded upstairs and noted that the lamp in Zane's room was still burning—a sliver of light showed beneath his closed door. She didn't bother knocking, but twisted the knob and found Zane, wearing only the worn Levi's, leaning back on the bed, almost as if he were waiting for her.

His head was supported by two pillows, and his eyes were the color of slate. His chest was covered with a mat of dark, swirling hair that covered a tanned skin and a washboard of rigid abdominal muscles before disappearing enticingly beneath his waistband.

The back of Kaylie's throat went dry. She forced her gaze back to his face. His lazy smile flashed white against a day's growth of beard.

"You room's to the *right,* remember?" His lips curved speculatively. "Unless of course you want to stay with me."

The shepherd, lying on the floor near the foot of the bed, lifted his head and cocked it to one side, as if he were sizing up Kaylie.

Kaylie turned her attention back to Zane. "I just want control of my life again."

Reaching over to the lamp, his shoulder muscles gliding with easy, corded strength, he clicked off the light. "Your choice," he said in the darkness. "Here—" he thumped on the bed "—or down the hall."

"I have a job to get to—"

"Forget it."

"They'll miss me."

He chuckled, as if he knew something she didn't. "Alan will be thrilled to have a chance to show the whole world he doesn't need you."

"You'll regret this, Zane," she muttered as she fumbled in the dark, then finding the door, walked quickly out of the room, slamming the door behind her.

What had she been thinking of? She'd been out of her mind to walk into his room and see him half-naked on the bed. A warmth in the pit of her stomach curled invitingly, and she remembered how lying next to him had been safe, secure, loving. The scent of his body lingering on the bedsheets, the feel of a strong arm wrapped around her waist.

"Stop it," she told herself as she marched to the room designated as hers and closed the door behind her. She surveyed her surroundings with a critical eye. The bedside lamps were lit, and golden light glowed warmly against the pine-paneled walls. The hand-stitched quilt on the double bed had been turned down. "How thoughtful," she grumbled, as if he could hear her as she stared at the plumped pillows. "But you forgot the mints!" She kicked off her sandals and padded barefoot against the smooth floor. The room was inviting, in an elemental sort of way, but she couldn't forget that she had been shanghaied here against her will, even if, as Zane so emphatically insisted, her life were in danger.

She groaned at the thought of what would happen tomorrow morning when she didn't arrive on the set of *West Coast Morning*. There would be chaos; her boss would be furious, and the phones at her apartment in San Francisco as well as at the beach house, would be ringing off the hook. Someone would call her sister, and Margot would worry herself sick.

"Oh, Lord, what a mess! She grabbed a handful of hair and flung it over her shoulders as she padded to the closet and, out of curiosity, opened the door. An array of clothes—women's clothes—filled every available space. Skirts, sweaters, jeans and slacks were draped on hangers or folded neatly on the shelves. So she hadn't been the first, she thought cynically. Disappointment welled up in her, and she slammed the door shut. No time for sentimentality.

So Zane had a woman—or women. So what? She didn't really believe that he'd lived the life of a monk, did she? It was only surprising that he would expect her to buy that whacked-out story, what with this closet chock-full of women's things.

Flopping onto the mattress, she tossed one arm over her eyes, trying to relieve the headache that was pounding at her temples. Too much wine, too much fear and way too much Zane Flannery, she thought. But tomorrow she'd find a way to force him to take her back to Carmel or straight to San Francisco, back to her home, her job, her life without him.

She only had to get through one night of sleeping under the same roof with him. One night with him lying, stripped bare to the waist, on a king-size bed only a dozen feet away.

Stop it! she thought, squeezing her eyes shut against the pure, sensual vision of him sprawled lazily across the smooth eiderdown quilt.

She didn't want him! She didn't! And yet there was something so provocatively male and charming about him, that she wondered, just for a fleeting moment, what it would be like to love Zane again.

Tossing the quilt over her shoulders, she started counting slowly, hoping that sleep would envelop her and that by morning Zane would come to his senses!

Zane climbed out of bed and stared out the window. He wondered if he'd made a big mistake. He'd known she'd be angry, of course, even expected her temper to boil. But he hadn't been prepared for her accusations cutting so close to the bone. Nor had he expected to want her so badly. Already he ached for her, and the thought of a night alone in the bed, with Kaylie only a few steps down the hall, would be torture.

From the foot of the bed, Franklin whined.

"Shh." Zane patted the big dog's head, then resumed his stance at the window, his thoughts drawn, as ever, to the only woman he'd ever loved.

She'd changed in the past seven years, he realized, placing one hand high on the window casing and leaning the side of his head against his arm. She'd grown up.

Gone was any trace of the naive young woman he'd married—the teenager who had made a string of semisuccessful movies before *Obsession*.

No, this new woman was strong, forceful and well able to control her own life. He'd have to be on his toes, he thought as he stared moodily into the dense, inky forest, because if he let down his guard for a second, she'd find a way to escape and throw her life in jeopardy. She didn't really believe that Johnston would be set free soon.

But Zane did.

He knew what it was like to have death take those he loved, and he was bound and determined that this time he'd thwart the grim reaper. Even if he had to keep Kaylie locked away for the next six months!

Chapter Four

The first few streaks of dawn crept across the bed. Groaning, Kaylie roused herself.

She was in an isolated cabin. With Zane.

God, what a mess!

Climbing out of bed, she stretched and looked out the window. The sun was rising behind a wall of sharply spired mountains. Golden light shone through the stands of pine, glittering in the dewdrops. What was she doing here?

"Oh, Zane," she murmured, grabbing the quilt and wrapping it around her. What was she going to do? Zane had always been an enigma of sorts, and she'd never learned how to handle him—just, she supposed, as he thought he'd never learned to handle her.

Smiling at the thought, she sat on the window seat and drew her knees under her chin. She remembered the first time she'd seen Zane and the tiny knot of apprehension that had coiled in her stomach, the same warm knot she felt now as she thought about him in the next room. She should be angry with him and she was, but the morning took the edge off her anger.

Had it been ten years ago when she'd first laid eyes on Zane Flannery? She'd only been seventeen at the time, and yet, the first time she'd seen him seemed as though it had occurred only yesterday....

A bodyguard! She, Kaylie Melville, with a bodyguard! She almost laughed at the thought. Just because she'd made a couple of pictures and she'd been receiving fan mail—some of it not so nice—didn't mean she needed a bodyguard!

"It's a bodyguard or nothing," her father warned her. "We can't be following you off to God-only-knows where every time you make a movie. So, you tell that producer of yours that you get your own personal bodyguard or you won't be making any more films for him!"

Her father, a short, wiry man with a temper that could skyrocket, wasn't about to take no for an answer.

"That's right," her mother had agreed, as she did with any of Dad's rules. "You listen to your father." Her mother had winked broadly. "No reason to give up your career. Just have the studio hire a guard. I'll talk to them myself."

Kaylie didn't argue. She loved making films. Her first picture had been mildly successful—a teen horror flick that made the studio more money than had been expected. Her second film was meatier, as she played a teenager who fell for the boy from the wrong side of the tracks and had to deal with unsupportive parents and pregnancy. Her third movie, *Carefree,* was a teen comedy that surprised the critics and earned the director, as well as Kaylie, glowing reviews. The film had grossed over a hundred million. Triumph Studios was ecstatic. Barely sixteen, Kaylie had become a household word, a budding star who received fan mail and was asked to do interview upon interview to promote her forthcoming projects. She was compared to other young actresses of the time. People sought her autograph. And the fan mail kept pouring in. Letters of undying love, proposals of marriage, and a few not-so-kind missives from a few tortured fans.

Soon the powers-that-be at Triumph Studios agreed with her father and insisted she retain a bodyguard.

But, at seventeen, she hadn't expected anything like Zane Flannery to walk into the offices of Triumph Pictures and announce that he would be looking after her. Not by a long shot! She had thought she'd be protected by some husky ex-football player with a couple of teeth missing. Or by some man with a huge belly and unshaven jaw who had once been the bouncer at a bar. But oh, no, Flannery was nothing like either man she'd envisioned.

He was younger than she'd expected—in his early twenties, by the looks of him, and much cuter—well, more handsome than any of her costars. His hair was longer than stylish and sable brown, curling over his collar and falling over his forehead in shiny, windblown waves. His face, though rough-hewn, took on a boyish quality whenever he flashed a rakish, devil-may-care smile that turned her inside out.

"Miss Melville," he said, extending a work-roughened palm. They were seated in the cluttered office of Martin York, the producer of her latest film, *Someone to Love*.

Flannery's large palm dwarfed hers as he shook her hand, then released her fingers. Wearing only a leather jacket, jeans and a T-shirt, he looked as if he were one of the stagehands or construction workers on the set, but his eyes gave him away. Gray and penetrating, they seemed to take in all of the office at once as he turned back to the producer.

Martin tossed his Dodgers baseball cap onto a chair behind him. Grinning beneath his beard, he reached over a desk piled high with scripts, reels of film and overflowing ashtrays, and clasped Zane's outstretched hand. "How the hell are you?"

"'Bout the same," Zane drawled, dropping into the chair next to hers and slouching low, his jean-encased legs stretched out in front of him.

"That bad, eh?"

Both men laughed, and Kaylie repressed the urge to giggle. Their easy camaraderie caused her to feel like an outsider, and when she was nervous, she often giggled. But she didn't want Zane to see her as the least bit girlish. He looked like the kind of person who wouldn't easily suffer fools, and she didn't want to get on his bad side.

"I've known Flannery here for more than a few years," Martin said, looking at her as if suddenly remembering she was in the room. "We knew each other in the navy. So don't let his appearance fool you. He's the best in the business."

Kaylie trained her gaze on the man who was to be her protector. The best in the business? So young?

"Zane's worked on some top-secret stuff for the armed services, then he landed a job at Gemini Security. Now he's starting his own company—right?"

"That's the rumor," Zane replied lazily. He glanced at Kaylie again, and his smile faded. "I'll take care of you, Miss Melville. You can count on it."

"Kaylie," she replied with a shrug. "And I'll call you Zane. Okay?"

"If that's the way you want it."

She looked from Zane to Martin, but Martin, too, lifted a shoulder. "Whatever works."

Kaylie grinned and tried not to be lost in the power of Zane's gaze. But she felt giddy and conspicuous and—What was wrong with her? He was just her bodyguard. No big deal. Or was it? This man—well, he looked as if one hot look from him could melt a glacier.

"Okay, okay," Martin said, handing Zane an address book. "Now, here's Kaylie's address. She still lives with her folks and her sister, and she'll be working here as well as on location in Mexico and Australia. Her folks won't be going along, so Kaylie will be your responsibility. She's been getting a few crank letters...." He tossed a stack of mail, bound by a rubber band, to Flannery just as he finished copying her address into his own book. "I want you to check them all out—"

"Hey, wait a minute," Kaylie cut in, surprised. "That's my mail, right?"

Martin nodded, his expression growing peevish.

Objecting, Kaylie reached for the small bundle. "Don't I get to read it?"

Martin waved off her request. "Don't worry about it. The secretary will respond."

"No way. I always read—"

"You don't have time," Martin said, obviously irritated. "You've got a plane to catch in three days and—"

"And it's mine," Kaylie said, hoping not to sound too petulant. But she wasn't going to let this new guy think he could boss her around. She'd agreed to the bodyguard but that was all. To Zane, she said, "If there's something else you want to know about me, just ask."

He arched one dark brow, and a smile tugged at the corners of Flannery's lips, though he tried to keep his expression grave as he slapped the stack of envelopes into her hand. "When you're done with them, I'd like to see them again."

Martin was fit to be tied. "We don't have time—"

"It's cool," Kaylie assured him, and Martin rolled his eyes.

"Women," Martin muttered under his breath, but Kaylie, cheeks burning, jaw tight, refused to rise to the bait. She just wanted this bodyguard to understand that she wouldn't be treated like a little kid. As for Martin's bad mood, he'd get over it.

From that point on, Zane was all business. He was with her constantly, but never obtrusively, and she began to relax around him. He helped her with her studies and taught her card games and even ran through her lines with her. Once in a while he'd show her a different side to him—a side that proved he did have a sense of humor. While going over her lines, he'd ad-lib, all very seriously, and she'd foul up her lines and they'd both end up laughing. Once in a while she'd catch him looking at her intensely, his eyes darkening, and she'd feel a tightening in her stomach, a warmth that seeped through her whole body.

When they were together, she felt secure. Even when they went out at night, he was cool and calm, almost relaxed. But at the slightest hint of danger, if any fan got too close and he sensed her unease, every muscle would flex and his eyes would glint with warning.

Being so close to him, closer than she was to any other male, she began to rely on him and fantasize about him. He was as handsome as any of her costars and seemed much more virile and worldly. He didn't party, nor try to impress the stars.

He was just there—steady as a rock—with his sexy smile that turned her insides to jelly. They spent month after month together.

In Australia, after grueling hours on the set, he'd swim with her in the ocean, and walk with her as the warm sand squished between her toes. He never touched her, though she'd caught his gaze drifting over her body as the wind teased the hem of her dress or the drops of saltwater dried on her skin.

Once, she caught him staring at the dusky hollow between her breasts. She couldn't breathe for a second. Instinctively she placed her hand over the halter of her swimsuit and his gaze moved, but not before she saw the flame in his eyes. Without a word, he tossed her a beach towel and kept his distance from her for the rest of the day.

It wasn't until the next year, after the success of *Someone to Love,* when they were filming in Victoria, British Columbia, that their relationship changed. Her parents had stayed with her on the set for two weeks, then flown back to California.

Kaylie, feeling restless, paced in her room. From her window, she spied the storm clouds gathering to the west, reflecting her own mood as they shifted in dark patterns on the water. She opened the window, feeling a stiff breeze, smelling the heavy scent of rain. There was electricity in the air, currents as charged as her emotions, and she couldn't think of anything but Zane and what it would be like to kiss him.

She told herself she was crazy, that her mother would tell her she was in the throes of puppy love, that her feelings for Zane were nothing more than a schoolgirl crush.

Nonetheless, she was wild for him.

For the first time in her life she had sexual fantasies, and they always involved Zane. Sometimes she blushed just looking at him.

After filming, she and Zane decided to walk back to the hotel. The wind picked up and the clouds overhead opened. Huge raindrops peppered the ground, forming puddles. "Come on," Zane said, turning up his collar and grabbing her hand as he dashed across a street. "We'll catch a cab."

Laughing, she followed, raindrops catching in her hair and

running down her cheeks. They hurried past other pedestrians fumbling with umbrellas, carriages pulled by huge horses and double-decker buses rumbling through the slick streets. But each cab that passed was full.

As a final cab roared past, Zane muttered an oath. Then, tugging at her hand, he said, "I think this is a shortcut." He pulled her through a park. They ran down gravel paths, their shoes crunching, their breath fogging in the air.

Kaylie's legs began to ache. "Hey, slow down," she said, gasping from his quick pace.

He slid her a disbelieving glance. "Out of shape?" he mocked, but tugged on her arm and pulled her beneath the leafy cover of a willow tree. The smell of damp earth and ferns filled the air. Magenta azaleas and pale lavender rhododendrons splashed color through the mist that seemed to rise from the loamy soil.

Zane threw his arm across her shoulders and wiped a drop from the tip of her nose. "I guess even I can't protect you from Mother Nature," he said with a crooked grin. His dark hair fell across his eyes, and raindrops glistened, jewellike, in the blackened strands.

His gaze touched hers, and in one breathless instant Kaylie knew he was going to kiss her. The arm around her shoulders tightened, his fingers wound in her hair, and, as she tilted her head back, his lips found hers in a kiss that was gentle and fierce.

She responded, opening her mouth to the tender insistence of his tongue. He moved closer to her, his suede jacket smelling of leather and rain, his after-shave tingling her nostrils.

She moaned his name and strained against him—intimately.

Zane stiffened as if he'd been hit by an electric current. Quickly he stepped backward until the heel of his boot scraped against the scarred trunk of the willow. "Damn." Running a shaking hand over his wet forehead, he stared past her, over her shoulder, to a point in the distance. "I can't let this... This just can't happen," he said raggedly, passion in his eyes as he attempted to fixate on anything but her.

"But—" She took a step closer.

"No!" Holding up his palm, he shook his head. "My job is to protect you, not seduce you." His gaze found hers. "Your parents—"

"Are in L.A.," she blurted out.

"—trust me."

He was right, of course, but she was too young and stubborn to admit it.

"Come on, let's get out of this downpour...."

Throwing caution to the wind, she flung her arms around his neck and pressed her anxious lips to his. She felt him shudder. From his shoulders to his knees a shiver of desire possessed him.

"No, we can't.... Oh, God," And with that desperate prayer, he kissed her, long and hard, his arms surrounding her, his mouth exploring. Turning quickly, he pinned her against the rough bole of the tree, but she barely noticed as she kissed him with all the wild abandonment she'd dreamed of.

His hands moved upward until the weight of her breast filled his palm. His hips shoved tight against her, and she felt the rock-hard force of his desire creating an answering awakening in her. Warm and moist, like the spring shower, she experienced a want that was dark and dusky and so demanding she ached for him, wanting him as she had no other.

He kissed her eyes, her nose, her cheeks, her throat, his tongue licking away the raindrops as his hands found the zipper of her jacket. The bleached denim opened, and he lifted her blouse until his damp fingertip plundered beneath her bra, touching and delving, causing her nipples to crest into small, hard buds.

Desire crept up her spine, spilled into her blood, causing her to moan and kiss him feverishly.

Beneath the drooping branches of the willow tree, with the wind sighing and the rain creating a moist curtain, Kaylie wanted to be loved.

"Oh, I should be hanged for this."

"Don't stop—" she cried, feeling him pull away.

"You're barely eighteen," he whispered, once again moving away from her.

"But I love you."

The words seemed to sting. He stepped backward and sucked in a long, slow breath while Kaylie, her breasts still aching, her jacket draped off one shoulder, felt suddenly bereft and empty. Didn't he want her? She had only to look at him to know.

"Those are strong words," he said, his voice so low and rough she barely recognized it.

"But—"

"Shh!" Stepping forward, he placed a finger to her lips, and she kissed his knuckle, touching it with her tongue. He grabbed her roughly. "Stop it, damn you!" he growled. "Don't you know you're playing with fire?"

"I'm—"

"You're eighteen. Eighteen! And I'm being paid to keep you safe!" In frustration, he straightened her jacket. "Let's get out of here before we do something we'll both regret."

"This is what I want," she pleaded, as his fingers clamped around her wrist and he yanked her toward the path again.

"You're too young to know what you want."

"I'm not—"

"And you're too used to getting anything you desire. On a whim," he said with more than a trace of remorse. "I'm not a rich man, Kaylie. And I'm not going to blow this job by getting involved with you." Casting her a dark look over his shoulder he added, "And I'm not some toy that you'll experiment with, lose interest in, then discard when you're bored."

"What?" she cried, planting her feet and trying to pull free of his grasp.

He stopped and then, as if he were searching for a way to throw away her feelings, he said, "Grow up."

She slapped him. With all the force of offended youth, she hauled back and smacked him across his wet cheek.

"You spoiled brat," he muttered, and she couldn't tell if he were angry or relieved. Maybe he'd baited her on purpose. But this time, when he took hold of her wrist, his grip was punishing, almost brutal as he half dragged her through the park, mindless of the muddy puddles that splashed her boots.

The path cut through a rose garden and a thicket of oaks before spilling onto the sidewalk that flanked the hotel. "Thank God."

Furious, she couldn't resist taunting him. "So what're you going to do with me, Zane?" she baited, still reeling from his assessment of her as a "brat." "Turn me over your knee and spank me?"

He stopped dead in his tracks. His face went stark white. His fingers slackened, and he squeezed his eyes shut, pinching the bridge of his nose between thumb and forefinger, as if in so doing he could call up his fleeing patience. "No, Kaylie," he said, slowly opening eyes as hard as glass. "As soon as you're safely back at the hotel, I'm getting the hell out of here."

"Meaning?"

"That you'll just have to find yourself another bodyguard."

No! Desperation tore at her. "But I don't want anyone else." She coiled her fingers around the lapels of his jacket and held on tightly, as if afraid he might run. "Don't you understand, Zane. I want you. *You.*"

Staring down at her upturned face, he let out a groan and dragged her closer still, kissing her over and over again. She felt him shudder against her, as if he were trying and failing to rein in impossible emotions.

Oblivious to the pedestrians hurrying, head and umbrellas tucked against the wind and rain, they held each other, she clinging to him as if to life itself, he embracing her as if she were a rare and fragile creature he was afraid to release for fear of never seeing again.

The wind and rain blew past, but they didn't care.

Finally he stepped away, his expression tortured and grim. He took both her chilled, wet hands in his. "This can't happen, you know."

"It already has."

He shook his head, though his eyes betrayed him. "Then it has to stop."

"No!" She knew what she wanted. Zane, Zane, Zane!

"Come on. You're getting drenched," he muttered, twining

his fingers through hers as he pulled her up the steps to the glorious old hotel. Built to resemble an English castle, the hotel stretched a full city block. Gold brick, leaded glass and tall, narrow windows created seven stories. Lush gardens and brick courtyards surrounded the sprawling building.

Zane, propelling Kaylie by her elbow, hastened her through the lobby and into an elevator. Once on the seventh floor, he unlocked the door to her room and made a sweeping search of the suite.

"Take a hot shower and I'll meet you downstairs for dinner."

She wouldn't let him go. "Stay with me."

"Kaylie—"

"Please!"

He groaned and pulled his hand from hers. "I can't. You can't. *We can't!*"

"But—"

"Don't you know this is killing me?" he finally admitted, as she reached for him again, trying to kiss him, feeling tears fill her eyes.

"I love—"

"Oh, God, Kaylie, don't!" he whispered, his voice raw as he left her and closed the connecting door between their rooms.

Later, at dinner, he refused to talk about their relationship. Instead, he was all business, sitting stiffly across from her, his gaze moving restlessly over the other guests, looking, searching for danger that didn't exist.

The meal, in Kaylie's opinion, was a disaster, and upstairs in their suite again, things didn't improve. He closed the door between them and refused to kiss her.

"I don't understand," she cried against the door panels, slamming her fist against the wall in frustration, but she received no answer.

The next few days were torture. Zane acted like a complete stranger. He was distant and proper to the point that she thought she might scream. She tried to draw him into conversation, but his replies were quick monosyllabic answers. No more laughing. No more jokes. No more ad-libbing to her lines. Stiff and businesslike, he became the antithesis of the man with whom she'd fallen in love.

On the set three days later, she cracked. She blew her lines for the third time when the director waved everyone off the set and called for an hour break.

Kaylie, cheeks burning, walked straight to the docks. Zane was near her side, though, of course, he didn't say a word. Not one solitary word.

She clamped her hands over the rail and, without looking in his direction, shouted, "What's wrong with you?"

Zane leaned against the fender of a car as she pressed her nails into the painted railing and stared at the rippling blue waters reflecting against a clear, cerulean sky.

Gulls floated on the air currents near the docks, while sailboats and fishing trawlers skimmed across the horizon. Kaylie barely noticed, her concentration centered solely on Zane.

"Well?" she demanded, wanting to shake him.

"Nothing's wrong."

"Like hell! You've changed, Zane!"

"I'm just here to do a job."

"You care about me!"

"You're my client. My responsibility."

She flew at him. Emotionally strung out, she raised her fists as if to pummel his chest, but he captured her wrists and pinned them together over her head before she had a chance to strike. So close she could see her own reflection in his sunglasses, she felt helpless and tired. Tears welled in her eyes and she crumpled against him. "There's more—we both know it. Tell me there's more," she pleaded, her throat closing against the pain of his rejection.

"There can't be." But the corners of his lips turned down, and she knew he was fighting his own ragged emotions.

"I *love* you."

"Kaylie, no!" But his face was pained, and he sighed loudly…sadly. "God, help us," he whispered, releasing her and shoving one hand through his wind-ruffled hair. Looking toward the heavens, he swore. Was he angry? At her? Or himself?

"I do love you, damn it, and I always will." Sobs choked her. "I love you, Zane. Please, just love me back."

"It won't work."

"We'll make it work!" she cried, reaching up and lifting his sunglasses to see the agony in his eyes.

With a moan, he wrapped his arms around her and dropped his mouth on hers in a kiss that nearly strangled her with promised passion.

She closed her eyes to the storm of desire overtaking her. He did care! He did!

When he raised his head, she saw the torment on his face. "This *can't* happen. We can't let it."

But she kissed him again and again. Only when she knew the director would send someone looking for her did she pull back.

That night she expected Zane to come to her. She lay on her bed, wearing a soft pink nightgown, trembling at the thought of what she intended.

She watched the clock as the hours passed. Ten. Eleven. Midnight. Still the light beneath his door shone. At twelve-thirty, she could wait no longer and knocked softly. "Zane?"

The door opened. He stuck his head into her room. "What?"

She swallowed hard. Though she'd played the role before, she'd never seduced a man, never been in bed with a man. "I—I uh, thought, you might like to come in...." Oh, Lord, why did her voice sound so high-pitched and trembling—like a child's?

"Are you all right?"

"Yes, but—"

"Then let's just leave it, Kaylie," he said, his voice as rough as sandpaper.

"I can't."

"Go to sleep." He shut the door firmly, and she wanted to die of embarrassment.

She couldn't sleep that night, nor the next. She was a failure at rehearsals, and the director, running behind schedule, was in a foul mood.

Zane was adamant. Cool and distant again. And no amount of anger or pleading would change his mind.

Until the phone call.

It came through at eleven o'clock on a rainy Monday night. Kaylie, restless anyway, picked up the receiver only to hear Margot's frail voice on the other end. "Kaylie?" Margot cried, her voice breaking. "Oh, Kaylie..."

"What?" Kaylie's heart leaped to her throat. Fear engulfed her.

"Oh, God, Kaylie. It's Mom and Dad...." Margot wailed. Nearly incoherent and sobbing uncontrollably, Margot cried on and on. Kaylie's insides turned to ice as she understood part of what Margot was saying—something about an accident and Mom and Dad and another car.

Trevor, Margot's boyfriend, took control, and his voice was firm as he explained about the accident. As he spoke, Kaylie understood. The room went out of focus. The floor tilted. Blackness surrounded her as she realized both her parents were dead, killed in a hideous accident on a winding mountain road in northern California.

She wasn't aware that she'd screamed, didn't realize that she'd sunk to the floor, couldn't feel the tears drizzling down her face, but all at once Zane was there, holding her, cuddling her, calming her as he spoke to Trevor.

He hung up and tried to get her to talk, to drink some water, to do anything, but her grief eclipsed all else.

"Shh, baby, shh," he said rocking her, but she was inconsolable.

He must have called the producer, who sent over a doctor, because she was given something to help her sleep. Even in her drugged state, images of her mother and father and a fiery automobile fused in her mind.

When she finally roused twelve hours later, Zane was there, his flinty eyes regarding her carefully, his jaw unshaven, his clothes wrinkled from sitting in the chair near her bed.

"I—I can't believe it," she said. Her head thundered, and

her eyes burned with new tears. Her throat was hot and swollen and she felt as if she'd aged twenty years.

He came to her then. Took her into his arms and stretched out on the rumpled bed with her. "Oh, Kaylie, I'm so sorry," he whispered, his voice cracking. "But I'll take care of you," he vowed, kissing her crown. "I promise."

And he had. From that moment on, he'd never left her side. Through the funeral and resulting media circus, Zane was there, protecting her, sheltering her, being her rock in her storm-tossed sea of grief.

When the pain had finally lessened and she was able to put her life back together, Zane had come to her bed as a lover, not a protector. He held her and made love to her and became her reason for living. His caresses were divine, his lovemaking glorious, and she was certain she was in love.

They married in June, and for months Kaylie was in heaven. Living with and loving Zane was perfect. Their happiness knew no bounds, and though Zane sometimes seemed a little more concerned about her welfare than she thought was necessary, she loved him with all her heart.

Then the letters started arriving. Letters about love and lust and weird rituals. An anonymous person wrote her every day, pledging his love, promising that he would "perform an act of supreme sacrifice" for her. These letters were much more frightening than any others she'd received and the fact that the terrifying missives arrived daily put Zane on edge.

Kaylie wasn't concerned, and even thought Zane was overreacting. And he started calling her day and night when he wasn't with her, asking about her friends, checking into their backgrounds.

She began to feel smothered.

Terrified for her safety, he spent every waking hour trying to locate the man who was invading her life. He spent days with the police to no avail, and he transformed their home in Malibu, where they were living at the time, into a veritable fortress, with guard dogs, an electronic security system and remote-controlled gates.

Kaylie, always a free spirit, felt as if she were withering. Her home began to seem like a military compound.

Zane even tried to secure the cottage in Carmel, but Kaylie put her foot down. They needed some normalcy in their lives, she reasoned, and against his better judgment, he'd acquiesced.

But they grew further and further apart. Hell-bent on protecting her, Zane refused to see that she was dying inside.

At nineteen she wanted an independence she'd never tasted, a freedom to make her own decisions, to live her own life, and all she wanted from him was his love.

They had worked on the marriage. Oh, Lord, she thought now, as she realized that they had both tried and fought to save their dying union. But they just hadn't tried hard enough.

Zane had become autocratic, and she'd become fiercely independent.

The letters had gotten worse, and when Lee Johnston, the anonymous person, finally accosted them at the premiere of *Obsession,* Zane had lost all control.

Now, seven years later, Kaylie swallowed the taste of fear that still touched the back of her throat as she remembered Johnston's blank face, his unseeing eyes, his hard body thrust up against hers. And the knife. God, she'd never forget the feel of polished steel against her throat.

If not for Zane, she might have died that night.

But Zane turned paranoid on her. Even though Johnston was locked up and the letters no longer made their way to her mailbox, Zane installed bigger and better security systems and used his best men to constantly patrol their home.

The marriage dissolved in its prison, and Kaylie had no option but to file for divorce.

At first he fought it. And he even tried to change. But he couldn't, and she doubted that he ever would. Even now, after seven years, he was still trying to run her life. Like Don Quixote fighting windmills, Zane was still grappling with the ghost of Lee Johnston.

And so was she.

Now, staring at the sunlight streaming over the mountains,

Kaylie tossed off the old quilt. Today she'd talk some sense into him—today when she wasn't tipsy, when she was rational and calm.

She'd find a way to convince him that they couldn't stay up here alone together. Her heart couldn't take it.

Chapter Five

It was time to take the offensive, Kaylie decided when she heard him rattling around downstairs. With renewed determination, she swept down the stairs and into the kitchen to find him seated on a bar stool, one booted foot propped on the bracing of the matching stool as he lazily flipped through the pages of a magazine.

"'Morning," he drawled with maddening calm. "Sleep okay?"

"As a matter of fact I didn't sleep much at all," she said, irritated, struggling to remain calm and rational. "So you've enjoyed your little joke," she said, shivering in her wrinkled sundress. "Now, let's get back to the real world."

Motioning around him, he said, "This, Lady Melville, is the real world."

"I can't stay here, Zane, even if I wanted to," she said, hoping to sound logical. "What do you think is going to happen when I don't show up on the set?"

He shoved the magazine aside. "Not much."

"Not much?" she repeated, hardly believing her ears but

his expression didn't change. She glanced pointedly at her watch. "We have exactly forty-five minutes to get to the city."

"We won't make it," he said, climbing off his stool long enough to pour two cups of coffee. "Even if we wanted to."

"We do want to."

"Correction. You want to." He handed her one of the cups and took an experimental sip from his. "Careful. It's hot."

Kaylie's temper soared. "And I have no say in the matter— right? All my citizen's rights have been stripped since you brought me here to this...this prison! Well, I'm warning you, when my producer figures out that I've been kidnapped, there'll be hell to pay!"

He looked maddeningly unconcerned. "Relax. He won't guess."

"But when he calls—"

"He'll get your answering machine."

"Not good enough, Zane," she said, crossing the room and glaring straight into his eyes. For an instant, a flicker of pain crossed those gray irises, and Kaylie thought there was hope. He wasn't as immune to her feelings as he'd like to pretend.

"Crowley won't call."

"Of course he'll ca—" she started to say, but stopped short. Obviously Zane had taken steps to prevent anything from going wrong with this ridiculous plan of his! Of course! Fury caused her heart to surge wildly. "What'd you do, Zane?" she demanded. "I mean besides becoming a major criminal now wanted by the FBI. What *else* did you do?"

"I made sure that you wouldn't be missed." He settled back on his bar stool and propped his elbows on the counter, eyeing her over the rim of his cup.

Now she was worried. "How?"

"By making the appropriate calls."

"What calls?"

"To the station."

"No—"

"And your sister." He took another long swallow from his coffee.

"You called Margot?" she whispered, disbelieving.

"No, but my secretary did."

She believed him, and her heart sank. Finally she realized that this was no joke. He was dead serious. He intended to keep her captive for God-only-knew how long! She slumped onto the nearest bar stool and wrapped her suddenly chilled fingers around the hot cup of coffee. Was he really that worried about Johnston? Licking dry lips, she tried to think and stay rational. "No matter what you think might happen to me," she said, her voice uneven, "you had no right to bring me up here against my will."

"I know."

"But you don't care," she said, seeing him wince. She took a gulp of her coffee. It was hot and burned a path to her stomach. Avoiding his gaze, she glanced around the room and noticed the phone jack. "You took out all the phones," she said. "Afraid I might call for help."

"Afraid you might do something stupid."

"Nothing could top this trick of yours," she said, and to her surprise he laughed.

"I need to make some calls."

He eyed her speculatively, then finished his coffee in one swallow and walked out of the room and headed upstairs. The floorboards creaked overhead. He was down in a few minutes, cellular phone in hand. "Okay. Who do you want to call?"

She couldn't believe her good luck. "First the station, then Margot—"

"How about the hospital again? Or Henshaw's home—I've got the number."

"But—"

"No one else," he said firmly, his gaze hard. "I brought you up here for your safety and we're not blowing it."

Angry, she watched as he dialed a number, then handed the phone to her. Henshaw's answering machine clicked on, and she left a message that she would call back. Zane connected with Whispering Hills Hospital again, but Henshaw wasn't available. Again, Kaylie was stymied in her requests about Johnston.

Then it was Zane's turn. As he drank a second cup of coffee, he called his office and received an update from Brad Hastings.

"Nothing new yet," Zane said, hanging up. "Look, I know you're furious with me for bringing you here, but it's for your own good." When she started to protest, he held up a palm. "And don't give me any grief about treating you like a child. I don't mean to. I—I just don't want to lose you."

The honesty in his eyes cut straight to her soul. Her mouth worked, but no sound came out. *Don't,* she reminded herself, *don't trust him again. It's too easy to get lost in him.* All too vividly she remembered just how much she'd loved him; how she'd waken every day looking forward to his kiss, his laugh, his touch.... She cleared her throat as well as her mind. She wanted to tell him that he'd already lost her, but she held her tongue because there always had been and always would be a frail connection between them.

Phone in hand, he grabbed hold of the back door. "I have to take care of the stock."

"The what?"

"Horses and cattle."

She glanced out the window to the hills. Blue-green pine and spruce were interspersed with thickets of oak and maple. Through a break in the trees she noticed a weathered barn and split-rail fence. "What is this place?"

"It was an old logging camp, then it was turned into a ranch of sorts. I bought it a couple of years ago." He glanced at her, and one side of his mouth lifted. "Kind of a spur-of-the-moment thing. I decided I needed a place to get away from it all. I knew the guy who owned the property, and we struck a deal."

"This guy—your friend—did he abduct women against their will and bring them here, too?" she baited, unable to keep from smiling. There was a modicum of humor in this situation, after all.

His grin was slightly off center. "Not that I know of," he replied, "but you never can tell. Anyway, I sold some of the timber rights, but I decided to keep this house and a few acres for vacations.''

"I didn't know you knew the meaning of the word."

"I'm learning," he drawled, "though no one ever accused me of being quick on the uptake."

Kaylie couldn't help but laugh. This was a new side to Zane, a side that was definitely appealing. She'd never thought of him as a person who was willing to kick back. That he, too, needed time to unwind and enjoy life touched her.

She eyed the big kitchen with its hanging copper pots, gleaming brass fittings and butcher-block counters. The room was airy and light, the windows sparkling clean. "So who keeps everything up when you're not here?"

"A retired couple—Max and Leona." Zane opened the door.

"And where are they?" Kaylie asked, hope springing in her heart. If she could just get the woman alone, explain her predicament, maybe Leona would understand and help her....

"Don't even consider it," Zane said, as if reading her mind. "I gave them an extended vacation and said I'd look after everything myself."

Kaylie's hopes crashed to the floor.

His gaze turned tender as he stared at her. What a sight she must be in her wrinkled dress, no makeup and tangled, unruly hair—a far cry from the famous teenager he'd once married, she thought ruefully.

"I'll be back in a minute." He walked through the door, leaving Kaylie alone. She took advantage of her short-lived freedom, hurrying from room to room, looking, with the help of daylight, for any means of escape. He took the phone with him and there was no CB radio! No living soul for miles!

She worked her way from the kitchen, dining room, living room and ended up in the den. A huge river-rock fireplace dominated one wall, and a bank of windows opposite offered a view of the sloping hillside and valley far below. A river, silver-gray against the blue-green pines, glinted through the trees. Autumn had touched the maples and oaks, turning the leaves gold or fiery red. Wild flowers bloomed in vibrant yellow, pink and blue, providing splashes of color in the dark forest.

"Beautiful, isn't it?" Zane asked, lounging in the doorway.

Kaylie whirled to see him staring at her. Goose bumps appeared on her skin. "I suppose it could be, were the situation different."

"It can be different, Kaylie. All you have to do is accept the fact that you're here and enjoy it."

She hesitated. It sounded so perfect. And too good to be true. "I can't."

He shrugged. "Then you're probably going to have a miserable couple of weeks."

A couple of weeks! she thought in horror. She had to get back now, today, as soon as possible. She couldn't be gone for two days, much less two weeks, for God's sake! For the first time she noticed the duffel bag hanging from his fingers. Her bag! "What's in that?" she asked, dreading the answer.

"I thought you might need a change."

"But how—"

"While you were swimming," he said, then his smile twisted. "I didn't have much time, though, so I just threw some things into the bag. It was hidden beneath the tarp in the back of the Jeep."

"You went through my drawers?" she asked, furious as she conjured up the image of him pawing through her clothes, her stockings, her lingerie....

"It wasn't anything I hadn't seen before," he reminded her softly, then cleared his throat. "I didn't think you'd wear anything I bought you."

"You bought me?" she queried.

"There are clothes in the closet upstairs. Surely you saw them—"

"They don't belong to some woman you're involved with?"

He smiled sadly. "They're yours."

"Mine?" Her heart stopped. "Then this was planned, right? For *days?*" So angry she was shaking, she started for the door.

Zane was quick. His hand shot out, and strong fingers

wrapped around her wrist. "Kaylie," he said softly, "slow down a minute—don't go jumping to conclusions." His hands were gentle, his gaze fastened on hers. "Yes, this took a little time to arrange," he admitted. "About ten hours, give or take a few minutes. I found out about Johnston yesterday morning. I had my secretary run out and buy clothes—size six, right?— and ship them here via a company van. At the same time I called the Browns—Max and Leona—and offered them a dream vacation that they well deserved and told them to take the telephones with them."

"And what about me, Zane?" she asked, pressing her face closer to his, standing on tiptoe to stare at him. "Did you ever wonder how I'd react? Did you realize that there's a good chance that I'll never forgive you for hauling me up here against my will?"

His jaw slid to the side, and his eyes searched her face. "That would be a shame, Kaylie," he said, his voice husky, and she knew in an instant that he intended to kiss her. She tried to yank away from him, but his fingers tightened around her arm. "Whether you admit it or not, we're good together." In one swift motion, he tugged impatiently on her wrist, lowered his head and captured her lips with his.

Kaylie struggled, but his arms closed possessively around her and his mouth moved sensually against hers. No! No! Her mind screamed, though her body began to tingle and familiar emotions tore at her heart. With all her strength she pushed away from him, away from the seduction of his body against hers. But he held her tighter, kissing her and stealing the breath from her lungs. The harder she struggled, the stronger he became, his will as unbending as steel.

His hands were hot against her bare shoulders, his mouth demanding. His tongue pressed hard against her teeth and gained entrance to her mouth.

A thousand memories—glorious and loving—flitted through her mind.

He groaned softly, and her blood turned to fire. Heedless of the danger signals, she began to kiss him back, passion exploding from anger. He smelled and tasted and felt so right.

His hard, anxious body, pressed tightly to hers, caused an ache to burn deep in the most feminine part of her. As if in a dream, she wondered how it would feel to make love to him again.

The thought hit her like a bucket of cold water. Realizing just how easily she could be seduced, she recoiled inside and shoved hard against his shoulders, struggling and breaking free.

"Don't—don't ever," she gasped, trying to think rationally and failing miserably, "do that again!"

"Why not?" he asked, his eyes gleaming, a satisfied smile plastered across his jaw. "Didn't you enjoy it?"

"No!"

"Kaylie, don't lie!"

She backed up, her cheeks flaming, her feet nearly stumbling over an ottoman. "You took me by surprise, that's all."

He cocked a disbelieving dark brow. "Maybe I should plan some more surprises."

"Maybe you should go out and feed the cows or horses or chickens or whatever it is you've got here and leave me alone!"

One dark brow arched in skepticism. "Leave you alone. That, I'm afraid, will be hard to do."

"Consider it a challenge!" she said, though she knew that being locked in close quarters with him would make it as difficult for her as it was for him.

He didn't leave. Instead he crossed his arms over his chest. To her consternation, he actually grinned—that boyish and adorable grin that wormed its way straight through her cold facade. "We *should* declare a truce. You know, wave the white flag—try to be civil to each other instead of always lunging for the jugular."

"In this situation?"

"It'll make things easier."

"For you!"

"For both of us," he said softly. "Come on, give it a rest. You might just find that you'll enjoy yourself."

She swallowed hard. That was exactly what she was afraid of—enjoying herself. Why couldn't she just hate him? It would be so much easier than fighting these lingering feelings that she couldn't quite forget. "I—I don't know."

"I'll be good," he promised, but a gleam sparked in his eyes.

What would it hurt? She was tired of the constant battle, though she still bristled at the thought of his high-handed technique of kidnapping her. She had rights, rights he had no business ignoring. "You know, Zane, I'd like to trust you—to get along with you, I really would," she admitted honestly, "but it'll be hard."

"Try," he suggested. "I'll be on my best behavior—charming and good-natured and...as fair as possible."

She blew her bangs out of her eyes in frustration. Fair? Impossible. But there was something beguiling about his smile, something she couldn't resist—something she had never been able to fight. "A truce, hmm?" she said, picking up a crystal paperweight and tossing it into the air only to catch it again. "Okay—on one condition."

"Name it."

"That as soon as we find out that Lee Johnston won't be allowed out of the mental hospital, you release me."

His mouth tightened imperceptibly, but he rounded the desk and extended his hand to her. "It's a deal," he said, wrapping strong fingers over hers.

"Deal," she agreed, shaking his hand, then trying to retrieve her palm from his grasp.

But he didn't let go. Instead he tugged slightly and, lowering his head, dropped a gentle kiss across her mouth. Soft as a whisper, his lips lingered against hers. Tenderness flooded her and she felt weak inside.

"I promise you," he reassured, lifting his head and staring into her eyes, "I won't let anything happen to you."

Her throat clogged. "I—I don't need a bodyguard."

One side of his mouth twisted wryly. "I hope you're right." He scooped a felt Stetson from the brass tree near the door and sauntered out of the room.

She touched her lips with her fingertips. Her pulse was thundering, her knees weak. She sagged against the desk and ran trembling fingers through her hair. Oh, Kaylie, girl, you're in a mess this time! You thought he was out of your system for good, but just one kiss and you melted inside.

She closed her eyes, squeezing them shut, forcing her breathing to slow, her heartbeat to quiet. This would never do. She had to think, be on her toes every minute. Or else she would end up falling in love with him again! "Oh, God," she whispered, afraid of the pain and heartache.

She heard the back door slam shut. Taking a deep breath, she moved to the window and saw Zane, his stride lazy and sensual, as he walked to the barns.

After watching him disappear into a weathered building, Kaylie pulled herself together. Hauling her bag with her, she climbed the stairs again. She needed to shower, change and think. But being around Zane made rational thought nearly an impossibility.

In her room, she opened the walk-in closet and studied the clothes neatly folded and stacked on the shelves. Once again, Zane had surprised her. Slacks, blouses, sweaters, shorts, skirts and dresses—all in her size! Now it was blindingly clear that the outfits, purchased from upscale department stores in San Francisco, were intended for her. How could she have thought otherwise?

As Kaylie gazed at the wardrobe, her heart sank. There was certainly more than two weeks of clothes here!

She intended to shower and change, then she'd put escape plan A into action.

"And what's that?" she asked herself as she stripped and stepped under the shower's steamy spray. But she had no answer. She just knew she couldn't let Zane dominate her again. She could handle her life by herself, but the thought of Lee Johnston turned her insides to ice.

Lolling her head back, she forced herself to relax. Warm rivulets of water ran down her shoulders and back. She closed her eyes and thought about Zane again, the power of his kiss flooding her senses.

Unconsciously she licked her lips and shivered deliciously at the memory of his mouth sliding seductively over hers.

Her eyes flew open, and she silently cursed her own weakness. Truce or no truce, she had to get out of here and fast. And it wasn't only because of the way in which he'd shoved himself back in her life. No, she realized fatalistically, she had to get away from him! Because, like it or not, he was right. It wouldn't take long before she might let herself fall in love with him all over again.

Chapter Six

Two can play at this game, Kaylie thought, buffing her body with a towel. If Zane intended to charm her to death, well, she'd just charm him right back, lead him to trust her enough to let down his guard.

And then she'd make good her escape, somehow leaving him high and dry, his plans foiled. A part of her yearned for that satisfaction; she was just plain tired of him trying to run her life, and yet she couldn't fault him completely. He was, or so he claimed, only looking out for her own good.

A breath of wind slipped through the window, and Kaylie shivered. Wrapping the towel around her body, she strode into the bedroom and surveyed it with new eyes. It was a prison, yes, but not a horrible place to stay. Zane could have made the accommodations much worse; as it was, she had a little freedom, which, she supposed, she should savor. He wasn't breathing down her neck twenty-four hours a day, and she wasn't sleeping with him. Opening the closet, she remembered how much she'd loved Zane in the past, how she'd trusted him with her life. In all truth, he'd saved her once before just as he thought he was saving her now.

Her eyes narrowed thoughtfully as she pulled a pair of stone-washed jeans and a peach-colored T-shirt from the shelf.

"Breakfast's ready," Zane whispered from behind her.

She nearly jumped out of her skin. Clutching the bath sheet around her, she turned to find him in the doorway. She'd been so lost in thought she hadn't heard him climb the stairs or push open the door. "Do you mind?" she asked, arching a lofty brow. "I'm trying to get dressed."

"Don't let me stop you," he drawled, an amused smile toying with the corners of his mouth.

"You're pushing it, Flannery," she warned.

He lifted his palms. "We agreed to a truce, remember?"

"Ahh. The truce. Don't you think we should set down some rules to this agreement? And I think the first should be that you quit sneaking up behind me and scaring the living daylights out of me." She tucked her towel more securely over her breasts. "I'll be down in a minute. And next time…knock, okay?"

He rubbed a hand around his neck and cast a devilish glance over his shoulder. "And miss seeing you like this?" He shook his head, and a lock of hair fell over his forehead. "No way. If you want privacy, next time lock your door."

She finished dressing and hurried downstairs where the scents of sausage and coffee wafted through the rooms. The kitchen table had been set for two, and a huge platter of eggs, sausage links and toast was steaming on the counter.

Zane waved her into a chair and poured black coffee into their cups. "I'll be right back."

"Where're you going…?" But he was already out the kitchen door.

A few minutes later he returned carrying a portable television. "Where'd you get that?" she demanded.

One side of his mouth lifted cynically. "There you go again, hoping to get me to divulge my darkest secrets."

"I thought we had a truce," she reminded him.

He plugged the TV into the counter outlet, snapped it on,

then fiddled with the antenna. "We do. That's why I'm being so irresistible."

"So *that's* the reason," she remarked dryly.

"Aha!" he said, finally satisfied with the reception.

Kaylie heard the familiar lead-in music to *West Coast Morning*.

"Oh, no," she said, her appetite nearly forgotten as the camera closed in on Alan Bently's handsome face.

"There he is—your fiancé," Zane said good-naturedly, though Kaylie thought she saw a muscle tighten in his jaw. "What a guy! Look at that! Even his makeup is perfect."

"He's not my fiancé." Kaylie shot Zane a warning glance, just as Alan made eye contact with the camera.

"Good morning!" Alan said. His brown eyes didn't blink, and his smile seemed a little forced. "You may have noticed that Kaylie Melville isn't with us today," he said half-apologetically. "She won't be with us for the rest of the week as she was called away from the city for personal reasons...."

"I was *what?*" Kaylie cried, astounded.

"Sick aunt," Zane explained, fiddling with the dials at the bottom of the set.

"What?"

"Your aunt. Very ill. Needs care."

"I don't like the sound of this," she said, pinning him with a glare that was meant to bore holes through solid steel. "I don't even have an aunt!" She reached for a piece of toast and thought aloud. "So you must've told Margot something else. She wouldn't buy into the sick-aunt scenario."

"Nope. But your sister thought it was romantic that I was whisking you away to a private hideaway."

"You *told* her?"

"Of course I told her."

"Just wait 'til I see her again," Kaylie muttered, feeling betrayed by her own flesh and blood. Margot might not know it yet, but when Kaylie saw her again, there was going to be trouble. Big trouble! She ripped off a piece of toast and popped it into her mouth.

"Margot will probably defend me," Zane predicted. "In

fact, she said she wished some 'knight on a white steed would carry her away to some romantic hideaway.'"

"Oh, give me a break!" But Kaylie could almost hear Margot uttering those exact words. Whereas Kaylie had always been sensible when it came to men—well, men other than Zane—Margot had been the dreamer, the romantic.

"Besides, she's concerned about your safety and she let me know that she doesn't much like Alan."

"She *knows* how I feel about Alan. No two-bit scandal sheet would change her mind."

As Zane buttered toast and scooped eggs onto his plate, Kaylie turned her attention back to the set. Didn't Zane know that Alan wasn't her type? Even years ago, when they'd filmed *Obsession* together and Alan had shown some interest in her, Kaylie had told him in no uncertain terms to keep his distance. She had been married to Zane at the time, and she wasn't interested in a steamy off-camera affair with Alan or anyone else for that matter. In fact, she had been so head over heels in love with Zane that she had actually laughed at Alan's sleazy attempts at seduction. Fortunately, Alan had taken the hint. Long ago.

"Old Alan looks pretty comfortable without you," Zane observed, taking a bite. "He kind of glossed over your absence, don't you think?"

"What was he going to say?" she countered. "He's not exactly dealing with all the facts, is he?"

Zane stopped chewing. "When you and Alan did your last picture together, he was the one ranting and raving for top billing, higher salaries, a bigger dressing room."

"A lot has changed since we filmed *Obsession.*"

Zane's eyes darkened. "Amen." He shoved his plate aside, half his food uneaten, and touched the tips of her fingertips with his. "So if you're not involved with Bently, who is the man in your life?"

Her lungs grew tight, and she quickly pulled her hand away. "Why don't you tell me? You're the one who seems to know everything about my life." She wished he'd just drop the subject; she didn't want to admit that she wasn't romantically involved with anyone, nor had she been since Zane. The dates and publicized relationships over the past few years had never become serious. She hadn't let herself become involved with any one man. However, she wasn't about to tell Zane about her less-than-fulfilling love live. If Zane knew she was entirely unattached, the feelings hovering in the shadows would only intensify the emotions already charging the air between them. No, it was better if Zane thought she was involved with another man.

"There is something more I should tell you," he admitted, his finger slowly rimming his cup in suggestive circles.

Kaylie's throat went dry. "What?"

The honesty honing his features disarmed her, his fingers quit moving on the rim of his cup. "I've missed you, Kaylie. I've missed everything about you."

"Zane, please—"

"You wanted the truth, didn't you? Well, you're going to get it."

She watched as he shoved his chair back and walked to the window. Staring out, his rigid back to her, he said, "I missed coming home to you at night. I missed hearing you sing in the shower. I missed your lingerie draped in the bathroom, I missed your perfume on the pillows, the feel of your hair brushing my face at night, the way you kicked your shoes into the closet.... I missed..." He turned and stared at her, his expression pensive and tormented. "I missed you, Kaylie. All of you."

Her throat tightened, and for a second she thought the tears burning behind her eyes might spill. He sounded so sincere and a part of her longed to believe him.

"So...you've taken advantage of this...situation. Is that what this is all about?" she whispered, her voice shaky, her hands clenched so tightly around her napkin her fingers ached.

The muscles in the back of his neck tensed. "No." Without another word, he walked out the door and it slammed behind him with a bang.

Kaylie tried to eat but the food stuck in her throat. Her appetite was gone. Angrily shoving her plate aside, she attempted to think rationally, to tell herself not to fall under Zane's spell again, but the simple truth was that she still cared about him—maybe loved him.

"You're the worst kind of fool," she muttered, blinking back tears. She ran up to her room, snagged a jacket from the closet and struggled into boots that were a little too tight. Clomping back downstairs, she headed out the front door and nearly ran over Franklin, who, upon spying her, growled.

"I hope your bark is worse than your bite," she said, side-stepping the dog.

The morning air was crisp. Drops of dew glistened on the sun-bleached grass, and sunlight streamed through the trees, warming the ground in dappled patches. Craggy mountains towered over the forests, and a few stray clouds drifted lazily in the blue sky.

This place was a touch of heaven, she thought reluctantly, remembering Zane's description last night as he hauled her up here. And it did seem heavenly compared to her hectic pace in the city and the job she'd left. "The job you were hijacked from," she corrected herself. "Sick aunt, indeed!"

She stopped at the Jeep and checked to see if it was unlocked. But the shiny rig hadn't moved since Zane had parked it and the cellular phone was nowhere in sight. Every door, including the tailgate, was secured. The windows were rolled up and even the hood was latched. "Wonderful," she sighed, dusting her hands.

She headed around the corner of the house and down a gravel lane to several outbuildings. The first small building was locked, so she balanced on her tiptoes on a chunk of wood and brushed aside the dust which had collected on the windowpanes. Shading her eyes, she squinted into the darkened interior. This particular building was a storage shed of sorts. Bags of feed and drums of oil, wheelbarrows and rakes, chain saws and other tools were stacked against the walls. In her peripheral vision she saw movement—a shadow. She braced herself.

"Find what you're looking for?" Zane asked, propping one booted foot against the bottom rail of a fence. Franklin had linked up with him again and flopped down in the shade cast by the barn.

"Here, maybe this will help." He reached into his pocket, withdrew a key ring and tossed it to her.

Kaylie snatched the ring in midair. She couldn't believe he'd give her his keys. Now, if she could make it to the Jeep....

As if reading her thoughts, he extracted a second ring. "These are to the equipment," he said, jangling his keys in the air. Kaylie watched as sunlight glinted against the sharp piece of metal. "But those—" he motioned to the keys gripped tightly in her fingers "—will get you in and out of most of the buildings on the place. Just be sure to lock all the doors behind you."

The man was absolutely infuriating! "Oh, yes, *master*," she mocked. "And when I leave the room, I'll bow at your feet."

"That would be nice," he drawled, with the hint of a smile.

"You're insufferable and overbearing—and a bully to boot!"

Zane's smile disappeared. "Let's get out of here," he said, striding across the gravel that separated them and grabbing hold of her wrist.

"Sounds good to me. This wasn't my idea in the first place!"

"Then you won't object?"

"Me? Object to anything you say? Never!"

"That's more like it!"

Insufferable. That's what he was! But she didn't protest as he tugged on her arm. Though she had to half run to keep up with him, she let him pull her along the short lane to the barn she'd spied earlier from the den. The exterior of the old building was weathered, the metal roof rusted in places, but the fenced paddocks still held a few head of white-faced cattle.

Zane shoved on a huge door of the barn, and it creaked open. They stepped inside. The interior was dark. It smelled of horses and new hay, dust and cobwebs.

"Over there," he said, taking her arm and propelling her across the worn plank floor to the back of the barn where two horses, on the other side of the manger, stood, tails switching, bridled and saddled. "I thought we'd take a ride."

Kaylie cocked a brow. "And what makes you think I won't just take off?"

"On Dallas, here?" he asked, nodding toward a rangy bay gelding. "Not much chance. He knows when it's feeding time and no matter where he is, he hightails it back here."

The horse looked docile enough. Big brown eyes blinked as the gelding studied her without much interest.

"Unless you've taken a few riding lessons in the past seven years, you won't get two miles from this place on Dallas." He grinned deviously in the half-light. "Besides, even if you try, this boy, here," he said, hooking a thumb at a muscular chestnut stallion, "will catch you. Meet His Majesty."

She looked pointedly at him and deadpanned, "I thought I already had."

Zane's lips twitched. "He's second in command."

"Oh." Kaylie looked thoughtful. "Let me get this straight. I'm riding a horse named Dallas and you're on His Majesty?"

"You got it." Zane opened the stalls and led both animals out of the barn.

"Figures," Kaylie muttered, blinking against the sudden brightness as Zane shouldered open the door.

They mounted the horses and rode through a series of paddocks holding several other horses and a few head of cattle. The grass was dry, the ground hard, but still the animals grazed, plucking at the few yellow blades, flicking flies with their tails, or standing in the shadows of the nearby forest.

A few spindly legged foals hid behind their mother's rumps and one feisty white-faced calf bellowed as they passed. Zane, surprisingly, seemed relaxed in the saddle and Kaylie, not much of a horsewoman, pretended that it was second nature to sit astride a huge animal with a mind of his own.

"Where're we going?" she asked, shading her eyes and wishing she had thought to bring along a pair of sunglasses.

"To the ridge."

"Why?"

He glanced over his shoulder, and his gray gaze touched hers. "For the view."

Zane was riding a horse up to a ridge in the mountains in order to show her a view? If anyone had told her two days ago this would be happening, she would have laughed in his face. And yet she found Zane's newfound laid-back, get-away-from-the-rat-race attitude appealing.

The ride took nearly two hours as the horses picked their way up an overgrown trail. Kaylie's legs began to ache, and her eyes burned from squinting against the sun. She took off her jacket and tied the sleeves around her waist as Dallas plodded after His Majesty.

As she swayed in the saddle, Kaylie tried to find interest in the wildflowers sprinkled among the trees, or in the flight of a hawk circling high overhead, but her gaze, as if controlled by an unnamed force, continually wandered back to Zane. His dark hair shimmered in the sunlight and curled seductively over his collar. His shoulders stretched wide, pulling at the seams of his shirt. His sleeves were pushed over his forearms, exposing tanned skin, a simple watchband and a dusting of dark hair.

There was something earthy and masculine that surrounded him, an aura she found captivating. She noticed how his shirt bunched over the waistband of his jeans, the way his belt dipped in back as he rode.

Right now all she could think about was one man—the one man who had once been her husband, the man who had loved her so thoroughly she'd been sure no other could take his place.

Maybe no one could.

That thought caused her to draw back on the reins. Dallas sidestepped, snorting and prancing, his ears flicking as Kaylie eased up on the bit. How easy it would be to fall in love with Zane again. *If you're not in love with him already.* "No!" she cried, and Dallas reared.

Zane yanked his horse around. His face was grim. "What?"

"Nothing," she said quickly, feeling her cheeks flame as she settled her horse. "I—I just lost control for a minute."

She couldn't fall in love with him again! Wouldn't allow herself the painful luxury!

"You're okay?" He didn't seem convinced, and the concern in his eyes touched a forbidden part of her soul.

"Just fine," she answered with only a trace of sarcasm.

One side of his mouth lifted. "Good. We're almost there."

The path curved sharply north, and the tall pines gave way to a rolling meadow of dry grass. A creek cut into the dry earth as it raced downhill to pool in a lake that reflected the blue of the mountain sky.

Kaylie, as she slid from the saddle, couldn't help but be enchanted. "It's gorgeous," she murmured, looking past this little alpine valley and over the ridge, where mountains steepled and gray-green forests covered the lower slopes. Zane tethered the horses, and the two dusty beasts sipped from the stream.

"That's the house," he said, standing behind her and pointing over her shoulder. His sleeve barely touched hers, and yet she was all too aware of him, his earthy scent, the warmth of his skin, the clean, sharp angle of his jaw. He extended one long finger, and Kaylie was mesmerized by the tanned length of arm and hand stretched in front of her.

She followed his gaze and saw, far below, nearly obliterated by fir trees, the roof of the old log cabin.

"You know," she said, "I never saw you as someone who would retreat up here."

He glanced down at her, and his lips pressed tightly together. "I learned a few years ago that some things are more important than business."

Her heart nearly stopped beating. "Did you?"

"You taught me that lesson, Kaylie." The look in his eyes grew distant and guarded. Tension controlled his rugged features. "Seeing you with Johnston on the night of the premiere brought everything into sharp focus. Nothing mattered but your safety. But, of course, it was too late." She watched as his naked pain dissolved to a cynical expression. He swept his hair back with the flat of his hand. "But you've never understood that I only protected you because I loved you and I was afraid of losing you. And I drove you away—did the one thing I was afraid someone else would do.''

The air between them hung heavy with silence. Only the lapping of the water, the twitter of birds in the surrounding pines and the painful cadence of her own heartbeat broke the stillness. Kaylie knew the devastating grief of losing people she loved. Hadn't she lost her parents when she was young? And Zane had been there to pick up the pieces.

He leaned closer, so close that she saw flecks of blue in his gray eyes. ''Losing you was the hardest thing I've ever experienced.''

Kaylie's eyes burned. When Zane's hand slid upward and strong fingers wrapped around the back of her neck, she didn't resist, but tilted her face upward.

His lips brushed intimately over hers, and she parted her mouth expectantly.

The wind swept through the trees, soughing through the scented pine boughs. Shadows shifted in the sunlight as Zane's arms wrapped tightly around her.

Kaylie closed her eyes and tried to think of all the reasons she should push him away. But the pressure of his mouth on hers, the intimate caress of his tongue, the feel of strong fingers splayed possessively along her back were too seductive to ignore. With the sun warm against her back, she succumbed, winding her arms around his neck.

Desire surged through her, and she moved closer to him, felt his anxious thighs against hers. The sweet pressure of his arms wrapped around her and held her so close that her breasts were crushed and she could barely breathe.

Her feet left the ground. He carried her to a thicket of pines and laid her on a bed of needles near the water. Then he stretched out beside her and his lips found hers in a kiss that was hot and wild and filled with emotion.

His hands moved downward, sculpting each of her ribs, his thumbs brushing the swell of her breasts.

Kaylie moaned softly as her nipples hardened and a moist heat in the depths of her womanhood swirled. Lost in battling emotions, she clung to him, laid her head back and felt the warm moist trail of his tongue as he kissed her throat and tugged on her shirt, exposing more of her skin.

Her breasts ached for his touch, her body quivered in a need that was overpowering.

He rolled atop her, and the weight of his body was welcome, the feel of his skin against hers divine.

She ignored all the voices in her head that still whispered she was making an irrevocable mistake, and she wound her hands in his hair, then let her fingers trail down the strident muscles of his back and shoulders.

"Make love to me, Kaylie," he whispered against her ear, and she could barely think. Blood was pounding at her temples, desire creating an ache so intense, she only wanted release.

He stroked the front of her T-shirt, resting the flat of his hand over her pounding heart.

"You want me."

She stared up at him. His handsome face was strained, perspiration dotted his brow. Above him, branches shifted against the blue, blue sky.

"You want me," he said again.

"Y-yes." She couldn't deny what was so patently obvious. She ached for him, yearned for him, burned deep inside with a longing so intense, she could think of nothing but the feel of his sweat-soaked body claiming hers in lovemaking as savage as it was sweet.

"And I want you," he whispered hoarsely.

He wasn't lying. She could feel his hardness through his jeans, rubbing against her hips, causing a friction that seared to her very core. She moved with him and sighed when he pulled her T-shirt from the waistband of her jeans and reached upward, the tips of his fingers grazing her lace-encased nipples.

"Oh, Zane," she whispered, her mouth finding his as she arched closer, wanting more.

He kissed her again, then his tongue slid down the milk-white skin of her throat, past her breasts, to the sensitive flesh of her abdomen.

"Zane," she whispered, and he buried his face in her.

A strangled sound escaped his lips, his breath fanned against her skin, and when he dragged his head upward and met her gaze, his eyes were glazed and stormy, as if he were fighting an inner battle that tore at his soul.

She reached upward to clasp her arms around his neck and drag his lips to hers, but he grabbed her hands. "Don't," he said, clenching his eyes shut and sucking in a swift breath.

"Zane?"

"Just don't!" The skin across his cheeks was stretched taut, and he dropped her hands, pushing himself upright. He swore violently.

"Is something wrong?" she asked as he rolled away, sitting with his back to her as he drew in long, steadying breaths.

"Everything."

"I don't understand."

"Don't you?" He twisted around, facing her again. "I intended to seduce you, Kaylie. I've planned it ever since I knew we'd be together again."

She could barely keep her eyes raised to his.

"But it's not enough."

"What—?"

"Physical lust isn't enough," he explained, the brackets near the corners of his mouth showing white. "It has to be more!" His fist pounded the dusty ground and he swore at himself between clenched teeth.

"But—I mean, I thought—"

"I know what you thought. And you were right. I planned to have you—right here and now. But I need more than a quick, hot session in the forest, Kaylie!"

She gasped and blushed to the roots of her hair. "I don't understand—"

"Sure you do. I want it all." He pulled her close to him, roughly jerking her against the rock-hard wall of his chest. His face was warm and close, his breath scented with coffee. "Let's go—"

"But—"

He whistled for the dog and climbed onto his mount. Kaylie

straightened her clothes, confused and bereft and feeling like a complete fool. Good Lord, she'd nearly made love to him and he'd rejected her!

She gathered up Dallas's reins, and slapping the leather against the gelding's withers, she wondered how she was ever going to survive the next few days being trapped up here alone with Zane.

Chapter Seven

"It's just not like Kaylie to leave us in the lurch like this," Jim Crowley, producer of *West Coast Morning,* grumbled. He stepped over the thick camera cables as he made his way off the cozy set, which was designed to look like the living room in one of San Francisco's charming row houses.

He headed down a short hall to his office, with his assistant, Tracy Montclair, following one step behind.

"Even Kaylie Melville has a personal life, you know," she pointed out.

"All of a sudden? In the past six and a half years, Kaylie hasn't missed one show. Not one. This just isn't like her." He shoved open the glass door to his office and stalked to the desk.

The ashtray was overflowing, and he dumped the contents into a wastebasket, then settled into his creaky leather chair.

"Call that sister of hers—Marge, isn't it?"

"Margot."

"Whatever." Jim winced as a nerve in his lower back twinged, the aftermath from a game of racquetball. "Phone

Margot and see if there's a number where we can reach Kaylie.''

"Oh, come on, Jim. You're not serious, are you? She's with her aunt in a hospital somewhere, for God's sake!''

"Well, even hospitals have phone numbers." Jim tried to ignore his craving for a cigarette and unwrapped a stick of gum. "I need to talk to her. We've got a helluva schedule next week and I don't think Alan can handle it alone.''

"She may be back by then.''

"Well, let's not leave it to chance, okay?" He wadded the gum into a small clump and tossed it into his mouth just as there was a quick rap on the door. Through the glass he spied Alan Bently.

"I swear that guy's got radar," Jim muttered under his breath. Alan had the annoying habit of showing up every time his name was mentioned. "What's up?" he asked, as Alan slid into the chair next to Tracy's.

Alan flashed his thousand-watt smile. Though no longer a leading man, he still had an on-camera charisma that attracted the female viewers. "I just thought we'd better discuss the next couple of shows. Unless Kaylie gets back soon, we've got to rethink the format. Starting with Monday.''

Jim scowled. "Reformat? How?''

"Well, I assume I'll have to do all the interviews as well as the news." Alan leaned forward, resting his elbows on his knees, looking earnest as he proceeded to explain to Jim that he could host the hour format of *West Coast Morning* all by himself.

For Kaylie, the next few days were torture. Torn between her life in San Francisco and the excitement of this adventure with Zane, she alternately formed plans of escape and talked herself out of them.

She felt as if she were on an emotional battlefield. One minute they were at each other's throats, the next, waving the white flag.

Zane's office hadn't come up with any new information on Lee Johnston. "Ted" hadn't called again. Dr. Henshaw was still out of town, though Brad Hastings promised to visit him at Whispering Hills the minute he returned. He also had an appointment scheduled with the administrator of the hospital.

Zane's nerves were strung tight. He admitted that he felt useless up here, that he should be in San Francisco checking things out for himself, but at the mention of returning to civilization, he blew up. Kaylie was safe here—at least temporarily.

It almost seemed as if they were married again, except of course, they didn't go to bed together. And, as in their marriage, Zane was dominating the relationship.

Half the time Kaylie was furious with him, and yet she could feel her emotions swaying and she was softening bit by bit. Often in the past seventy-two hours she'd caught him watching her when he'd thought she wasn't looking, and she had noticed how he'd avoided even the briefest physical contact. That was the hard part—being so close to him and yet not touching.

During the days, they took horseback rides, mended the fence, worked on the house, took care of the stock, and Kaylie found herself fantasizing about Zane—remembering the good part of their marriage, the love that had been so special. In the evenings they talked, watched television, played cribbage or petted the dog. Franklin still wasn't crazy about her, but he accepted her and even thumped his tail on the floor when she walked into a room. And that was progress.

To her surprise, she discovered Zane had changed, just as he'd said he had—he'd mellowed with the past seven years, and she couldn't help wondering what life would be like now, were she married to him.

But that was an entirely irrational thought.

Now, as he knelt at the fireplace and laid firewood in the grate, she watched the pull of his jeans at his hips, the slice of skin that was exposed as his sweater inched upward. He glanced over his shoulder and motioned to the empty wood basket. "You could help, you know."

"Could I?" She laughed. Seated on the couch and swirling a glass of wine, she added, "And here I thought you were going to treat me to a life of leisure—you know, pamper me to death.''

"No way." He dusted his hands. "I thought you were a fiercely independent woman who wouldn't let any man treat you as less than an equal."

"Well, I am, but—''

"Then get some wood," he suggested, nudging the empty basket toward her with the toe of his boot.

"Slave driver," she whispered, taking a last swallow of wine. "You'll pay for this, Flannery." Smiling good-naturedly, she grabbed the basket and marched out the front door.

"I don't doubt it," he called after her.

Outside, a cool breeze swept over the mountainside and a thin stream of moonlight guided her. A few stars winked jewel-ellike in the black sky and an owl hooted from a nearby stand of pine. The wind picked up, and the air was heavy with the promise of rain.

Kaylie walked past the Jeep and noticed that the interior light was on.

Her heart skipped a beat.

She reached for the door, and it opened.

She hesitated for a second. This was her chance, but did she really want to leave? She chewed on the inside of her lip and glanced at the house. Of course she had to leave—she had no choice! As long as Zane tried to control her, she had no will of her own. And she was falling for him again. That was dangerous.

Swallowing hard, she dropped the basket and slid into the interior, realizing that she didn't have his keys. Crossing her fingers, she silently prayed that he'd left the keys in the ignition. No such luck. Even though Zane had made several trips carrying grain from the storage shed to the barn in the Jeep, he hadn't forgotten his keys. Nor the phone. It, too, was missing.

"Damn!" she muttered, sneaking a glance at the house. Light spilled from the windows but she couldn't see Zane. It didn't matter. He was busy with the fire. He wouldn't miss her for a good five minutes. But how in the world did one go about hot-wiring a car?

"Think, Kaylie," she said, deciding that she had to look behind the ignition and try to find two wires that when touched, would create an electrical charge. Or at least that's what she guessed. It seemed logical. And she didn't have time for any other speculation. It was now or never. Do or die.

She lay on the driver's seat, her head under the dash, eyeing the wires that ran every which way. Biting her lip, she tugged gently on a tangled group that seemed to feed into the ignition switch. There was a red wire and a black one—if she pulled them out of the dash, unwrapped the plastic coating, then touched the wires…?

Hopefully she wouldn't detonate the engine or shoot herself into orbit, she thought ruefully.

She pulled on one of the black wires.

A low growl erupted from the woods.

Kaylie's heart leaped to her throat.

"Don't tell me. You've decided to take a crash course in auto mechanics," Zane guessed, his voice so soft she barely heard him. But Franklin, lurking in the shadows, barked loudly.

She froze, dropping the wires as if they were indeed hot.

Feeling like a fool, she tilted her head so that she could see him, and took the offensive. "I think I've already mentioned your vile habit of sneaking up on people." She pinned the dog with her glare. "The same goes for you."

Franklin wagged his tail, proud of himself, and Zane threw back his head and laughed. "And you, Ms. Melville, have a *vile* habit of trying to run away." He eyed the interior of the Jeep, and his mouth quirked. "So you were trying to start the Jeep without the aid of a key. Well, don't let me stop you." Gesturing grandly to the dash, he swallowed an amused smile. "Go right ahead."

"And have you stop me the minute the engine turns over?"

"A risk you'll have to take."

Her temper started to soar. What she wouldn't do to start

this damned Jeep and take off, leaving him in a spray of gravel.

Zane leaned his hip against the fender. "And of course, you could shock yourself while you're at it."

"I realize that!" Sitting upright, she slid out of the car. "If you're done belittling me—"

"And if you're done with this teenaged prank."

She shot him a withering glance. "Prank? After the stunt you pulled by kidnap—"

He held up a palm, and she clamped her mouth shut, determined not to break their fragile truce.

"I thought we'd gotten beyond that," he said, his brows beetling.

"I—we—I thought we had to," she said, knowing he didn't believe her. "But the opportunity to leave just presented itself. You can't blame me for—" She bit her tongue.

He grabbed her by the arm and propelled her toward the house. "Oh, no? Then who should I blame?"

"Yourself! For hauling me up here in the first place. It's been three days, Zane! Three days of being away from the real world!"

"And it's been great, hasn't it?" he said, pressing his face close to hers.

"Just spiffy," she shot back, not letting him know for even a second that he was right, that being here with him was a little touch of heaven.

He picked up her discarded basket and glanced up at the sky. "*I'll* go get the firewood. It's safer. You'd better go inside. It's gonna rain soon." Swinging the damned basket, he strode to the woodpile with Franklin trotting after him.

Later, once the fire was burning in yellow and orange flames, Zane left the room for a few minutes. When he returned, he was carrying a small tape player, a bottle of wine and two glasses.

"Okay, it's time to get serious," he said, uncorking the wine and pouring them each a glass.

"About what?"

"This." He punched a button, and the tape of his phone call with Ted started playing.

Kaylie couldn't take a sip.

"Does this sound like anyone you know, anyone you've ever met?"

"I—I don't think so," Kaylie replied, her skin crawling at the sound of the raspy warning.

"Think, Kaylie! This is important." Zane rewound the tape and played it again and again until Kaylie could repeat the conversation word for word.

"I don't know," she admitted, biting her lower lip.

Zane snapped the recorder off and plowed angry fingers through his hair. "Obviously Ted knows you and your connection with me. He also knows all about Whispering Hills and Lee Johnston. And he knows that you and I are together."

"He does?" she cried. "How?"

"You weren't on the show, but that doesn't necessarily mean that you were with me. However, the fact that Ted's quit calling makes me think he's got a line on us."

Kaylie's fingers slipped on her glass. She spilled wine on her pants, but quickly mopped it up. "A line—"

"Well, maybe that's a little drastic. Maybe he would've quit calling anyway. He only called a couple of times. But it's a coincidence and I don't believe in coincidence."

"So, what—what does that mean?" she asked, not feeling safer knowing that some other nut case might guess where they were.

"It means we stay put until Hastings gets some more information."

"Don't you think this Ted, if he's so smart, might find us?"

Zane frowned into his wine, swirling the glass thoughtfully. "I don't think so. Only a few people know I own this place."

"But he could find out." Fear strangled her. "Do you think Ted is Johnston?" she asked, her thoughts racing ahead wildly. "And that he placed the call to you, knowing that you would drag me up here?"

Zane shook his head, but his expression remained grim. "I doubt it. You were too visible in San Francisco. He could find you more easily. If he's going to be released, he wouldn't want to tip you off." His gaze moved from his glass to search her face. "Don't worry, I'll take care of you."

Surprisingly, that thought was comforting.

"But it would help me a lot, if we could figure out who Ted really is."

He played the tape again, and a headache began to pound at Kaylie's temples. She finished her wine and, before she began feeling too cozy and safe with Zane, set her glass on the coffee table. "I think I'll turn in."

She started to stand, but Zane placed a restraining hand on her shoulder. "Just remember one thing," he said, his voice firm.

"What's that?"

"If you try to escape again, I'll have to make sure that it doesn't happen. And that means I'll stick to you like glue."

Shrugging off his hand, she couldn't help but rise to the bait. "You'll have to catch me first."

"I know." One side of his mouth lifted, and his eyes glowed in the firelight.

She knew then that she loved him with all of her foolish heart. And if she didn't leave him soon, she never would be able to. She would have to give up her freedom and independence for the sake of love.

She hurried upstairs to her room. "Oh, Zane," she whispered, her throat aching. She had no choice but to escape— for both their sakes.

Zane drained his glass and wondered how long he could keep up this charade. Soon he would have to go back to the city and he couldn't, even in his wildest fantasies, keep her locked away forever. Tomorrow morning she'd miss another taping of her program and sooner or later the producer would start checking. Margot wouldn't be able to keep Crowley at bay forever.

And he couldn't force Kaylie to love him.

That thought tore open old wounds. He'd lost her once, and

the surest way to lose her again was to keep imposing his will on her.

Absently, he flicked on the tape again, and Ted's hoarse voice filled the room. "Who are you?" Zane said aloud. "Just who the hell are you?"

And what about Johnston?

An icy knot curled in his stomach. Maybe this Ted character was wrong. Surely the courts wouldn't set a psychotic like Johnston back on the streets. But it had happened time and time again. He shivered inside. He loved Kaylie; he'd never stopped. But he wasn't going to sacrifice her life for any-thing—not even for a reconciliation. So, if it meant Kaylie would hate him for the rest of her life, so be it. At least she would be safe.

Or would she?

Even here, Zane wasn't completely at ease.

He walked outside to a shed where he kept his phone and, despite the late hour, dialed Brad Hastings. Something had to happen soon. He couldn't keep Kaylie up here forever.

Kaylie didn't waste any time. The situation was intolerable. She was getting in much too deep with Zane, and she'd have to leave him soon, or she'd never find the willpower. As for Lee Johnston, she'd take care of herself—hire a bodyguard if necessary.

A bodyguard like Zane?

Her heart turned over and she had to fight the strong pull of emotions.

Upstairs she tossed a pair of jeans, her running shoes, a sweater and jacket over the end of the bed. She drew the covers to her neck and waited, listening to the sounds of the old house: timbers creaking, wind rattling windowpanes, clock ticking in the hall.

Go to bed, Zane, she silently prayed.

An hour passed before she heard his footsteps on the stairs. He paused at the landing, and she wondered if he'd check on her. How would she explain her clothes? The fact that she was still awake?

Chewing on her lip, her heart pumping crazily, she heard his footsteps retreat and the door to his room open and close.

She let out her breath. Now she could get started. She gave him a half hour to get to sleep, then fifteen minutes more for good measure. At a quarter to one, she slid out of bed and dressed in the moonlight streaming through her window.

Tucking her shoes under her arm, she headed in stockinged feet through her door and into the hallway. Her footsteps didn't make a sound, but her pulse was thundering in her brain.

Slowly she started downstairs, wincing on the third step when it creaked beneath her weight.

She waited, holding her breath, but Zane's door didn't bang open, so she hurried down the rest of the flight, picked her way through the living room to the kitchen, then dug in the pantry where she had discovered the old jacket and flashlight. Carefully she switched on the portable light and was rewarded with a steady, if pale, beam.

Good enough, she thought, unlatching the back door and slipping outside. She closed the door behind her, slid into her Reebok tennis shoes and, using only the faint light from a cloud-covered moon as her guide, made her way to the barn.

Inside, the horses snorted and pawed at the stalls. "Shh," Kaylie whispered, flashing her light until she found His Majesty. "It's all right."

Dallas poked his silken nose over the stall door and Kaylie petted him fondly. "Not tonight," she whispered, feeling a little like a traitor. "Tonight I need speed. I can't take a chance that you-know-who will catch me."

With surprising quickness, she bridled and saddled His Majesty, then led him from the barn. He danced and minced as the wind rushed through the trees, and Kaylie felt the first drop of rain fall from the sky. "Oh, great," she murmured. She tried hard to disregard the fact that she wasn't horsewoman enough for him if he were spooked.

His hoofbeats seemed to echo through the night as she unlatched the main gate and guided him through.

She had no idea where she was going, but intended to follow the long lane until daylight. Hopefully, by then, she'd find a crossroad or two and be able to lose Zane, because, if and when he caught up with her, all hell would break loose.

She didn't pause to consider the consequences of his wrath now. Instead she swung into the saddle and shoved her heels into His Majesty's sides. The horse picked up speed, trotting down the drive as the cold wind rushed against her face.

Kaylie squinted in the darkness, hoping beyond hope that His Majesty had some vague idea where civilization would lie, because she didn't.

The sky was dark—no bright lights over the hillside guiding her. Nope, this time she'd have to let common sense and her mount's instincts lead the way. *And I need a little luck,* she thought with an inward smile as she shone her flashlight toward the sky and caught the reflection of heavy cable. She'd follow the electricity and telephone wires. Eventually, she reasoned, the cables would lead to civilization.

The road was steep, the switchbacks hairpin curves, but His Majesty picked his way along the gravel without faltering. Kaylie, tense, forever listening to the sounds of the night, prayed that Zane would sleep in and not wake until after nine. By that time she'd be well on her way to San Francisco. Clucking her tongue, she encouraged the stallion to pick up his pace as rain beat down in a steady drizzle.

She'd ridden for nearly an hour before she came to the first road of any significance. Her shoulders had already begun to ache, and her fingers and cheeks were slick with rain. "Okay, boy, what do you think?" she asked, patting the chestnut's sleek neck and frowning when she noticed the wires overhead were strung in both directions. One way would lead to a city, the other could lead to another isolated, and perhaps abandoned, house in the forest.

"Great," she mumbled to her disinterested horse. "Just fine and dandy!" No doubt Zane would expect her to head west, for that was the most likely way to reach civilization. And, blast it, she didn't have much choice as the mountains to the north and east were forbidding and there were no roads that led south.

"West it is," she ground out, refusing to think about the cold water seeping through her collar and running down her neck. She urged His Majesty forward, her ears straining for the sound of an engine behind them. But all she heard was the sigh of the wind, the steady drip of rain and the rhythmic plop of the stallion's hooves. Occasionally a rustle in the undergrowth would startle the horse as a hidden animal scurried through the woods flanking the gravel road. "Squirrels and raccoons and rabbits," she told herself. "Nothing bigger or creepy. No bats or snakes or cougars...."

As the night wore on, Kaylie shone her flashlight whenever there was a crossroads, but otherwise followed the road by using the thick power cables as her guide.

Lightning struck in jagged flashes that illuminated the distant hills for a few sizzling moments. His Majesty shied and reared at the eerie light and the growl of thunder as it echoed over the hills.

"Hold, on, boy." Kaylie's hands tightened over the reins. "Steady."

The night closed in around her, and she felt the silence of the woods, the breath of the wind against her fingers and bare neck, the cold damp touch of the rain. She considered turning back a couple of times, but pressed on. Being with Zane was just too dangerous. Some women were cursed to love the wrong men. She just happened to be one of them.

Eventually, the road grew less steep. Kaylie's heart soared. She closed her eyes and thought she heard the hum of traffic on a faraway interstate. Or was it the rattle of a train on distant tracks? No matter. It meant she was approaching some sort of civilization.

Suddenly His Majesty tossed back his head and snorted violently. Stopping short, he rolled wide, white-rimmed eyes backward. His nostrils distended, and his wet coat quivered under her hands.

"Hey, whoa—" The hairs on the back of Kaylie's neck rose as her mount minced and sidestepped. "What is it?" she whispered, hoping she didn't convey her fear to the horse.

She shone her flashlight ahead, and its tiny beam landed on

Zane, half lying on the hood of his Jeep, soaked to the skin, his back propped by the windshield, his arms crossed over his chest, his expression positively murderous.

"Oh, God." Kaylie's heart plummeted.

Lightning flashed over the hills, and His Majesty reared, but at the sound of Zane's voice, the horse quieted, nickering softly.

"Well, well, Ms. Melville," Zane drawled in a tone so low and angry it rivaled the distant thunder, "I was wondering when you'd finally show up."

Chapter Eight

"But how—" Kaylie sputtered, shivering as she stared past Zane to the road beyond. Maybe she could make a run for it—or maybe His Majesty could find a path through the woods, a path the Jeep couldn't follow....

"Don't do anything crazy," Zane warned, shoving himself upright and hopping to the wet ground. "And the way I found you is simple. Most of the side roads around here are old logging trails—roads that crisscross over the mountain but eventually end up here. I knew if I waited long enough, you'd turn up."

"You heard me leave?" she asked, swiping at a drip of rain on the tip of her nose.

"Take my advice—don't apply for a job with the CIA."

"You tricked me!"

"No, you tricked me." He strode over and reached for the bridle, but she pulled hard on the reins and His Majesty's broad head swung away from Zane. Kicking sharply into the stallion's sides, Kaylie tried to spur past Zane, but he was too quick.

With an oath, Zane sprang like a puma and grabbed hold of

the reins, ripping the wet leather straps from Kaylie's chilled
fingers. "That was a stupid thing to do! Even worse than trying
to hot-wire the Jeep!"

A ragged streak of lightning scarred the sky.

The horse reared, and Kaylie, thrown off balance, grabbed
wildly at the saddle horn and His Majesty's wet mane.

"Whoa—slow down." Zane soothed the stallion, murmuring
softly until the anxious beast slowly relaxed. "That's it, boy."
Zane patted the chestnut's shoulder.

Kaylie, her hair tossed around her face, accused, "You pretended to be asleep! You heard me leave and you followed
me!"

"Of course I heard you leave. Do you think I'd trust you
after I caught you tampering with my ignition?"

"Tampering?" she repeated, furious and cold and hurt. "I
was just trying to regain my freedom—you know, one of the
basic constitutional rights guaranteed to every citizen!"

"I've heard this all before."

"Well, you're going to hear it again!"

"Get down, Kaylie."

"No way."

"Get down. Now!" he roared.

"You have no right to order me around!" she yelled, tossing
her head imperiously.

"Probably not," he admitted, "but it's late and I'm tired and
wet. Now let's go home."

"That log monstrosity is *not* my home!" she shot back, frus-
trated and angry that he'd caught up with her twice. Why, when
it was so hard to leave him, didn't he make it easy for her and
just let her go?

"Not your permanent home maybe, but for now—"

"Don't you know I'll hate you forever for this?" she hurled
down at him, glaring.

Moonlight washed his face, and a sliver of pain slashed
through his silvery eyes. "So hate me," he replied, his mouth
tightening at the corners. "But while you're hating me, get
down." When she didn't budge, he glanced up. "Okay, have
it your way. You can ride His Majesty all the way back in this

damned rain while I lead him in the Jeep, or you can enjoy the relative comforts of a heater, radio and padded bucket seats. Your choice.''

"Get in that Jeep with you?" she challenged, though it did sound inviting, and she wished for just a second that loving Zane were simple. "That's what got me into this mess in the first place!''

"Fine." He tugged on the reins, and His Majesty followed docilely.

"Traitor," Kaylie whispered to the horse, and Zane rolled down the driver's window, climbed into the Jeep and fired the ignition.

His Majesty sidestepped. Kaylie patted the stallion's sleek neck. "It's okay," she said, lying, as Zane rammed the vehicle into gear.

"Last chance," he called, and Kaylie, though she longed to climb down from the saddle and sit in the warm interior of the Jeep, didn't move. Zane shook his head in disgust as the rig crawled slowly forward.

Kaylie grabbed hold of the saddle horn as His Majesty started the long trek back at a fast trot. The brisk pace jarred her, and the cold, wet air seeped through her jacket, but she'd be damned if she'd complain! Gritting her teeth, she tried to keep her mind off her discomfort, though her muscles were already aching, her teeth chattering.

As the incline grew more steep, Zane slowed, letting the horse walk. Kaylie was chilled to the bone, and her arms and thighs burned mercilessly, but she refused to call out and ask Zane to stop. Rain dripped down her nose and neck. Clenching her teeth, she endured the painful journey, head high, jaw thrust forward.

After about twenty minutes, Zane muttered something unintelligible, then stood on the brakes. The Jeep ground to a halt in the gravel and mud. "This is insane," he growled, opening his door and splashing through the puddles to His Majesty's side. "Maybe you don't give a damn about yourself, but you could give the horse a break!"

He pulled her from the saddle, and she landed on the ground

so hard, her knees nearly gave way. Zane kept a strong arm around her. "A little wobbly?" he mocked, but there was a kindness in his features as he helped her to the Jeep. And the rain seemed to soften the hard lines surrounding his mouth. He touched her forehead, shoving a wet strand of curling hair from her eyes. "Come on, Kaylie," he whispered, his voice so tender it nearly broke her heart, "give it up for the night."

"I—I can't," she stammered.

"Sure you can."

"But—"

"Please, love," he insisted gently, opening the door. "It isn't worth it."

"How would you know?"

He rolled his eyes, and a self-effacing smile tugged at the corners of his mouth. "When it comes to stubborn pride," he admitted, "I think I wrote the book."

His unexpected kindness pierced her pride. Tears filled her throat, and she had to grit her teeth to keep from crying as he gently lifted her into the Jeep. She sagged against him. The warmth of him, the fact that he so obviously still cared for her, perhaps loved her, caused more tears to burn in her eyes. She wanted to cling to him and never let go. Inside the Jeep, she could barely stretch out her cramped, cold muscles.

Before he slid behind the steering wheel again, Zane unsaddled the horse and tossed the saddle and blanket into the back. He found a clean, thick towel, and a worn sheepskin jacket. "Here, dry off a little," he said, handing her the jacket and towel and turning up the heat as he shoved the rig into first.

Kaylie glanced his way as the vehicle rolled forward. Blotting her face with the towel, she leaned her head back against the seat and tried to ignore the cramps in her shoulders and legs as she fought back tears and the overwhelming urge to fall against him and be held and comforted; to let him take control.

His narrowed eyes were trained on the winding gravel road. Every so often he would glance in the side-view mirror, checking his stallion. It was romantic, in a way, she thought, how he kept chasing her down, swearing to protect her, saying he loved her. If only she dared believe him...trust him a little...love him a lot.

"Did you really think you could get away with it?" Zane asked, as the silence grew thick around them and the gloom of the forest seeped into the interior.

Shivering, she rubbed her arms, trying to keep her teeth from chattering. "I thought it was worth a shot."

"You cold?" He worked with the knobs of the heater, then, still driving, eased out of his own jacket and laid it across the blanket. "I'll probably end up taking you to the hospital."

"I'll be fine," she replied, still chilled to the bone.

Zane sighed. "And what would you have done if you had, by some miracle, found the freeway? Ride the horse down four lanes?"

"No," she said, her spine stiffening involuntarily, "I intended to stop at the first house and call."

"Whom?" he asked.

"Jim maybe—or Alan. Not Margot since she's in cahoots with you."

"And what would Alan have done?"

"Rescued me!"

"Ha!" He barked out a laugh and twisted hard on the wheel. "So now you want to be rescued?"

"No, I just want my life back," she said, staring out the window and watching the wipers slap away the rain.

"A life without me."

She drew in a steadying breath and tried to lie, but couldn't. The words stuck in her throat. She didn't want him completely out of her life—not anymore. And that was the problem. There was no letting Zane in a little bit. With him it was all or nothing. "All" meant giving up her hard-fought independence. "Nothing" meant never seeing him again. Her heart squeezed painfully at the thought. These past few days had been exhilarating and romantic, and her life back in the city seemed colorless in comparison.

"I thought Alan didn't mean anything to you."

"He's a friend. A co-worker and a friend."

He snorted and fiddled with the heater as the windows began to fog. "So what about us?"

"I don't know what to do about us," she admitted, her emotions as raw as the dark night. "Part of me would like to see you burn in hell for what you've put me through."

"And the other part?"

She slid him a glance. "The other part tells me you're the best thing that ever happened to me."

Zane drew a slow breath, then smiled painfully. "I definitely think you should listen to part two."

"How can I," she asked, turning to face him, "when all you've done since you showed up at my house is bully me into doing things your way?"

The honesty in her eyes cut deep into his soul. He knew that he'd gone too far. But now there was no turning back. He'd considered letting her leave, pretending not to hear her sneak out of the house and into the barn. But what then? Let her show up in San Francisco with his horse and never see her again? The thought was unbearable. "I'll let you go, Kaylie," he promised, forcing the words through his teeth. "Once I'm assured that you'll be safe." He swallowed with difficulty and almost tripped over the lie. "That's all I really want for you."

As the rain stopped, he turned off the wipers and checked the side mirror. His Majesty was tiring. "I think we'd better pull over for a little while," he said, frowning. "Give the old guy a break. He's had a hard night."

"Haven't we all?" she said, but climbed out of the Jeep when it slowed to a halt. Both she and Zane checked the horse, who was sweating and starting to lather. Zane walked him slowly for a while, until the stallion's heavy breathing returned to normal. Zane slanted a glance at Kaylie, and his gut twisted.

She caught his gaze, and her lips moved a little—so seductive and innocently erotic. He wondered how much more of this self-induced torment he could stand.

Time seemed to stand still as they stood, not touching, gazes locked, the earthy, rain-washed forest surrounding them.

"We'd better get going," he said, his voice gruff.

She glanced away, breaking the spell. Nodding, she replied, "I'll lead His Majesty."

Zane didn't argue. Once she was safely inside the Jeep, he handed her the reins, then climbed behind the wheel. The rest of the ride was tense and excruciatingly slow. Several times his fingers, gripping the gearshift, brushed against her knee, and she looked sharply up at him, but there weren't accusations in her gaze. If anything, there was an unspoken invitation.

Zane's fingers tightened over the wheel, and he thought he'd go out of his mind battling the urge to stop, take her into his arms and make love to her right then and there!

Finally, after agonizing minutes, he steered the vehicle around the final corner, and the log house loomed in the darkness ahead.

"I'll take care of the horse," he said as he parked the rig and looked long and hard at Kaylie. "And you should take a hot bath, drink something warm and then find the heaviest nightgown in the closet and wrap yourself up in about a thousand blankets." She reached for the door, and he couldn't let her escape. He grabbed her and pulled. She fell against him. As she did, he covered her mouth with his, pressing hard, insistent lips to hers and surrendering to the emotions that had warred with him ever since he'd seen her walking out of the water on the beach in Carmel.

His blood thundered, his body burned, and all those vows he'd sworn to himself—vows to stay away from her until she was ready—vanished.

She seemed to melt against him, her supple lips responding, a quiet moan escaping her throat. "Why?" he rasped, when he finally lifted his head from hers. "Why do you continue to fight me?"

"Because you fight me," she responded, eyes glazed as she slowly disentangled herself. "And that's what it is with us—a battlefield—your will against mine. It's always been that way, always will be."

She opened the door and stepped into the darkness, and Zane, wishing the throbbing in his loins would subside, struggled out of the Jeep. Pocketing his keys, he said, "I'll only be a few minutes."

She stared at him with wide, vulnerable eyes, then hurried into the house.

He should have just let her go back to the city, he realized, knowing that he couldn't hold out much longer. Sooner or later, he'd give in to the demands of his body, and then... Oh, God, then who knew what would happen?

There was a good chance that he'd lose her forever.

"If you haven't already," he reminded himself grimly. With a gentle tug, he led the tired stallion to the barn.

Kaylie kicked off her soiled clothes and made a beeline for the shower. She let the hot spray soothe her throbbing muscles and loosen her sore joints, while the warm water restored feeling in her fingers and toes. She felt as if she'd been in the saddle for a millennium.

"As a pioneer woman you're a failure, Melville," she said, chiding herself as she squeezed water from a sponge and lathered her body. "And as a modern woman, you need some lessons on the male of the species." What was wrong with her? she wondered, twisting off the faucets and snatching a bath towel from the rack. Every time Zane touched her or kissed her or looked at her, she turned into jelly.

"Don't let him know that," she warned her reflection as she rubbed away the moisture from the mirror. "You're supposed to be strong, independent and in control!" But the green eyes staring back at her accused her of the lie. When it came to Zane, whether she wanted to admit it or not, she was in love. Always had been.

"And you're a fool," she whispered bitterly, toweling dry her hair.

She flung open the closet door and picked out a white cotton nightgown and a robe.

She'd go downstairs, get something to eat and then try to get to sleep. Right now, she knew that sleep was out of the question.

She started downstairs, only to stop short at the doorway to

Zane's room. The door was open a crack, and she could see him, standing in front of the mirror, wearing only low-slung jeans.

His eyes caught hers in the reflection, and the look he sent her stopped her breath somewhere between her throat and lungs. "I thought you were going to rest," he said.

"I'm not tired."

He cocked a disdainful brow. "You should be dead on your feet."

"Nope," she replied, hoping to sound chipper, though she had to stifle a yawn.

Turning to face her, he smiled, a small, lazy grin. "So, how're you going to plan your next escape attempt?"

"Next time it won't just be an attempt," she replied, unable to resist teasing him.

"Oh?" One dark eyebrow cocked in interest. He crossed the room and held the door open. "So next time you'll dupe me."

"That's right."

"I can hardly wait," he drawled, baiting her.

"Oh, you won't have to wait long," she promised, though she had no idea how she'd ever pull it off.

"No?" His eyes narrowed speculatively, and Kaylie could feel the air charge between them. "You know, Kaylie, I wonder about all those reasons you concoct to go back to San Francisco." He studied his nails. "The job, the empty apartment, your co-worker, that all-fired important life."

"It is important."

"No doubt, but I think there's another reason you can't wait to make tracks out of here." He looked up at her and his gaze was so intense, she could barely breathe.

"And what's that?" she asked, swallowing hard.

"I think you're afraid of me—or at least of being alone with me."

"That's silly."

"Is it?" His gaze accused her of the lie. "I think you're less afraid of dealing with that madman who would like to slit your throat than you are of facing your real feelings for me."

"My feelings?" she asked, licking her lips in unwitting invitation.

"Right. I think you're afraid that if you stay here too long with me, you won't have the willpower to leave."

Though his guess was close to the truth, she laughed nervously. "You always did have an incredible ego."

His smoldering look accused her of the lie. She knew he was going to kiss her. In the intimate room, alone in the wilderness, he was going to take her into his arms and she wouldn't be able to resist. "Please, Zane, if you care about me—"

"I do. I told you that. I also told you that I love you."

"Then, if you love me, take me home."

He hesitated, pain shadowing his eyes. "This is home, Kaylie. You and me together—that's home."

"Not anymore, Zane," she said, forcing the words out. "And never again."

"You're kidding yourself."

"I—I think you're the one doing the kidding."

"Am I?" His expression darkened, and the lines around the corners of his mouth grew tight. He grabbed her wrist and slowly tugged, pulling her toward him. Deliberately he lowered his head, until his lips hovered over hers. "I can't leave you alone," he admitted hoarsely, his face only inches from her, his breath stirring the wet strands of her hair, his gaze moving to the pout of her lips. "Damn it, I want to, but I...just...can't." He tugged on her arm, and his mouth claimed hers in a kiss that burned deep into her heart.

Though a thousand reasons to run flitted through her mind, her love for him still lingered. His lips were warm, his body, hard and long, his arms strong. Tilting her head upward, she wrapped her arms around his neck and kissed him with all the pent-up desire she'd tried so desperately to suppress. Lost in the wonder of his male body pressed urgently against hers, she didn't stop him when one hand tangled in her hair, the other splaying possessively against her back. He kissed her throat and eyes and cheeks, and she tingled everywhere, aching for him.

Slowly he lowered her onto the bed and she didn't protest.

His tongue slid between her teeth, flicking against her tongue, causing thrills to chase up her spine.

Her nipples grew hard, and dark peaks pressed against the thin cotton of her gown. Her breasts ached for his touch, and she moved intimately against him, rewarded by the feel of his hands slipping past the cotton, sliding the nightgown over her shoulder, exposing her white skin.

His thumb grazed her nipple, and she moaned. Zane lowered his head, suckling on the tiny dark bud, flicking it with his tongue, igniting her blood. Wanting so much more, Kaylie writhed against him. Impatiently his hands slid the nightgown over her other shoulder, baring both breasts.

With a primal groan he kissed both white mounds and buried his head in the cleft between them, alternately suckling from one, then the other.

"Oh, Kaylie," he rasped, kneading one soft mound as he kissed the other. "Don't ever stop." Slowly his hand lowered to the hem of her nightgown, his fingers grazing her thigh, skimming her skin that already felt on fire.

"Please…" she whispered.

He groaned, ripping the nightgown from her body and dropping to his knees, his hands on her bare buttocks as he touched her heated flesh with his tongue, kissing her breasts and abdomen and lower. Sucking in her breath, she leaned against him, her hands tangling in his hair as he explored and probed until she could think of nothing but the swirling hot void, a vortex of want, an emptiness only he could fill.

"I love you," he vowed, his hands still massaging her buttocks as he stood.

Oh, God, if she could only believe him. The words rang in her ears. But did he know that love and possession weren't the same? Could he learn?

Unable to resist, she boldly touched the waistband of his jeans. He made a primal sound deep in his throat, then tilted her head up to his. "Yes, love," he whispered, eyes glazed with passion.

She slid his jeans over his legs and he kicked himself free of them and wrapped strong arms around her middle. In one swift motion, he whirled her onto the bed and was lying over her, his gaze locked with hers, his tongue rimming her lips. "Just love me," he whispered.

"Oh, Zane, I do."

Closing his eyes for a second, he parted her legs with his and entered her swiftly. She sucked in her breath as he began to move, slowly at first, then with an ever-increasing rhythm that drove all thoughts from her mind.

She was here with Zane, making love, and that was all that mattered. They moved together, fusing, loving, spiraling upward and soaring above the clouds. Heaven and earth seemed to splinter before her eyes and she cried his name as she tumbled on a slow, heated cloud back to earth. "Zane, oh, Zane!"

"I'm here, love," he murmured into her hair. "I always will be."

"I know," she whispered, more content than she'd ever been, snuggling deep in his arms, resting her head against the soft mat of hair on his chest, listening to the loud cadence of his heart. This seemed so right, so perfect.

As afterglow finally faded, his lips found hers again and they made love—more slowly this time—exploring and touching, rekindling old fires that flamed and sizzled, becoming intimate as naturally as if they'd never separated.

Afterward, Kaylie sighed contentedly against him as he drifted into a deep sleep. Closing her eyes, she knew that she loved him. It was that simple. And that complicated.

Moaning, he rolled away from her, then sighed, still sleeping. His face, in slumber, was carefree, his mouth a soft line, his lashes dark against his cheek.

Kaylie touched his hair, and her heart nearly broke. Why was she doomed to love a man who was so smothering? Pressing a soft kiss to his lips, she rolled over, intending to fall asleep and deal with her feelings in the morning with a clear head. Maybe she and Zane could work things out. He was a reasonable man, and she was now a mature woman. If she only explained....

She noticed a reflection of moonlight on the floor—a dazzling flash of silver in the dark pile of his clothes. Her heart stopped when she realized that she was staring at his keys as they poked from the pocket of his jeans.

She closed her eyes for a second, wishing the vision away, but when she lifted her lids, the keys still lay there. Beckoning. Offering escape and freedom.

Her mouth turned to cotton.

Oh, God, she thought, shaking inside. Could she leave him? She glanced at his peaceful, trusting profile, tanned skin in relief against the white pillow, and her heart felt as if it were tearing in two.

She had no choice. She had to control her own life. She couldn't allow him to manipulate her.

Holding her breath and fighting tears, she slipped slowly from the bedcovers and silently picked up his keys. As her fingers closed around the cool metal, she hardly dared breathe. They jangled softly, but Zane just snorted and turned over.

For a few precious seconds Kaylie stood silently in the room, staring longingly down at Zane. If only they could love each other again—if only...but it would never work. Wasn't the fact that he kidnapped her proof enough that he always intended to force her will to his?

She couldn't let him control her! Her heart in her throat, she grabbed her clothes and sneaked out of the room.

She dressed quickly on the landing and fought the overpowering urge to run back to him.

Instead she slipped silently downstairs and outside. The air was fresh from the rain, and the first streaks of dawn illuminated the eastern sky.

Kaylie braced herself, then strode off the porch.

The Jeep waited for her.

Chapter Nine

Rick Taylor jabbed at a broken piece of pottery with his broom. Rolling his eyes, he cocked his head toward the patient, "He's been this way ever since Friday."

Dr. Anthony Henshaw rubbed his chin as he surveyed the damage in the small room. Books were thrown haphazardly on the floor, the desk chair was overturned, a bulletin board ripped from the wall, papers scattered on the floor and the pieces of clay pottery and dirt smashed against one corner. "What's the matter, Lee?" Henshaw asked the patient with the flaming red hair.

"He won't talk about it," Rick said, tossing the trash into a plastic bag. "But it started the other day during that show he watches, *West Coast Morning*. The woman who usually does the interviews—Kaylie whatever-her-name-is—wasn't on that day; out for 'personal reasons' the other guy said, and ol' Lee, here—" he cocked his head toward the patient again "—went 'round the bend. I've been cleaning up this room once a day."

Henshaw frowned. This didn't sound good. He'd just returned from a symposium in Chicago and discovered from Dr.

Jones that Lee Johnston had relapsed. "You miss Kaylie, Lee?" he asked, but the patient, sitting on the end of the unmade bed, didn't reply, just stared blankly ahead, hands clasped prayerlike on his lap.

Dr. Henshaw scratched his chin. Lee was a difficult case; always had been. He sat next to the patient. "Does it bother you when Kaylie isn't on the show?"

No reply, just a slight movement of Johnston's thin lips.

"Even people who work on television take vacations. They need time off, too."

"He's not talkin' today," Rick said, shaking his head as he restacked books and magazines in the bookcase. "Won't say a word. Not one. Not to me, nor to Jeff or Pam, either. If you ask me, he's waitin' for the show." Shoving the last book on the bottom shelf, he glanced over his shoulder at the doctor. "Let's just hope she's back. Then maybe Lee here will calm down."

Rick left the room, and Henshaw tried communicating with Lee, but to no avail. Quiet, but obviously still upset, Lee refused to acknowledge the doctor's presence. After ten minutes, Henshaw gave up. He had other patients to see and a staff meeting in half an hour.

Ramming his hands deep into his pockets, he walked down the long hallway, rounded a couple of corners to the administrative offices. His own cubicle was near the back, with one window and a view of the gardens.

Dropping into his chair, he scowled to himself. Johnston obviously still had problems. Henshaw doubted if the man would ever fit into society. Yet there was talk that he might be released soon. Aside from a few incidents like the trashing of the room, Lee had been a model patient.

Henshaw picked up a pen and clicked it several times. Then there was the matter of Johnston's privacy. Several people were interested in his case and wondered about his freedom. Henshaw had been called by Kaylie Melville's ex-husband often enough. The man was obviously still hung up on her. As, apparently, was Lee. And then there was Kaylie's costar, Alan Bently, a man who seemed always linked with her. There were even rumors of their engagement. Not that Henshaw cared. What she did with her life was her business—until it involved his patient.

Henshaw had met Kaylie a couple of times and even he, happily married for twenty-seven years, a proud father and grandfather twice over, understood a man's fascination with Ms. Melville. Whether she knew it or not, she had a way of stirring up a man.

The doctor shoved thin strands of hair from his face and set his glasses on the table. He rubbed his eyes and wondered how he could get through to Lee. With a long sigh, he decided convincing Johnston that his obsession was pure fantasy and in no way reciprocated would take a miracle. Lee had been obsessed with Kaylie for over seven years. Making Johnston believe that Kaylie had no interest in him would be no easier than walking on water.

Returning to San Francisco took hours. During the long drive through the mountains as the sun climbed higher in the sky, Kaylie felt more than one twinge of guilt. Gritting her teeth, she shoved the ridiculous feeling aside. She couldn't start second-guessing herself. Not now. Not after seven years of living without Zane.

Her throat grew tight at the thought of the love they'd shared, the passion that had rocked her to her very soul. She could still remember his whispered words of endearment, smell the scent of him clinging to her skin, see in her mind's eye his body lying across the bed.

Glancing into the rearview mirror, she noticed shadows in her eyes. "Oh, Kaylie," she said with a sigh, "forget him." Then, her lips twisting at the irony of it all, she murmured, "He asked to be left up there alone—he *deserves* it for barreling back into your life again!"

But she couldn't forget the fire of their lovemaking, the tenderness with which he kissed her, the passion he used to try and keep her safe.

He was wonderful and horrible, and she didn't want him out of her life. To forget about him, she flipped on the radio and tried to catch up on the news, yet she couldn't shrug off the guilt of leaving him high and dry. "Remember," she told herself, "*he* kidnapped you. You owe him nothing!" But the guilt remained.

She followed the highway signs west toward San Francisco. She'd have to return Zane's keys and Jeep to the headquarters of his security firm. When she squared off with Brad Hastings, Zane's right-hand man, she'd tell him where to look for his boss.

At that thought, she grinned sadly. Zane would be furious! But at least she'd finally gotten the better of him, even if her victory seemed somehow hollow.

Kaylie's fingers tightened around the steering wheel just as the deep green waters of the bay came into view. Sunlight spangled the surface, and the San Francisco skyline stretched to the sky.

Once in the city, traffic slowed and clogged the main arterials. Pedestrians crowded the sidewalk.

The Jeep climbed the city's hills easily, and she parked in the lot of her apartment building. She yanked on the emergency brake, then switched off the ignition. The parking lot was quiet save for the ticking of the engine as it cooled, and Kaylie was left with the empty feeling that she'd left something important—something vital—back at the log house in the forest.

"Don't be a fool," she snapped, locking Zane's Jeep and making her way to the elevator that would take her to her third-floor flat.

Inside, her apartment looked the same as it had when she'd left it last week, but the atmosphere in the rooms was different—cooler, somehow. Vacant. Though Zane had never lived here.

"You're imagining things," she chided herself, stripping off her clothes and heading for the shower. She needed to clear her mind, make a few calls, and then, when she was refreshed, tackle the issue of Zane again.

Smiling at the irony of it all, she imagined returning the Jeep and explaining to Brad Hastings that Zane was stranded. She stepped under the shower's steamy spray and relaxed. Yes, she decided, Zane, for his high-handedness, deserved everything she'd given him and more.

So why, as she washed, did she still feel regrets that their idyllic time together had come to an abrupt end?

As she dressed and dried her hair, images of Zane flitted through her mind. She listened to her answering machine. Several people had called including Alan, Tracy and Dr. Henshaw. Dialing Whispering Hills, she waited, her stomach knotting, for the receptionist to put her through to Lee Johnston's psychiatrist.

Eventually he picked up. "I'm sorry it took so long to get back to you," he said, explaining that he'd been out of town. Kaylie asked him point-blank about Johnston, and there was a pause on the other end of the line.

"You shouldn't have to worry about him for a long while," Henshaw said slowly.

The relief she should have felt didn't wash over her. In fact, Henshaw's pregnant pause caused her mind to race in a thousand questions. Zane was right—Henshaw seemed to be holding back. "How long?"

"That's for the courts to decide."

"Upon recommendation from you and the other doctors at the hospital."

"Don't worry, Ms. Melville. Lee's not going anywhere. Not for a long, long time, I'm afraid."

"Well, I think you should know someone is saying differently," she said, deciding that confiding in him wouldn't hurt. But he already knew about the two calls from Ted and he dismissed them as a "twisted petty prank."

By the time she replaced the receiver, she was reasonably certain that Johnston would remain at the hospital for a while, and yet she wasn't satisfied.

It's because Zane isn't here, a voice inside her head insisted as she punched out the number for the station.

The receptionist answered and put her through to the producer of *West Coast Morning.* "Kaylie!" Jim shouted, bringing a smile to her face, "about time we heard from you! How's that aunt of yours?"

Kaylie's face fell. How was she going to deal with Zane's intricate web of lies? "She's—uh, improving," Kaylie finally replied, deciding to keep Zane's kidnapping to herself—at least for a while. "Incredible recovery," Kaylie forced herself to say, inwardly cursing Zane. "I'm sorry I didn't call you myself—everything got really crazy...." At least *that* wasn't a lie.

"Not to worry. Margot explained everything."

Not quite everything. In Kaylie's estimation, Margot had a lot of questions to answer.

"We've missed you around here," Jim joked good-naturedly. "The show just hasn't been the same without you. And we've been getting a lot of calls. People wondering how you and your aunt are doing. You might have to bring it up on the show tomorrow. Viewers really get off on all that personal stuff."

The thought of lying on the air curled Kaylie's stomach. But Jim was right. "About those calls," Kaylie asked. "Did I get any from a guy named 'Ted'?"

"I don't think so. What is it with that guy? Someone else called about him. Tracy took the call." She heard a muffled noise as Jim placed his hand over the receiver and talked to his assistant. "She says that a guy named Hastings called—a guy who works for your ex. Is something going on?"

"Just a crank call," Kaylie said, quickly explaining to Jim about the threats, though he didn't seem overly concerned when she explained that Lee Johnston was still locked up.

"Another nut. I tell ya, this town is full of 'em," Jim said before the conversation ended.

She hung up the phone, grabbed her jacket and purse and headed out the door.

The offices of Flannery Security were located on the fifth floor of a building not far from the waterfront. Bracing herself, Kaylie pushed open glass doors and recognized the receptionist. Peggy Wagner was a plump woman, somewhere near fifty, with tight gray curls and wire-rimmed glasses. Peggy had worked for Zane forever.

"Mrs. Flannery!" Peggy cried, a smile gracing her soft features as she glanced up from her word processor. "Are you here to see Mr.—"

"Hastings. The executive vice president," Kaylie replied, hoping that the couple waiting on a low slung couch in the reception area hadn't overheard. Peggy never had been able to use Kaylie's maiden name. Apparently she still thought of Kaylie as Zane's wife.

"You're in luck. He's in," Peggy said, flipping a switch on an intercom and announcing Kaylie. "I'll walk you back." She ripped off her headgear and motioned to another woman at a nearby desk. "I'll be right back," she said, then guided Kaylie through a labyrinth of corridors.

At the end of one hall, Peggy knocked, then opened a door to a small office. The floor was hardwood, the desk oak and the rest of the furniture was expensive and neat, but far from opulent.

Peggy motioned to a pair of leather couches. "Just have a seat and he'll be with you in a moment. Would you like anything while you wait? Coffee or tea?"

"I'm fine," Kaylie replied, wishing Hastings would suddenly appear so she could explain how he could find Zane, then get out.

Peggy crossed the room again. "It'll just be a little while," she assured Kaylie as she closed the doors behind her.

Kaylie, rather than sit anxiously twiddling her thumbs, walked to the windows and stared through the glass to the city beyond. Skyscrapers knifed upward against a hazy blue sky, and a jet circled over the bay. Below, traffic twisted and pedestrians bustled along sidewalks.

The door clicked softly behind her.

Finally! Grinning to herself, Kaylie reached into her purse for Zane's keys. "I'm so glad you could see me," she said, turning, only to wish she could drop through the floor.

Zane was locking the door behind him.

Her heart slammed against her ribs as she stood face-to-face with him. The keys fell from her hand, and her mouth went suddenly bone-dry.

"Me, too," he replied with more than a trace of sarcasm.

His expression was dark and murderous, and every exposed muscle contracted tightly. His eyes were the cold gray of the barrel of a gun, and his lips were razor thin. He looked dangerous and coiled—like a whip ready to crack.

Kaylie gulped, but stood her ground.

"Surprised?"

"I think the word is thunderstruck," she said, hoping to make light of the tension crackling through the room.

"Well, I've got to hand it to you, Kaylie. You fooled me." His jaw slid to one side, and he shot her a glance from the corner of his eye. "I thought we were making progress, but you decided to take one last gamble. And it worked. Almost." He tossed his leather jacket into his chair and shoved the sleeves of his blue sweater up his forearms. His hair was still wind-tossed and wild, and his pallor had darkened with the quietly repressed fury burning in his gaze. "I guess I should offer you a job. You're the only person who's been able to pull one over on me in a long while."

Slowly he advanced upon her. "You lifted my keys, then stole my car—"

"I warned you, Zane," she said, refusing to back up, though she wanted to retreat desperately.

"Warned me?" He shook his head, and he was so close that the movement fanned her face. "That's a good one." The skin over the bridge of his nose was stretched taut, and his nostrils flared. Little white lines etched the corners of his mouth. He was furious—his eyes flared with savage fire, but she couldn't let him know that he frightened her at all.

"I trusted you," he said quietly.

"So that's why you had to keep me prisoner? Because of your 'trust'?" she tossed back at him.

His lips compressed. "We made love, damn it!"

"I—I know."

"And it meant nothing to you!" he charged, his rage exploding.

"No, Zane, I—"

"You slept with me, toyed with me, then the minute I let down my guard, you took off in the night, like some cheap…"

He let the sentenced dangle between them—unspoken accusations cutting deep.

"Like some cheap what?" she threw back at him.

"Oh, the hell with it!" His arms surrounded her suddenly, crushing her against him as he kissed her angrily, passionately, desperately. When he lifted his head, some of the fury had faded from his gaze. "What kind of a game are you playing with me, Kaylie?

"Me? Play a game with you?" she whispered as he searched her face.

"I thought last night meant something."

"It did."

"What?"

"That—that—there's still something between us," she admitted.

"And what's that?"

"I don't know, Zane!" she said in exasperation, her nerves stretched tighter than piano wires as he held her so close that she was all wrapped up in the warm feel and smell of him again.

"You deliberately tricked me!"

"And you deliberately seduced me!"

His lips twisted at that. "If I remember correctly, you seemed to enjoy yourself. And there might be some argument about who seduced whom?"

That much was true, she thought, wrenching herself free so that she could think clearly. Her heart was knocking painfully in her chest, her ears rang with the rush of her own blood. When she reached upward to push a strand of hair from her eyes, her fingers trembled so, that she balled her fist and crammed it into her pocket. "How did you get back here?"

His eyes narrowed. "A helicopter. Less than a mile from the cabin," he said, clipping his words. "I was back in the city hours ago!"

"I told you I'd escape—"

"Ahh! But you didn't warn me that you'd sleep with me to lull me into trusting you, did you?"

"You must have expected— Ohh!"

Snagging her wrist in his strong fingers, he pulled her roughly against him. "I didn't expect to be *used*, Kaylie. I didn't think you'd stoop so low as to go to bed with me just to get what you wanted."

"I didn't!" she declared furiously.

"You couldn't prove it by me."

She stared into his eyes and saw a flicker of pain, a shadow of just how deeply she had wounded him. Her heart wrenched painfully, and she wondered if all love were this agonizing.

"I trusted you," he whispered, his breath caressing her face.

"But I gave you ample warning, Zane," she said quietly. "I told you over and over again that I wouldn't be coerced, threatened, kidnapped or held hostage. But you didn't believe me, did you? You know, maybe if you'd just have asked me—invited me to spend a few days with you—things would have been different."

"You would have come with me?" he asked, one dark disbelieving brow arching skeptically. "Do you really expect me to believe that you'd give up your precious job, even for a week or two, to spend time with me?"

"Yes!" she cried. "If I would have thought there was any chance that we could have recaptured the good parts of our marriage. If I'd believed for an instant that we could create something wonderful again, I'd have come with you!"

"But you don't believe we can recreate that happiness, do you?"

She shook her head, her heart twisting. "You showed your true colors by kidnapping me, Zane. You'll never change. You'll always smother and overprotect and try to force me into doing everything you want."

"Like I forced you last night?" he whispered, and her gaze was drawn to his Adam's apple as he swallowed.

Mesmerized, Kaylie was vaguely aware that he smelled of soap and a cologne that brought back far too many memories of lying naked with him. She noticed the rise and fall of his chest. Only a few hours ago, she'd touched that chest, a chest that had been bare and taut, with strong, strident muscles and covered by a mat of dark, swirling hair.

When she glanced up, his features had softened. "Oh, Kaylie..." He sighed. "What am I going to do with you?"

"Nothing, Zane. *You* can't do anything with me. That's the whole point. It's not *your* choice. You don't own me!"

"I've never wanted to own you."

"That's not the way I remember it," she said, though she felt a flicker of doubt. For seven years she'd thought of her short marriage as a prison, but now she wondered if she had only been stronger during the time that she was Zane's wife, if she had stood up for her rights, would those prison walls have crumbled?

"You didn't stick around long enough to know, did you?" he flung back.

Stung, Kaylie said, "I think I'd better leave before we say things we'll regret."

"Leave. And what about Johnston?"

"I talked with Dr. Henshaw. Whoever this Ted character is, he's all wet. Henshaw assured me that Lee Johnston will be locked up for a long, long time."

"And you believe him?"

"The man has no reason to lie."

Zane's expression grew thoughtful. His fist clenched as he attempted to control himself. He didn't trust Henshaw. No, he put more stock in crank phone calls than medical opinion. "I should never have let you escape."

"*Let* me?" she mocked.

"I was crazy to trust you. To let down my guard." A muscle worked in his jaw. "You know," he said slowly, "I had the ridiculous idea that if you and I spent enough time alone together, we could work things out. No matter what it was, we could handle it."

"We didn't before," she reminded him.

"I know. But we're older—wiser, I'd hoped."

"More mature?" she pointed out sardonically. "Think about the past few days! Nothing we've done can qualify under the 'mature' category."

He shrugged. "I guess we haven't acted much like adults, have we?" Shoving his hands into the back pockets of his jeans, he added, "Maybe I was wrong. I thought there might still be a chance that you could love me."

Her throat closed. If only he knew. A tide of emotion swept over her, and she realized she had to get away from him and fast, while she still could. She picked up his keys from the carpet and dropped them onto the desk. "Goodbye, Zane," she said, and the words, as if barbed, stuck in her throat.

"Why are you always running from me?" he asked suddenly. "Do I scare you so much?"

She couldn't lie. "Yes," she said, her voice raw.

He closed the distance between them, and his lips crashed down on hers so swiftly, she gasped. Her breath was trapped in her lungs, and immediate traitorous heat fired her blood. He pressed her back against the door, and his thighs fit familiarly over hers, his chest crushing her breasts. Memories of the night before enveloped her, and desire swept through her bloodstream in wicked, wanton fury.

Her heart pumped gloriously, her blood rushed through her ears. She pressed her palms against his chest, intending to shove him away, but all her strength fled, and she found herself clinging to him instead.

When at last he lifted his head, his face was flushed, his eyes shining with a passion that seared right to his soul. "Dear God, why can't I get over you?" he rasped.

For the same reasons I can't forget you, she thought, but held her tongue. She tried to move, to slide away from him, but he trapped her.

His hands were pressed against the door, his arms blocking her escape. "Why, Kaylie?" he finally asked. "Why did you leave me?"

Feeling suffocated, she drew in a breath. "For all the old reasons."

His jaw grew tight, and any pain she'd seen earlier was quickly hidden. "Last night you weren't pretending," he said slowly, and one of his fingers traced the line of her jaw. "Last night you felt what I did. And yet you can ignore how good we are together, how we feel about each other and—" he touched her lips with one finger "—don't lie to me. I *know* you feel it, too. So how can you pretend that you don't care?"

"Because I can't care!" she said shakily, her hands scrabbling behind her for the handle of the door. Her fingers found cool metal and she shifted, tugging on the knob.

Zane didn't stop her. Instead he backed away. "Escaping again?" he mocked, bitterness tinging his words. "Maybe you should seduce me first so that I'll let down my guard."

"You bastard," she bit out, but shrank as if physically wounded.

"You certainly have grown up," he jeered.

"So have you," she replied, tugging on the door until it opened. Then she slid an icy glance his direction. "Goodbye, Zane," she said stiffly. Marching rigidly through the doorway, she told herself it didn't matter what he thought of her—she had a life of her own to worry about.

A life without Zane Flannery.

Chapter Ten

Zane slammed his fist onto the desk in frustration. The lamp rattled, a coffee cup rolled onto the floor, and his picture of Kaylie, a promotion shot for her second movie, toppled with a crash. The glass cracked, destroying the image of a smiling seventeen-year-old.

Her hair had been longer then, hanging nearly to her waist in luxurious golden waves, and her face had been more rounded, her cheeks fuller with adolescence, her green eyes filled with energy and the innocent sparkle of youth.

He'd fallen for her so hard, he'd felt as if the air had been knocked from his lungs. She'd been so young, so damned young, and he'd been hired by her agent as her bodyguard.

Now, running his finger along the crack in the glass, he remembered all too vividly how he'd come to love her. At first he'd resisted, of course, and she hadn't been aware of his changing feelings. But he, too, had been young, and keeping rein on his emotional downfall and charging lust had been impossible. He'd been with her constantly, to protect her, when, in fact, he'd often felt that he was the predator. He'd wanted her as he'd wanted no other woman, burning for her at night, hungering for her by day.

And though he'd sworn never to touch her, never to let her know that she was forever burning brightly in his mind, he'd succumbed at last, body and soul, foregoing his usually clear thinking and deciding that he wouldn't rest until he made her fall in love with him.

It hadn't been easy. Kaylie had as many reasons for not wanting him as he had for keeping his distance from her. But in time, all the walls disintegrated and they were married. And their marriage had ironically become the beginning of the end.

He frowned darkly to himself. She was right, he realized now, as he twisted a pen in his fingers and stared out the window. Clouds were rolling in from the west, converging over the bay, turning the murky waters as gray as his mood. He had been overprotective, near paranoid in his need to protect her.

He'd lost so many before. Both parents and his older brother had died in a mountain-climbing accident when he was twelve. Only he had survived, with injuries that should have killed or crippled him for life. But his mother's sister, Aunt Hilary, had been patient and caring and, with the reluctant help of her second husband, George, tried her best to raise him. George had referred to him as a teenaged hellion on wheels.

Four years after the mountaineering accident, a hit-and-run driver sideswiped Aunt Hilary's car, killing her instantly. At that point Zane dropped out of school, left home and joined the navy.

So when, years later, he'd fallen so hard for Kaylie, he'd been paranoid that he might lose her. In his efforts to keep her safe, he'd smothered her, and she'd demanded a divorce.

"Idiot," he ground out now, "damned bloody idiot." Shaking off his nostalgia, he reached for the phone, dialed the number of Whispering Hills Hospital and waited impatiently, drumming his fingers, for the receptionist to locate Johnston's psychiatrist.

Henshaw eventually answered, but the call was brief. Even though Zane was one of the biggest names in the security business and Kaylie's ex-husband, the doctor, as usual, was reluctant to give out any information on his patient.

"Damn patient confidentiality!" Zane growled, hanging up. Henshaw had been vague, as if he were holding something back, and the hairs on the back of Zane's neck bristled. Something wasn't right. Though Henshaw had assured Zane there were no plans for Johnston's "immediate" release, he hadn't ruled out that someday Lee Johnston might be stalking the streets again.

"Terrific! Just bloody terrific!" Zane's hands felt clammy, and he wished there were some way to get through to Kaylie. She was and always had been much too cavalier about her safety. Even after the horror of the opening of *Obsession*. Because Johnston was locked up, she had refused to worry, going about her life as if the terror hadn't existed, as if her life hadn't hung by a fragile thread that one man had nearly sliced.

He strode to the recessed bar and poured himself a stiff shot of Scotch. He'd bungled this and badly. Gambling that he could convince Kaylie to stay with him at the cabin, he'd thought he'd be able to protect her, if and when Johnston ever saw the outside of the hospital again. But now things were much worse. Kaylie wouldn't even talk to him.

A cold, tight knot of dread twisted in the pit of his stomach. He wasn't out of this yet. Come hell or high water, he intended to protect Kaylie, even if, in so doing, he might ram a wedge between them that could never be removed.

Her life was more valuable than his love. With that miserable thought, he drained his glass, pressed the intercom on his desk and told his secretary to arrange a meeting of his most trusted men.

On the darkened set of *West Coast Morning*, Kaylie guessed that Alan didn't like anything she was telling him. In fact, he was being bullheaded and stubborn about an issue that she considered very cut-and-dried.

Maybe, Kaylie thought wearily, Zane had been right about Alan all along.

"I don't get it," Alan complained, plucking a piece of lint

from his jacket. His mouth pinched together into a contrite pout. His auburn hair was brushed neatly, and his suit didn't dare have a single wrinkle. He sat on a bar stool in the kitchen of the set, his notes spread on the tile countertop of the island bar, near the gas range where Chef Glenn cooked up his Friday-morning concoctions. "What's the big deal about a little publicity?"

"It's not publicity, Alan, and we both know it. Who started the rumor that we were getting married?"

"Who knows? And who cares?" He lifted his shoulders in an exaggerated shrug. "If you're in the business and you're popular enough, eventually you find your name and face on the front page of *Up Front* or *The Insider* or some other rag."

"So you think we should be flattered?" she accused.

Alan forced a smile, and seeing his reflection in the copper pots hanging near the stove, smoothed his hair with the flat of his hand. "Well, I think the least we can do is go with the flow. Next week someone else will make the headlines and we'll be old news."

"That's not the point."

"Hey—just chill out, okay?" he said, irritated as he noticed a mistake in his notes, clicked open a pen and made a quick slash on the neatly typed pages.

"I'll 'chill out' just as long as both you and I deny this whole engagement thing to the legitimate press."

He lifted his palms. "Suits me." Looking back to his notes for the next day's show, he asked, "So what happened? Does Brenda take some rag that got you all riled?"

"Brenda?" she repeated, not understanding.

"Your aunt. The one who was so sick." Alan glanced up sharply, and a tiny line appeared between his thick brows. "The one you were visiting in the hospital for the past few days?" he prodded, eyeing her suspiciously from behind the wire-rimmed glasses he never wore on camera.

"Oh—no!" So Zane had gone so far as to name her supposedly seriously ill aunt. Kaylie cleared her throat. "No, I just had a lot of time to do some thinking...." Well, at least that wasn't a lie. She'd spent the past four days thinking, thinking,

thinking. And she'd gotten nowhere. Her thoughts kept turning back to Zane.

"So?"

"So I thought we should take a professional stand against all this tabloid gossip."

"Tell that to the station. It's my bet that our ratings went up while we were splashed across the headlines."

"Still—"

"So cool it," Alan cut in, chuckling. "No harm done. Right?"

She wasn't so sure. "I just like to keep my private life private, that's all."

Alan's eyes, behind the thick lenses, narrowed as he studied her. He shoved his notes together, straightening the pages on the shiny mauve-colored tiles. When he looked at her again, his expression had turned thoughtful. "Is something else going on with you?"

"Meaning?"

He rubbed his chin pensively. "Before you left to take care of your aunt, Flannery called here a couple of times."

Kaylie didn't flinch. "Right."

"So—does all this talk about privacy have something to do with him?"

"Of course not," she said, rubbing her palms down the sides of her skirt.

"You're sure? Because it seems like a big coincidence, you know, that Flannery calls a couple of times after leaving you alone for years. Then you don't show up for work the next day—and now that you're back, you're all worked up about your privacy."

"You're not making any sense," Kaylie countered.

"If you say so." He touched his pen to his lips. "You know what I think?"

"I'm not sure I want to."

"If you ask me, you never really got over him." Alan set his notes on the table and walked to the front of the cameras to the grouping of couches and chairs that created a cozy living room on the set of *West Coast Morning*. Hands deep in his pockets, he leaned a shoulder against the fake mantel on the brick fireplace.

"Zane has nothing to do with this."

"You always were a poor liar. And, unless I miss my guess, Zane has everything to do with it! Remember—I know you. I've known you as long as he has. I saw the hell you went through during your divorce."

"Let's not dredge all that up again—"

He ignored her. "The way I see it, you never were divorced from him—not emotionally. Oh, I know you went through all the legal hoops and you haven't seen him for a while. But it's glaringly obvious to anyone who knows you that you're still in love with him." He tugged on his tie and flicked open his collar button. She wanted to argue with him, but before she could say another word, Alan went on, "If Zane whistled, you'd go running. You might have wanted out of your marriage a few years ago, but that's changed."

"And how would you know?" she wondered aloud.

"Because I've worked with you, Kaylie—seen you grow. Don't forget, I was at the premiere of *Obsession*. I remember what happened when you were attacked, how Zane reacted. Can't say as I blame him, either. He was scared spitless—and he should have been. Johnston was a maniac."

Kaylie crossed the set and took a seat in one of the rose-colored chairs that she'd sat in for hundreds of tapings. So it was that obvious, was it? Even Alan, self-centered as he was, knew how she felt.

"You know, Flannery was just trying to keep you safe," Alan said, then muttered something under his breath and kicked at one of the ottomans on the set. "I don't know why I'm defending the guy—I don't even like him. But he was right in worrying about Johnston attacking you again."

Kaylie's head snapped up. "What does that mean?" she asked suspiciously, nervous fear burrowing deep in her heart. "Is Lee Johnston going to be released soon?"

Alan, not really interested, lifted a shoulder. "If he is, it's a well-kept secret. But he'll be out someday."

With that chilling prediction, he glanced at his watch and

shot to his feet. "Got to run," he explained, reaching for his briefcase and athletic bag he'd tucked near the island. "Got a tennis game with my agent. See ya later." With a wave, he was down the hall and out the door.

Kaylie spent the next couple of hours at the station, checking her messages, but there was no pink slip asking her to return a call to "Ted." She answered her mail, returned her calls and reviewed the shows she'd missed, talked with Jim and Tracy and got ready for the next morning.

Eventually Kaylie left the station in a car she'd rented for the week—until she could drive to Carmel and pick up her Audi. She had one last errand to run. One very important errand.

She drove over the Golden Gate Bridge, barely noticing that the steel-colored clouds were moving inland and that the sun was once again sprinkling the bay with golden light.

Driving by instinct, she was unaware of the traffic or the change in scenery as the highway was flanked by vineyards. In Sonoma, she guided the rented Mustang up a steep hillside and parked in her sister's driveway. She turned off the engine and listened to the radio as she waited for Margot to get home from work. The interior of the car was warm, so she cranked open the sunroof. At five-thirty, the garage door opened, and Margot's sporty little Toyota wheeled into the garage.

As Kaylie climbed out of her Mustang, Margot shoved open the door of her car and fairly ran down the drive to Kaylie's car. "Kaylie! You're back!" she cried, crossing the asphalt and throwing her arms around her younger sister. Margot's shining coppery-gold hair gleamed in the sunlight, and her sky-blue eyes danced. "So tell me all about your adventure with Zane!"

Kaylie rolled her eyes. "Adventure? Is that what you think it was? He literally kidnapped me and held me hostage for days—"

"Umm—sounds divine."

"That's crazy!"

"Is it?" Margot's eyes twinkled. "I can't wait to hear what happened and I want details, Kaylie. Very explicit details."

"You're an incurable romantic," Kaylie said, laughing nonetheless. Some of Margot's enthusiasm was infectious. "I came over here to do you bodily harm, you know."

"Why?"

Kaylie was speechless for a moment. "You know why! Because you were in on it with him."

"And proud of it," Margot teased. "And don't give me this offended victim routine. It doesn't wash. You're crazy about Zane. Always have been, always will be. I don't known why you just don't admit it and make things easier on everyone. Now, come on, help me carry these groceries into the house and we'll have a glass of wine to celebrate."

"Celebrate what?"

"That you're back in the city. Or back with Zane. Whichever you choose." She glanced over her shoulder, and a dimple creased her cheek.

"I'm *not* involved with Zane."

"Sure you are. You're just too bullheaded to admit it." Opening the hatchback, she eyed her sacks of groceries, chose one and stuffed the ungainly bag into Kaylie's arms. "There you go." Balancing a second sack, she led the way to the house, unlocked the door and was greeted by several yowling cats. "Miss me?" she asked the felines as she deposited the groceries on the kitchen counter.

She was rewarded with a chorus of loud mewing, which didn't stop until she petted three furry heads.

Kaylie set her sack on the counter. Margot's house, which she'd built with her husband, Trevor, clung to the side of a steep canyon overlooking the rolling hills and valley floor of the wine country. Margot loved this house, and though Trevor had lost his life in a boating accident nearly two years before, she'd never moved. The good memories outweigh the bad, she'd always say, when the subject of selling the house would come up.

"You know," Margot said now, pouring dry cat food into three separate bowls, "you're lucky Zane still cares enough to try to win you back."

"You think so?"

"Umm." Margot finished with the cats, washed her hands,

then pulled a bottle of zinfandel from the refrigerator. Splashing some of the liquid into two glasses, she said sadly, ''I just wish I had the chance to start over with Trevor.'' A tiny crease marred her forehead.

Kaylie felt a jab of remorse. ''But Trevor was different from Zane.''

''Not so much,'' Margot said, shaking her head. ''He was stubborn, arrogant, prideful and—'' her voice cracked ''—loving and wonderful.''

Wishing she could help Margot quit grieving for a man who'd never return, Kaylie said, ''I miss Trevor, too. He was a great guy.''

''The best.'' Margot's voice turned husky, and she blinked rapidly against gathering tears. She took a sip of wine and sniffed. ''I guess that's why it's just so hard for me to understand why you're willing to throw away something so precious as Zane's love when he so obviously still wants to work things out.''

''I just need to be independent.''

''Oh, that's a cop-out and you know it. Let's take these drinks and go outside onto the deck.'' Margot opened the sliding door with her back. ''Grab that bag of chips,'' she said, motioning to a sack of tortilla chips. ''And there's homemade salsa, Chef Glenn's best recipe, in the fridge.''

Kaylie poured the chips into a bowl and found the salsa. On the deck, she dropped the snack onto the round table and took a seat under the shade of the green-and-white umbrella. Margot was propped on the chaise longue, rolling her wineglass between her palms.

Kaylie dunked a chip in the salsa and took a bite.

''Believe me, I've had it with independence.'' Margot gazed dreamily over the rail to the sunset blazing in the west. ''If I could have just one more day with Trevor…'' She frowned and shoved her hair from her eyes. ''You know, the night he left, we fought.'' Her teeth sank into her lower lip. ''I never had a chance to take back all the horrid things we said to each other. But you—'' she glanced over at her sister and arched a fine, dark brow "—you have the chance to make things right with Zane."

"It's not that easy," Kaylie admitted. "He kidnapped me, remember? Took me away against my will. Thrust his will on me without the least little concern for me."

"Well, this might sound strange, but I'd give anything for Trevor to come back and try to protect me...." she whispered wistfully. Then, as if realizing she'd said too much, she cleared her throat and took a quick sip of wine. "Well, I guess that's not going to happen, is it?"

"I don't think so." Trevor's body had never been found. For months Margot had believed he was alive and would eventually show up, healthy and robust, but time and reality had finally convinced her that he had been killed.

They sat in silence for a while, listening to insects hum in the trees and watching the sun sink lower in the sky.

"Maybe you're too hard on him," Margot finally said, reaching into the bowl of chips and thinking aloud.

"No way. He lied to me, Margot. And that cock-and-bull story about Lee Johnston—"

"That wasn't a lie." Margot shook her head, and a tiny furrow creased her brow. "You and I both know they won't keep Johnston locked up forever. Zane's just being careful."

"Oh, save me."

"I mean it, Kaylie. So Johnston's not on the loose right now. He may be soon. According to Zane, there's been talk. Now, come on...." The sparkle returned to Margot's blue eyes. "Let's hear it, Kaylie. What was it like being whisked to some romantic hideaway with Zane?"

Kaylie's lips twitched. "I don't know," she said sincerely. "I can't decide. I felt like I was caught somewhere between heaven and hell."

Margot dunked another chip. "Uh-oh, that's passion talking."

"Maybe," Kaylie admitted, wrinkling her nose. "And I haven't forgiven you for your part in this, you know. You sold me out."

"I only tried to help."

"I don't think I need it, thank you very much."

"Oh, get off it, Kay." Margot grinned and leaned closer. "Let's hear all about it, and don't you dare leave out one tiny detail!"

It was after eight when Kaylie finally parked in her own garage. She and Margot had gone out for Chinese food, and after Kaylie had told Margot everything about her stay with Zane—well, almost everything—she'd returned to the city. Margot would never understand leaving a man after making love to him, and Kaylie wasn't sure she did herself.

She noticed Zane immediately. Leaning against his Jeep, his arms crossed over his chest, he was waiting for her, and from the looks of him, had been for some time.

"What're you doing here?" she demanded, ignoring the tug on her heart at the sight of him.

"Waiting for you."

"Why?"

"I just wanted to know how things went today at the station."

"Sure." She didn't believe him for a minute. He didn't give a damn about her job. "What is it you really want, Zane?"

"You did go to see Margot, didn't you?"

"How'd you know that?" Kaylie cried, and then a fresh sense of betrayal washed over her. "No, don't tell me, my sister called you!"

"The minute you left her house."

"Why?" Kaylie whispered, wanting to throttle her meddling sister.

"She's a romantic," Zane said, cutting her off. "She seems to think we're destined to be together." He started forward, advancing on her, and Kaylie didn't know whether to throw her arms around him or run for cover. Instead she unlocked the door. "Why did she call you?"

"She seems to think there's still a chance for us."

Oh, Margot, how could you? "She didn't hear our argument this afternoon."

"Look, Kaylie, I'm sorry," he said suddenly. "I went off

the deep end today at the office. I said some things I didn't mean, and I...I don't want to leave it like that.''

"I don't think there's any other way.''

"Sure there is,'' he cajoled, cocking his head toward his Jeep. "How about a drive?''

She laughed. "We tried that once before,'' she said, shaking her head. "I'm not going to make the same mistake twice.''

With a flip of the wrist, he tossed her the keys. "You drive. I'll let you take me anywhere you want to go.''

Her fingers surrounded the cold bits of steel.

"Come on, Kaylie. It'll be fun.''

"No tricks?'' she asked.

He lifted one hand. "On my honor.''

"Now we are in trouble,'' she said, but couldn't resist. "I must be out of my mind. We'll take my car. That way there's no mix-up with the keys. You seem to have a problem with that.'' He laughed and caught the keys she tossed back to him.

She climbed behind the wheel of her rented Mustang, and Zane folded himself into the passenger seat. "Anywhere I want to go?'' she repeated, ramming the car into gear.

"Anywhere.''

From the minute the car's wheels hit the pavement, she knew where she'd take him—a remote stretch of beach that she'd discovered on the other side of the peninsula.

Zane didn't say a word as she parked the car near the sea. He'd driven to her apartment on impulse, unable to let her go. Now, as she tucked her keys in her pocket, he knew he'd made the right decision.

The night-darkened ocean stretched for miles, disappearing into an inky horizon. Kaylie climbed out of the car. Rushing off the ocean, a breeze danced through the beach grass and trees, swirling and rustling leaves overhead. A pale moon, guarded by flimsy clouds, offered soft illumination and cast Kaylie's blond hair in silver light.

The scent of the sea mingled with Kaylie's perfume as they walked toward the frothy waves. They passed a few people, an elderly couple walking their dog and a group of teenagers bopping to the music cast from their radios.

As they neared the surf, Kaylie kicked off her sandals, cast an impish glance in his direction and taunted, "Bet you can't catch me."

Then she took off. Bare feet pounding on the sand, she laughed and headed for the pounding surf.

Zane grinned at the chance of a challenge. He struggled out of his shoes and socks, and though she had a huge head start, tore off after her, determined to catch her as he watched the wind stream through her hair and heard the soft tinkle of her laughter over the roar of the surf.

"You'd better run, Melville," he yelled, exhilarated as the distance between them shortened.

Kaylie felt the wet sand beneath her feet, smelled the briny scent of the sea and heard the slap of Zane's feet against wet sand as he shortened the distance between them. His breathing was loud, his footsteps pounding a quick, even rhythm.

Don't let him catch you, she thought, wondering why she'd started this stupid game. She should have known that Zane would rise to the challenge!

Hazarding one glance over her shoulder, she saw him bearing down on her. In the moonlight his features appeared more harsh, and the gleam in his eye made her already thudding heart slam against her ribs. She pushed herself farther, the air burning in her lungs, her legs beginning to protest. Several large rocks loomed ahead. If she could just make it past them....

With a laugh, he caught up to her, grabbed her around the waist and spun her around, toppling them both in one quick movement.

He landed on the wet sand with one shoulder and dragged her on top of him, twining his fingers through her hair. He kissed her lightly on the lips. "Did you really think you could outrun me?"

"I hoped."

"Foolish girl."

"Woman," she corrected, and he laughed again, his teeth flashing white in the black night. Screened by the boulders from the rest of the beach, they were aware only of each other and the night surrounding them.

"Woman," he replied just before his lips claimed hers in a kiss as wild as the violent sea. Kaylie could do nothing but kiss him back as he shifted, rolling over so that he was above her.

Any thoughts of denial receded with the tide, and she wound her arms around his neck and curved her body to his. Why was it always like this with him? she wondered as his mouth moved from hers. Softly he kissed her eyes and cheeks before his lips returned to the corner of her mouth again and his tongue delved and tasted, rimming her parted lips and touching her teeth.

Vaguely she was aware of the foam that touched her bare legs and toes, the cool sea against her skin. They were alone on this part of the beach, hidden by the rocks and the blackness of the night, as if they were the only two people on earth.

She shivered, but not from the water, as he slowly discovered the hem of her cotton sweater and his fingertips brushed the bare skin of her abdomen. His weight pinned her to the sand while his lips and tongue explored her mouth and neck, playing havoc with her senses.

Moaning softly, she kissed him back, her fingers coiling in the thick hair at his nape, her body arching to his. She didn't stop him when he lifted her sweater and dampened the lacy edge of her bra with his lips. Nor did she protest when his tongue dipped beneath the delicate fabric, gently prodding and wetting the edge of her nipple until her breast swelled and ached.

"Tell me you want me," he persuaded. His breath whispered across the wet lace, tantalizing her with its warmth.

"I—I want you."

"Forever?" he questioned, and in the moonlight she saw one of his dark brows cock.

He's playing with me, she realized, but couldn't control her body as he bent over her breast again and began, through the now-wet fabric, to suckle, gently tugging at her nipple with his teeth and lips. "Hmm, Kaylie?" he said huskily. "Forever?"

"Y-yes," she whispered, a familiar ache beginning to burn deep and hot.

He groaned and rubbed against her, suckling and petting, his breath hot and wet, his body lean and hard. She felt the grit of sand against her bare back, but she didn't care.

He shoved her strap over her shoulder, and her breast spilled out of her bra, translucent and veined in the moon glow, her nipple dark and standing proudly erect.

"You are beautiful," he murmured, reverently touching the hard bud before laving it again with his wet, hot mouth.

Kaylie closed her eyes and cradled his head against her, wanting more, feeling the hot ache of a void only he could fill. Anxiously she moved against him, and her fingers fumbled with the buttons of his shirt. With a growl, he ripped the offensive garment off, then returned his attention to her pants. Groaning, he yanked her skirt away and kicked off his trousers.

"Love me, Kaylie," he whispered, his hands on her shoulders, his gaze delving deep into hers and burning with a primal fire.

But before she could say anything, he moved over her, his perfect, sleek body poised above her, his knees parting her legs. "I can't help myself," he cried as he entered her and she arched upward to meet him.

Her fingers clung to the hard, strident muscles of his back as he moved, thrusting inside her with a passion so fierce she could barely breathe.

She met each of his impassioned lunges with her own. Time and space ceased to exist, and her mind spun out of control. The sound of the sea receded, and all she could hear was her own throbbing heartbeat and Zane's ragged breathing.

Staring up at him, watching the play of emotions across his strong features, she let her body control her until there was nothing in the universe save Zane and her. Hot and wild, she felt him stiffen, and a wondrous release caused her to cry out. "Zane— Oh, Zane!" Her world tilted out of control as spasm after glorious spasm enveloped her.

"I'm here, love," he answered, before falling in exhaustion into her waiting arms.

Chapter Eleven

She let him stay. Telling herself she was every kind of fool, Kaylie let Zane spend the night. She was allowing herself one more night of pleasure without thinking of the consequences, and they spent the early hours of the morning making love.

At five, she reluctantly rolled out of bed. Zane turned over and groaned but didn't wake up. She showered quickly. As she dressed, she glanced at him still sprawled across her peach-colored quilt and blankets.

Her stomach twisted painfully when she thought that this might be the last time they would ever be together. She couldn't afford to become emotionally tangled up with him again, but a part of her longed for the marriage they had once shared, the happiness they'd held for so brief a moment.

She loved him still. As much, if not more, than on the day they married. Now, as she gazed at his sleeping form, all tangled in her sheets, she felt a rush of hot tears in her throat. If only things had worked out differently....

"Stop it," she muttered, clasping a gold necklace around her neck and swiping at her eyes. She wouldn't cry now. Nostalgia would serve no purpose.

"What?" Zane growled, opening a sleepy eye. "Stop what?" His jaw darkened with the stubble of a beard, his eyelids drooping seductively, his bare muscles moving fluidly as he adjusted the covers. He looked so virile and male, she had to glance back to her reflection before she did or said anything stupid. "Were you talking to me?" he asked with a yawn.

She brushed her hair until it crackled. "No, I was talking to myself, but since you're awake, remember to lock the door when you leave." She adjusted her turquoise-colored skirt and slid her arms through a matching jacket. "And leave the extra set of keys on the table."

"You're throwing me out?" he asked, disbelieving. He stretched lazily, his skin dark against the sheets. His sable-brown hair fell rakishly over his eyes, and his lips twisted into a thin, sensual smile.

"I think it would be safer that way."

"For whom?"

"You," she quipped, seeing her eyes twinkle in the reflection as she added earrings and a dab of perfume. "You just never know when I might decide to have my way with you."

"So have it!" He tossed back the covers to display all too vividly his well-muscled body, his mat of dark curling chest hair, his firm legs and much, much more.

Kaylie's breath caught in her throat, and she had to swallow in order to speak. "It's, uh, tempting—very tempting, but really, I've got to go—"

"Call in sick," he suggested.

"Not on your life!" She slipped into bone-colored heels. "After already being gone while 'Aunt Brenda' was taken so ill, I don't think calling in sick would go over so well."

Zane grinned devilishly. "I could arrange it so that your aunt had a relapse."

"You're impossible!" Kaylie threw her brush at him, then strutted down the hall.

Zane scrambled off the bed, the glint in his eye unmistakable. Kaylie giggled as she half ran to the kitchen. Stark naked, he tore after her through the house and caught up with her at the back door.

"Zane, don't," she protested, fighting more laughter as his arms surrounded her and he kissed her passionately, holding her hostage against the back door. She squirmed and wriggled, but his kiss was warm and wet and reminded her of the way he'd felt the night before.

"Don't what?" he whispered, his tongue flicking sensually between her teeth.

She couldn't speak until he lifted his head.

"Don't muss my hair or clothes or..." The words faded away as he kissed her again, his tongue darting between her teeth, claiming her mouth, his hands moving downward to cup her buttocks and bring her hips hard against his.

"Or what?" he prodded, not abandoning his assault on her senses.

Kaylie's knees turned to jelly, and though she knew she should shove him away, she couldn't find the strength. "Or I might just—"

"Have your way with me?" he mocked, his eyes dancing with gray light as he lifted his head and stared at her.

"Or worse!" she tossed back.

"Worse?" A wicked grin slashed across his jaw. "Believe me, I'm ready."

"I can tell," she teased. Glancing over his shoulder, he noticed the time on the wall clock and groaned. She was already late! "You wouldn't want me to lose my job, would you?"

He growled and kissed her again. "Yeah, that would be a real pity!"

"I'd never forgive you!"

"No?" He lifted a disbelieving brow, and his eyes were alight with challenge.

"I mean it!" She reached behind him until she found the door knob, then sidestepped him and hurried onto the covered porch leading to the parking lot. "I don't expect you to be here when I get home."

"Not even if I make your favorite dinner?" he asked in a high, falsetto voice.

"Oh, you're impossible!"

She climbed into the Mustang. But as she adjusted her side-view mirror, she caught a glimpse of Zane, naked as the day he was born, standing in the open doorway, arms crossed over his chest, one shoulder propped against the frame, not in the least concerned that the neighbors might see him.

"It would serve you right if you get arrested!" she yelled through the window, missing his response as she slammed the car into reverse.

Zane laughed, and the rich sound lingered in her thoughts as she drove toward the heart of the city.

"Lee?" Dr. Henshaw took a seat in the chair next to his patient. But Johnston didn't look up. As if he were rooted to the cushions of the old couch facing the television in the rec-reation room, Lee Johnston sat, waiting, the blank screen reflected in his icy eyes.

"Lee, can you hear me?"

Johnston scratched at a scab on the back of his right hand. But still he stared at the TV.

"No use trying to talk to him," Rick said, walking in and switching on the set. Music blared. Rick adjusted the volume with the remote control. A children's cartoon show was in progress. Johnston didn't move. "Until *West Coast Morning* comes on, he won't say a word."

Henshaw exchanged glances with the orderly, and he thought about the messages he'd received and had to return. Flannery had called again, as had Kaylie Melville herself. He'd have to talk to them both, which didn't present any particular problems.

It was the other call that bothered him, a call he didn't want to return. But, of course, he had no choice.

Rick, still cleaning off a table in the corner that had recently been used for arts and crafts, shook his head at the doctor. "Let's just hope you-know-who is on the show today," he said, placing the palates, brushes, paints and other tools onto a cart. He wheeled the cart next to Lee's chair just as a heavyset orderly named Pam rushed into the room. "Dr. Henshaw? There's a problem in 301," she said breathlessly, her pudgy face red.

"Norman is upset—I mean really upset. He threw his breakfast all over the room and...and..." Seeing Lee for the first time, she gained control of herself. "Maybe you'd better come, too," she said to Rick.

Rick mumbled something inaudible under his breath, but gave the cart a shove. The corner caught on the edge of the couch, and several paint mixing tools and palates clattered to the floor.

"Son of a—" Rick caught himself and reached down, grabbing the paint-spattered knives and brushes. The floor was smudged with yellow ocher, Christmas green and scarlet. "Great—just great!"

Henshaw was already following Pam out of the room. Rick, in a foul mood, snarled at Lee, "Maybe you'd just better go back to your room until I clean this up. I don't want you messin' this up any more than it already is! Come on, get going! You'll be back for your stupid program!"

Rick prodded Lee on the shoulder. Johnston jerked away, his nostrils flared slightly. He didn't like to be touched. Not by Dr. Henshaw and especially not by Rick, the know-it-all with the smug smirk. Rick really thought he was crazy and he looked down on Lee, but Lee intended to show Rick and Henshaw and all the others just what he was made of. Reluctantly, he got to his feet.

"Hurry up, I don't got all day," Rick growled, looking around for a towel or mop.

Lee, spying a knife that had slid just under the couch, hazarded a sly look at Rick, whose back was turned as he unlocked a closet. Quick as a cat, Lee grabbed the dull knife, stuck it into the side of his shoe and pretended to be tying his laces.

"You still here?" Rick asked, facing him again. "Well, come on, come on." He touched Lee again, and Lee recoiled, his stomach turning over.

Only one person had the right to touch his body. And that person was Kaylie...sweet, sweet Kaylie. He licked his lips and scratched absently at the itch on his hand as he stepped into the hallway. He'd missed Kaylie the last few days, but her absence from the program had brought one thing into perfect focus. He had to see her again, touch her, smell her, taste her. Soon.

His bloodless lips curved into the faintest of smiles as he felt the knife, wedged tightly between sock and leather, rubbing against the side of his foot.

Kaylie's first full day back at work started the minute she shoved open the glass doors of the building. She waved to the receptionist and made her way through the series of hallways toward her office. On the way, Tracy flagged her down with a sheaf of papers.

"Today's guests?" Kaylie asked.

Tracy nodded and slapped the papers into Kaylie's outstretched hand. "Yep. Just a little more information that came in late. Isn't that always the way?" She lifted her slim shoulders and turned her palms toward the ceiling.

"Always." Kaylie laughed, glad to be back in her normal routine. She didn't even think about Zane standing naked in her driveway—well, she didn't *dwell* on the vivid image she'd seen in her side-view mirror.

She stopped by the tiny cafeteria and saw a couple of technicians and cameramen.

"Great to have you back, Kay," Hal said as he grabbed a doughnut from the box of pastries lying open on the glossy Formica table. Hal, thin and balding, was in charge of the sound booth.

"We missed you around here," his partner, Marvin, agreed.

"It didn't look like it," Kaylie replied, picking up a cinnamon twist and a napkin. "I saw the program."

Hal snorted. "Old Alan was in his element; no doubt about it. He was snapping orders around here like he owned the place."

Marvin, his slight paunch jiggling, chuckled. "The funny part was, no one paid him much mind."

"I bet that went over like the proverbial lead balloon."

"More like a lead zeppelin," Marvin said. "Hey, how's that aunt of yours anyway? What was wrong with her? Heart problems?" He dusted the sugar from his fingers.

Hal, wiping the last crumb of a jelly doughnut from his mouth, said, "I heard she was in an accident of some sort—ended up in a coma."

"She's fine. Her heart did act up after the accident, and she was in and out of consciousness, but she's fine now, out of ICU," Kaylie replied, improvising, mentally cursing Zane for his lies. She breezed out of the cafeteria, balancing a coffee cup, her pastry and napkin in one hand, her briefcase swinging from the other and the notes Tracy had handed her tucked under her arm.

"Welcome back to the rat race," she told herself as she dropped into the chair behind her desk. Sipping her coffee, she retrieved her notes from her briefcase. As she added in the information Tracy had handed her, she jotted down a few new questions and underlined background information she considered important.

She finished with the notes and her pastry just as the door of her office flew open and Audra, the hairdresser and makeup artist, scurried breathlessly inside. "Lord, what a day! Sorry I'm late. Alan's toupee, you know. He's never satisfied with that damned rug, and there's only so much I can do with it. If he hates it so much he should break down and buy a new one. Or go without. Hell, I think a man is much sexier in nothing than something, and that goes for hairpieces as well as clothes." She laughed at her own joke and unzipped her oversize makeup bag. "Well, anyway, I didn't mean to rush you."

"No problem," Kaylie said around a smile. Audra, with her fast tongue, stiletto heels and bloodred lipstick, was always a breath of fresh air in this conservative old building.

Audra eyed her critically. "Nope. You look none the worse for wear," she agreed, rifling in her bag with her red-tipped nails. "In fact you look pretty damned good for hanging around a hospital for four or five days." She frowned thoughtfully as she pulled out a comb and swirled it in some cleanser. "How's that aunt of yours? Heard she had a gallstone operation."

"Uh, it was her heart—no operation," Kaylie replied.

Thanks a lot, Zane, she thought as Audra smoothed a few errant strands of her hair into place.

"Well, at least you got away for a few days," Audra said, pointing an aerosol can in her direction and spraying a cloud of mist over her locks. "And don't be worrying about this—ozone friendly. See, right here on the can." She pointed to a symbol Kaylie couldn't read through the mist. "I'm an environmentalist now."

"Good," Kaylie said, coughing as she reached for her coffee.

Audra snatched the cup away, sloshing a few drops of brown liquid onto Kaylie's notes. "Oh, no, you don't. No, sirree! Your lipstick's perfect. Let's not be messing it up by leaving it on this here cup."

"Aye-aye, Captain," Kaylie teased, saluting Audra as the makeup artist picked up her gear, zipped her case closed and exited.

There was a rap on her door and the familiar sound of Tracy's voice. "Ten minutes, Kaylie!"

She scanned her notes one last time, then dashed to the set. Alan was already waiting. As Kaylie's microphone was pinned onto her jacket, she caught his glance and smile. He seemed genuinely glad to see her.

"Don't worry about a thing," he said, as she settled into her chair. He patted her hand affectionately. "I've got everything covered today. All you have to do is sit there and smile and be your gorgeous self."

"You're kidding," she replied. "Besides, I'm all set."

On the floor in front of camera three, Tracy was motioning for all quiet on the set.

At a silent signal to the sound box, the lead-in music filled the small auditorium. Kaylie took a deep breath, smiled and wondered if Zane was watching. Giving herself a mental slap, she forced thoughts of him aside.

The show went well. She interviewed a rock star named Death, a woman who grew an entirely organic garden, as well as the snake handler from the zoo, along with his favorite python and boa constrictor. She held the snakes and let them crawl across her shoulders as she spoke to their handler.

Alan handled the national news and talked with Hugh Grimwold, a pitcher for one of the bay area teams.

After the local news, and another sports update, both Alan and Kaylie spoke with two high school seniors who had started their own recycling business.

In the final segment, Alan announced the guests for the next show and reminded the viewers that on Friday, Chef Glenn was going to create his famous Cajun breakfast. The credits began to roll as music once again drifted from the speakers positioned around the set.

"Good job, Kaylie," Jim said, clapping her on the back and smiling broadly. "You know, the show just didn't feel right without you." He waved and sauntered toward the reception area while Kaylie headed toward her office.

From the corner of her eye she noticed the dark look that Alan passed her way, but she ignored Alan's foul mood and bathed in Jim's compliments. Jim Crowley didn't hand out praise often.

At her desk, she pulled the cap off her underlining pen with her teeth and started reading the bio information on the guests for the next day.

The door to her office opened and slammed against the wall.

Alan, face scarlet, eyes blazing, stormed into the room. "You don't even have an Aunt Brenda!" he charged, crossing his arms indignantly over his chest.

"What?" she asked, nearly dropping her pen.

"Don't lie to me, Kaylie. I checked."

"You did *what?*"

"I called around, checked with some of your friends. Eventually I even talked to Margot. *She* told me the truth. She didn't want to—at least not at first—but she came clean. Jeez, Kaylie, I think she gained some perverse pleasure in telling me that you'd lied." His red face turned almost purple.

"Oh."

"'Oh' is right! You let me and everyone else here think you were on some mission of mercy when all the time you were shacking up with Flannery!"

"Now, wait a minute—" Kaylie's voice rose indignantly.

Slowly getting to her feet, she wished she could throttle her meddling sister as well as Alan.

Alan made an impatient motion with one hand. "Oh, Margot didn't exactly fill me in, but she made enough broad hints that I figured it out. You were with Flannery last week, weren't you?"

This couldn't happen! Kaylie planted her palms on the top of her desk and tried her best to remain calm. "What I did or didn't do isn't really any of your business."

"You left us in the lurch, Kaylie!"

"You seemed to handle everything well enough without me. And if I remember correctly, I covered for you a couple of years ago—when you bruised your backside and your ego while snow-boarding."

Alan's face went white. "But I couldn't tell Jim or the rest of the crew that I'd..." His voice dropped off, and he swallowed hard.

"That you ended up with a broken tailbone trying some silly teenaged stunt with a ski bunny who'd been busted for drugs?"

"Oh, God." The wind disappeared from his sails. "You know about all that?" He ran a shaking hand across his hair, and his toupee slid a little. Kaylie almost felt sorry for him. Almost.

"So what happened?" he asked, his face puddling into a pout as he slid into a chair near her desk. "I thought it was over between you and Flannery."

"It was."

"But...?"

She was through lying. In fact, as soon as she was finished talking to Alan, she'd go and explain everything to Jim. If the powers-that-be in the station decided to fire her, so be it. At least she wouldn't have to walk this tightrope of lies any longer. "Zane stopped by the other night and we went to dinner. He persuaded me to go to the mountains with him for a few days."

"Just like that?" Alan snapped his fingers.

"Oh, no, it took a lot of convincing," she said, swallowing a smile as she remembered how Zane had fireman-carried her into the lodge. "A *lot* of convincing."

"For God's sake, why did you agree to have dinner with him in the first place?"

"It was part of the deal."

"The deal?" he repeated, shaking his head. He rolled his eyes and tossed his hands up. "So now she's making deals with her ex-husband! Kaylie, do you know that the press has us practically married?"

"We discussed this. It's a dead issue."

"I know, I know. But…well, I thought we could let it ride awhile. What could it hurt? But you running off with Flannery, well, that about kills it."

"Good!"

Alan left a few minutes later, and Kaylie marched into Jim Crowley's office to tell him the abbreviated truth. Jim took the news in stride. He wasn't happy, of course, and he warned her to "call next time—about ten days *before* you plan to leave." But she left his office with her pride and her job intact.

Hours later, she returned to her apartment. Zane was long gone, but the scent of him still lingered in the air. The bed was made, but she couldn't resist taking a pillow and breathing deeply. The feathers still smelled of his after-shave. "Oh, Melville, you've got it bad," she chided, still clutching the pillow as she fell back on her bed and stared up at the ceiling. "Real bad!"

Realizing that she sounded like an adolescent in the throes of puppy love, she tossed the pillow aside and walked into the kitchen.

The red light on the answering machine was blinking, and she played back the messages only to hear Zane's voice, as if he were there.

"I guess I'm hung up here at the office awhile," he said with a sigh. "So I won't be over."

"Too bad," she murmured, though she did feel a jab of disappointment.

"But I'll call you later and I'll see you soon."

He hung up, and she listened to a couple more messages—

one from Margot begging her to call and another from an insurance salesman.

After popping a dinner into the microwave, she dialed Margot's number.

"Hello?"

"I should tar and feather you," Kaylie announced.

"I guess you talked to Alan."

"Screamed would be the appropriate word."

"I know I shouldn't have said a word to him, but he had the nerve to call here asking about you, and I just had to set him in his place. If you ask me, that guy's got a screw loose."

"Alan?" Kaylie laughed.

"I'm not kidding. I bet he's the one that gave all those papers the idea you two were engaged. Anyway, I couldn't resist hinting around about Zane. He deserved it."

Kaylie couldn't stay angry with Margot for long. "It's okay, I guess. I was tired of talking about this fictitious Aunt Brenda and I told Jim the whole story—well, most of it. Fortunately I still have my job."

The microwave beeped, and as they talked, Kaylie pulled out her dinner—a pathetic-looking concoction of chicken, peas and potatoes—while Margot asked about Zane.

"He's not here," Kaylie said, nearly burning her fingers as she opened the plastic cover.

"No?" Margot sounded worried.

"He does have his own life."

"I know but—"

"Look, Margot, I know you think that Zane and I should reconcile and live this storybook existence, but it's not going to happen."

"Why not?"

Exasperated, Kaylie replied, "For one reason, he's not Prince Charming and I'm not Snow White or Cinderella or whoever it was Prince Charming was linked up with."

"Oh, Kaylie," Margot said cryptically, "if you only knew."

At eleven-thirty, Zane was finally caught up. His work, while he'd been off in the mountains with Kaylie, had piled up. He'd had to deal with a complaint about one of his men in the Beverly Hills office, double-check two new security systems in offices downtown, hire three more men as well as go over the books quickly to keep his accountant appeased.

And through it all, he'd thought of Kaylie, worried about her, wished to God that she was with him.

He reached for the phone, but decided not to call her. It was too late. She'd be exhausted. And he'd promised himself to let her live her own life.

Lifting his arms over his head, he felt his spine pop from hours of restless sitting. He stood, walked to the window, and stretching the muscles of his back and shoulders, caught a glimpse of the city at night. Cars rushed by, their headlights cutting into the semidarkness, their taillights small red beacons. A few pedestrians scurried along the sidewalks, black forms visible in the lamplight.

He'd called Whispering Hills earlier in the day and been assured by Dr. Henshaw that Johnston was going to stay locked up for a while. But, though the good doctor had been forthcoming, Zane had a feeling Henshaw wasn't telling him everything.

It wasn't anything Henshaw had said; it was the hesitation in his voice that had caused the hairs on the back of Zane's neck to rise—it was as if the doctor were trying to hide information.

"But why?" Zane wondered aloud, rubbing the day's growth of beard on his chin. Maybe Kaylie was right. Maybe, where her safety was concerned, he was paranoid.

Even the tape from Ted could be a hoax. But why? *Why?*

He'd had gut feelings before and he never second-guessed his instincts. Right or wrong, he had to be careful. This was Kaylie's life—her *life,* damn it. He wasn't about to fool around.

He rotated his neck, closing his eyes. She would be furious if she even guessed that he'd sent someone to watch her apartment, to follow her, to protect her when he wasn't with her.

"You're getting in deep, Flannery," he told himself as he grabbed his keys and snapped off the lights. No, that was wrong. Where Kaylie was concerned, he'd always been in deep, so deep that he felt that sometimes he was drowning.

He wanted nothing more than to drive to her apartment and stay the night, make love to her and awake with her wrapped around him. But he couldn't.

"Breathing room," he muttered as he locked the door of the building behind him. "She wants breathing room."

Alan Bently swirled his onion in his glass and stared broodingly at his drink. Seated at a private table in an expensive restaurant, he was alone with his own bleak thoughts. He was past forty—pushing forty-five—and his hair was little more than a memory. Though he worked out every day, his physique was suffering and his career looked as if it was on hold. Or worse.

For a while, with all the hype and speculation about Kaylie and him being romantically involved, things had started to look up. His agent had talked about a possible part in a movie, and there was even a rumor that a big-name producer was interested in putting Kaylie and Alan back on the silver screen together—to do a sequel to *Obsession*. True it had been over seven years since the original movie had been released, but that didn't matter. Sequels were the thing now.

But Zane Flannery seemed hell-bent on ruining everything. It didn't matter that he and Kaylie had disappeared for a while, though Alan would have liked to milk that disappearance for a little publicity, and he'd enjoyed being the star of the show. Now she was back and definitely not interested in anything but Flannery. Again.

So all his dreams seemed to be slipping away. Like a ghost from his past, fame eluded him. Alan Bently wanted the big time and he'd tasted a little of it once. Not that his job with the station was anything to sneeze at. *West Coast Morning* was big—at least on the West Coast. But it wasn't as glamorous as a successful movie. He wanted his name in the credits. He was still young enough to be a leading man, but he couldn't wait much longer.

Alan tossed back his drink. He knew that his career was teetering on the brink. One wrong move and the fickle public would forget him. But, with the right amount of publicity and interest, he could reach the big time again.

Smiling as the liquor slid through his system, sending a cozy warmth through his bloodstream, he motioned to the maître d' for a telephone and made the call that would ensure his fame again.

Chapter Twelve

The next morning Kaylie felt a pang of loneliness. Zane wasn't lying in the sheets, nor was he winking at her, nor making jokes with her, nor, as she headed for the door, tossing off the blankets and, without a stitch on, chasing her down the hall.

"This is what you wanted," she told herself as she grabbed a piece of toast, slapped some butter on it and munched as she locked the door behind her.

She felt restless and anxious. For seven years she'd lived without Zane, and now, she told herself as she drove toward the station, she couldn't stand one night away from him.

Her thoughts still clouded by Zane, she flipped on the radio, hoping to hear the news, and tried to concentrate on what was happening in the world—to no avail.

At the station's lot, she parked her rental, snatched her briefcase and climbed out of the car. In her peripheral vision, as she locked the car door, she noticed a silver Ford Taurus parked on the other side of the short hedge that separated the station's lot from the street. The driver didn't get out of his car, but pulled a newspaper from the seat beside him and began scanning it as if he were waiting for someone.

A car pool?

Had she seen the car before—yesterday morning? She couldn't remember, and deciding the man had every right to read his paper in the car, walked briskly to the station doors.

Inside, she poured herself a cup of coffee, and after talking with a few co-workers, none of whom asked about Aunt Brenda, fortunately, she made her way to her office where she sequestered herself with the intention to go over her notes on today's guests: a heart surgeon from Moscow, a woman who wrote a diet book for people who love chocolate, and a new young actor promoting his latest movie.

She'd no more than sat down when there was a tap on the door, and Alan, already in makeup, poked his head inside. "I'd like to talk to you after the show," he said, as Audra rushed by him with her huge case and a quick "'Scuse me."

"Sure. What about?"

He glanced at Audra then shook his head. "It'll wait."

"Good, because I can't!" Audra said, unzipping her case and eyeing Kaylie. "Now, you don't look as good as you did yesterday."

"Thanks a lot," Kaylie teased, but she knew the hairdresser was right. Two nights ago she'd slept soundly in Zane's arms, only to be awakened to make love to him. Last night she'd tossed and turned, angry with him one minute, missing him the next. She hadn't gotten much sleep.

"A few eye drops—a little blush, and you'll be good as new," Audra announced, but Kaylie wasn't convinced.

However, Audra worked her magic and Kaylie felt better. The show went well, and aside from Alan sending her silent messages she didn't understand, the segments passed without a hitch.

Afterward she had lunch in the deli across the street, then spent the rest of the afternoon in her office, reviewing the tape of the day's show and making preparations for the next program.

There was a quick knock on the door, and Alan once again poked his head inside. "Got a minute?"

"Sure. What's up?" She tossed her pencil onto the desk as Alan closed the door behind him.

"There's talk about a sequel to *Obsession*."

"I've heard."

"The producer's talking with the writer of the original script as well as to Cameron." Cameron James had been the director of *Obsession*.

Alan's face was split with a huge grin. "This could revive both our careers," Alan went on, pacing on the other side of Kaylie's desk.

"No one's approached me yet," she said.

"And if they do?"

"I—I don't know." A shiver of fear slid down her spine as she remembered the premiere.

"'Don't know'?" he repeated, aghast. "Kaylie, just think of it. You never had a chance to prove yourself as anything but a child star, but now you could show how you've grown up, how your character has matured!" He was excited. His eyes practically glowed, and his hands became expressive. "This is an opportunity we can't pass up."

"No one's shown me a script yet."

"It'll happen," Alan predicted, buoyed. "I spoke with my agent last night and again this morning. Sequels are all the rage. Look at *Back to the Future*, the *Rocky* films. Not every one is a blockbuster, but some are. And they don't have to be action films. There's *Texasville*."

Kaylie considered the idea. She'd been approached to do small parts in several movies over the years, but had always declined. "I'm happy here—doing what we do, Alan."

"Well," he said, rubbing his hands nervously, "it hasn't happened yet, but when it does, just promise me you'll keep an open mind. I know that the *Obsession* premiere was a real bummer, but it was a once-in-a-lifetime thing, and look at it this way, the publicity didn't hurt the ticket sales."

"Alan!"

He grinned as he reached for the door handle. "Just a little joke. You know, you're too serious, Kaylie. Much too serious. You need to lighten up.''

"I'll keep that in mind."

He left, and Kaylie, a headache beginning to pound behind her eyes, decided to call it a day. She was tired of Alan and his schemes. How could he talk about the premiere of *Obsession* as if the entire horrifying experience were nothing more than a publicity stunt?

If only it had been....

But the memory was too vivid, the images too terrifying and real. Frowning darkly, trying not to dwell on the brutal image of that night, she shivered and told herself to shake off the lingering fears.

She didn't see him, so much as feel his presence.

"Kaylie?" Zane's voice drifted to her as if in a dream. Standing in the doorway, filling it with his broad shoulders and narrow hips, Zane was watching her. His hair was mussed, and Kaylie guessed he'd sprinted across the parking lot.

"Is something wrong?" His features were taut with concern.

"Oh—no, nothing." She decided there was no reason to worry him just because Alan had mentioned the premiere of *Obsession.*

"Nothing?" He closed the door behind him and crossed the room. "Something's bothering you," he challenged, hooking one leg over the corner of her desk. "What happened?" Concern etched the lines of his face, and she thought guiltily that she should be thankful that he cared.

She couldn't lie. "Well, for starters, Alan seems to think I should jump-start my movie career by agreeing to costar in *Obsession II* or whatever it may be called."

Zane didn't move.

"Never mind that there's no script or director, yet."

"You couldn't—"

"And that was on top of a pretty bad week to begin with."

"Bad?" he said, a small smile tugging at the corners of his lips.

"Well, you see, I have this ex-husband, who has been ramrodding his way back into my life." She crossed her arms over her chest. "You probably know the type—pushy, arrogant, opinionated."

"But handsome, sexy and intelligent."

"That's the one," she said, her bad mood beginning to evaporate.

"And you don't like him pushing you around, right?"

She avoided his eyes for a second and fingered the strand of pearls at her throat. "Well, the problem is, I do like him—a lot. More than I think I should. But I don't appreciate him trying to dominate me. But he knows that—"

Zane reached across the desk and took her hand in his. "Kaylie, I love you." The words hung in the air suspended by unseen emotional threads.

Her mouth went dry, and she had trouble finding her voice. As she stared into his eyes, she whispered, "Love isn't based on possession, Zane, and you've tried to possess me for as long as I can remember."

"Hey, Kaylie, about tomorrow's show—" Alan said, opening the door without knocking. With one glance at Zane, he froze.

To Kaylie's surprise, Zane actually smiled, releasing Kaylie's hand and facing Alan. "Bently," he drawled, as if seeing a long-lost friend. "I was just asking Kaylie if she's seen the front page of *The Insider*.

"You what…?" Kaylie asked, feeling a cold lump form in her stomach. Alan licked his lips.

Zane reached into the inner pocket of his jacket and withdrew a folded piece of newsprint. He smoothed it on her desk, and she read the bold, two-inch high headlines: Lover's Spat Forces Kaylie Off Morning Show.

"What is this?" she demanded, skimming the article that insinuated that she and Alan, still planning marriage, had been involved in an argument that sent her running away, seeking solace for her wounded heart. "This is absurd. I did no such thing!" she said, glaring first at Alan, then at Zane. "You're the reason I left. You kidnapped me!"

"Kidnapped?" Alan repeated, his mouth falling open, his

gaze moving from Kaylie to Zane and back again. "Wait a minute. Let me get this straight. He *kidnapped* you?"

Zane shot her a look that cut to the bone.

Alan lounged one shoulder against the wall. "Is that what you call *persuading* you to go to the mountains?"

Zane pushed himself to his feet and said quietly, "Kaylie and I need to talk. Alone." He grabbed her jacket from a hook near the door. "Let's go."

Alan was amused and couldn't help the grin that toyed with his lips. "Well, Kaylie, what happened to all that independence you were so hell-bent to earn, hmm?"

"Oh, give it a rest, Alan," she snapped as she and Zane walked out of the building. Still stung by Alan's remark, she said, "I'll drive."

To her surprise, Zane didn't argue, just slid his long body into the small interior of the Mustang. As she cocked her wrist to twist the key in the ignition, he slanted a sexy, knowing smile in her direction. "I suppose it would be too much to expect you to kidnap me to a private lodge in the mountains."

"Way too much," she said as the engine started. But she laughed. "Okay," she said, and eased out of the parking lot and into the late-afternoon traffic, "talk."

Sighing, he stared out the window. Evening shadows stretched across the town as traffic moved sluggishly along the hilly streets. "Well, I've spent the last—" he checked his watch "—thirty-six hours staying away from you, giving you some space, and it's been hell. I just wanted to be alone with you again."

Kaylie's heart turned over.

"I'm trying to give you space—breathing room—all those things you figure are so important, but, if you want to know the truth, I don't like it much."

"Neither do I," she admitted, trying to concentrate on traffic as she switched lanes and stopped for a red light. As the light changed, she tromped on the accelerator and the car sped forward again.

"Then let's change things," he said quietly.

"How?"

"Pull over—"

"What?"

"Over there." He pointed to a side street near a park. Kaylie found a parking spot and turned off the car. Zane climbed out of the Mustang, and she followed, not sure what he was going to say.

The sun, partially obscured by a few flimsy clouds, was low in the sky and shadows lengthened over the ground. Leaves danced across the grass, pushed by a cool breeze. In the distance, children played football while dogs bounded in the thickets of trees nearby. Women pushed strollers, and squirrels chattered in the high branches of the oaks and maple trees.

Kaylie's heels scraped against the path. Zane took her hand, his warm fingers linking through hers. "I think we should try again," he said quietly, his voice rough with emotion as he looked down at her.

"Try?" she repeated, but she knew what he meant, and happiness and fear surged through her.

He brushed a strand of hair from her forehead, his fingers warm and gentle. "Marriage. I want you to be my wife again. Marry me, Kaylie."

She wanted to say yes, to throw her arms around his neck and kiss him and tell him that they could live together happily ever after. Tears sprang to her eyes, and she bit her lip. "I—I don't know," she whispered, blinking rapidly.

"Why not?"

"We tried marriage once before—"

"And we were young and immature. Both of us. This time it would be different. Come on, Kaylie." He drew her into the protective circle of his arms, and his lips brushed gently over her forehead.

God, how she loved him! Her arms wrapped around his back, and she laid her head against his chest, hearing the steady beat of his heart. She closed her eyes for a second. Living with Zane would either be ecstasy or torture—heaven or hell.

When her eyes opened, she focused on the street, where the cars whipped by, wheels spinning, horns blaring.

"Well?" he asked, holding her at arm's length.

Say yes! Don't be a fool! This is your one chance at happiness! "I just don't know," she admitted, and the pain that surfaced in his eyes cut through her heart. "I love you, Zane," she confessed. "I always have." His arms tightened around her.

"So what's the problem?"

"I just don't want to fail again."

"We won't," he promised, kissing her crown.

"Then...I...I need a few days to think it over."

Zane sighed, his breath ruffling her hair. "Why? So you can analyze our chances?"

"Last time we rushed things—ran on pure emotion. This time—if there is a this time—I want to make the right decision."

For a second she thought he'd be angry. His face clouded, and he dropped his hands. "Okay," he finally said, shoving a hand through his hair in frustration. "You have time to think it over, but don't take too long, okay?" He strode back to the car and climbed inside. She followed and slid behind the wheel.

"Why don't you take me to dinner?" he remarked as she checked her side-view mirror and tried to pull into traffic.

"I have a better idea—you take me."

"Only if I can persuade you to marry me."

She grinned inwardly. At least he wasn't furious with her. Signaling, she eased the car into the right-hand lane and noticed that a silver car about a block behind her followed suit. She frowned as she realized the car was a Taurus, but so what? The city was crawling with them.

Zane placed a hand on her knee. "How about someplace elegant—French dining overlooking the bay."

"How about pizza?" she countered, and he laughed.

"You're the driver, Kaylie. You can take me anywhere you want."

"You did *what?*" Margot nearly dropped her glass of Chablis as Kaylie finished her story about her relationship with Zane.

Margot had driven Kaylie to the house in Carmel so that she could turn in the rental and pick up her car. "I told Zane that

I'd consider it. Then we went out for pizza and I took him back to his car.''

"Oh, boy, are you crazy.'' Margot took a long sip of wine and shook her head. Seated at a round umbrella table on the back deck of Kaylie's house in Carmel, she eyed her sister as if she had truly lost her mind. "Some women spend their entire lifetimes looking for a man like Zane Flannery. And you know what?''

"What?'' Kaylie asked, not really interested in Margot's big-sister wisdom, but knowing she was going to hear it one way or another.

"They never find him, that's what! Men like Zane Flannery don't exactly grow on trees, you know!''

"Thanks for the advice.''

Margot smiled. She was on a roll. "And you got lucky and found him twice! If I were you, I'd march right into the house and call him right now.''

"And say what?'' Kaylie teased.

"That you've already found the preacher, for crying out loud!''

Kaylie twisted the stem of her wineglass. She'd thought the very same thing and had even made it as far as the telephone a couple of times, but in the end she'd backed down. "I don't want to make the same mistake we did before.''

"You won't. You're older now. And, most importantly, the man loves you, with a capital *L*. So why are you fighting it?''

Kaylie let her gaze wander out to sea. Margot had a point, she admitted to herself.

"And you miss him, don't you?''

Kaylie sighed and shrugged. "Yeah,'' she admitted, trying to sound indifferent when deep inside she missed him every minute of every day. She hadn't stopped thinking about him, couldn't sleep, plotted ways of bumping into him.

"Look, if it's a matter of pride—''

"It's more than that,'' Kaylie admitted, remembering the way Zane kidnapped her—just hauled her into the woods without even asking her first. "I can't accept a man who insists on dominating and pampering me."

"You did once."

"That was before."

"Right," Margot said, as if she'd just made her point. "Before that damned premiere of *Obsession!* Until then, you and Zane were comfortably ensconced in marital bliss. To tell you the truth, I was envious."

"You?" Kaylie's eyes rounded on her sister. "But you and Trevor—"

Margot waved impatiently, and sadness stole over her features. "I know, I know. But the truth of the matter was, my marriage wasn't perfect."

This was news to Kaylie. For as long as she could remember, Margot had been in love with Trevor Holloway.

"Oh, don't get me wrong. I loved Trevor more than I should have and I know that he loved me. But—" she lifted a shoulder "—we had our problems, just like anyone else."

"What kinds of problems?" Kaylie asked.

"It doesn't matter—they seem stupid now and petty. I'd gladly take all our problems back if Trevor were still alive." Margot sighed and squinted out to sea, watching the sun lower in a blaze of brilliant gold that scorched the sky and reflected on the water. She seemed to focus on a solitary sailboat that skimmed across the horizon—a sailboat not unlike the one on which Trevor had lost his life.

Kaylie thought she was finished, but Margot settled deeper into her deck chair and continued, "No marriage is perfect, but some are better than others and some are the best. I have a feeling that you and Zane had one of the best—at least until that creep Lee Johnston decided to mess things up." Margot shuddered.

"Even before the premiere, Zane was...autocratic."

"He was scared. You'd been getting those letters and he was terrified that something might happen to you—which it did." Margot leaned across the table, her gaze touching her sister's. "Give the guy a break, Kaylie. All he's ever done is love you too much. Is that such a crime?"

"I guess not."

"I know not!" Margot finished her glass of wine. "The point is, that Zane's crazy about you. Also, he's handsome, successful, caring, dependable, honest, intelligent and has a great sense of humor. What more do you want?"

"Someone who'll let me make my own decisions," Kaylie replied before smiling and adding, "but of course he'll have to be handsome, successful, caring, dependable—and all the rest of those qualities you reeled off."

"Then if I were you, I wouldn't look any farther than your ex-husband," Margot said as she climbed out of her chair and stretched. "Mark my words, Kaylie, you'll never find a man who loves you more than Zane does. And, if you'll stop long enough to be honest with yourself, you'll realize that you'll never love a man the way you love him." She reached for her purse and concluded, "You just have to ask yourself what you really want in life—to be lonely and independent or to take a chance on love—real love. I'll see you later. Think about what I said."

Kaylie figured she didn't have much choice. She watched Margot leave and knew her older sister was right. She'd never love a man as she loved Zane.

Zane paced around his office. He'd spent the better part of the afternoon listening to his accountant argue that another office, located in Denver or Phoenix, was just what the company needed. Zane wasn't interested. Expanding the business suddenly seemed trivial.

For the past week he'd tried to stay away from Kaylie. He hadn't called her, he hadn't visited her, he hadn't even shown up on the set of *West Coast Morning*, though he had tuned in every day and had sworn under his breath whenever Kaylie and Alan shared a smile or a joke.

"It's just her job," he told himself, but he couldn't stem the stream of jealousy that swept through his blood. More than once, he had snapped off the TV in disgust, only to click it on again.

But he was giving her time to come to a decision—the most important decision of his life!

He slumped back into his chair, picked up the accountant's proposal, then tossed it into his wastebasket. He didn't need another office to stretch the corporate tentacles of Flannery Security. He didn't really care if he never made another dollar. He just wanted Kaylie.

"You're obsessed," he told himself, not for the first time, as he strode to the bar, found a bottle of Scotch and poured three fingers into his glass. Then he checked his watch. Barely one-thirty in the afternoon. Disgusted with himself, he tossed the drink into the sink, strode back to his desk and fished the figures for the new office from his wastebasket.

"Concentrate, Flannery," he ordered himself as he picked up a pencil to jot notes. But the letters and numbers on the pages jumbled before his eyes, and Kaylie's face, fresh and smiling, framed in a cloud of golden hair, swam in his mind.

His pencil snapped.

Muttering an oath aimed at himself, he grabbed his jacket and marched out of the office. "Cancel all my appointments this afternoon," he told Peggy as he headed toward the elevator.

"And where can I reach you?"

"I wish I knew," he replied. The elevator doors whispered open, and he climbed inside. He thought of a dozen schemes to contact Kaylie again, but dismissed them all. He'd just have to wait.

The following few days Kaylie was nervous as a cat. Margot's advice kept running through her mind. She half expected Zane to fall back into his old pattern—and she suspected that he might have her under surveillance.

But he never showed up at her apartment or the beach house again. Nor did he call or leave a message on her machine.

It was as if she'd finally gotten through to him and he was going to leave her alone.

"That's what you wanted, wasn't it?" she asked herself one evening. It was Friday and had been raining all day. Alan had been in a bad mood on the set, and the taping hadn't gone well.

By the time Kaylie reached the beach house, she'd acquired a thundering headache and her shoes were soaked from her walk across the television station parking lot. All she could think about was a hot shower, a cup of tea and a good book.

And Zane of course. She let herself in with her key and smiled sadly. She never had bothered to change the locks; she hadn't had the heart to lock Zane out. And yet he'd never so much as tried any of her doors since the night he'd spirited her away.

And now he wanted to marry her. She was warmed by the thought. Her only hesitation was the thought of failing again, of the pain of divorce. She would never put herself, nor Zane for that matter, through all that pain again. Stripping off her clothes, she continued toward the bathroom.

The phone rang and she grabbed the bedroom extension, half expecting the caller to be Zane. "Hello?" she answered, smiling.

No answer.

"Hello?" she asked again, and there was still silence on the line. "Zane—is that you?" She waited, but heard nothing, and her nerves stretched taut. "Is anyone there? Look, I can't hear you. Why don't you try again?" She hung up slowly and waited, staring at the rain sheeting against her bedroom window and the dark, threatening clouds rolling in from the sea.

The only sounds were the distant rumble of thunder, the rain peppering the roof and the sound of her own heartbeat. The minutes ticked slowly by. "It was probably just a wrong number," she thought aloud, then continued toward the bathroom. She'd hoped the caller had been Zane, and her heart tripped at the thought that he'd tried to reach her.

Maybe Margot had been right, she finally decided, maybe it was her turn to reach out to Zane. Maybe there was a chance that they might start over again. If given the chance, surely Zane would treat her as an intelligent, mature woman.

He had to.

Because she loved him. With all her heart, she loved him and always would. There was no other man for her—no white knight lurking in the wings ready to dash up and carry her away. Zane was the only man in her life—always had been, always would be and she'd been a fool not to realize it before.

Wrenching off the faucets, she heard the phone ring again. She barely took the time to wrap a bath sheet around her before she dashed into the bedroom, leaving a trail of water behind her.

"Hello?" she called into the phone, her voice breathless, just as the caller hung up. "No! I'm here!" she yelled, feeling in her bones that the caller had been Zane. "Well, there's only one way to find out," she decided, throwing open her dresser drawers and yanking on her underwear. Tonight she was going to drive all the way back to the city, back to Zane's apartment and tell him she loved him. They'd have a chance to start over again.

Rick Taylor groaned. His hand went to his head and he felt something sticky and wet on the floor where he lay. Blinking hard, he forced his eyelids open only to close them again at the glare from the single shaft of light near the floor. He slipped back out of consciousness before jerking awake. His skull pounded, the pain creating orbs of light behind his closed lids.

"Wha-what the hell?" he muttered, licking his lips. He remembered walking into that loony patient Johnston's room. But Johnston had not been in his bed. Turning to sound an alarm, Rick had felt the hot flash of pain in his abdomen and, doubling over, the crash of something against the back of his head.

Now he propped himself on one elbow, feeling the wound in his side tearing open. "Help," he tried to cry, but the sound was barely a rattling whisper. How long had he been here? Seconds? Minutes? Hours?

But surely he'd be missed. Trying to push himself upright, he fell back and attempted to call for help again. The narrow sliver of light, coming from the hall outside the door, wavered in front of his eyes.

"Help me! Please!"

Using all his strength, he pulled himself toward the door and the hallway. Pain ripped through his body, pounding at his temple. The room, barely ten foot square, seemed to stretch on forever as he inched his way to the door.

With each agonizing tug, his muscles shuddered and sweat poured over his bleeding head. "Somebody help me!" he said again and again until he reached the door. His bloody fingers surrounded the knob and he tugged. But the door didn't budge. He tried again, then realized that the door was locked from the outside.

Swearing, Rick fumbled on his belt for his keys only to discover that his entire key ring—the keys to the hospital, his apartment and his car—was missing.

"Oh, God," he cried, using his last ounce of strength to pound on the door before slipping into unconsciousness again.

"Answer, Kaylie, answer!" Zane whispered, before giving up. "Damn it all to hell!" He swore violently as he slammed the receiver into the phone cradle. His heart was thudding, his palms sweating as he stared at the phone message stating that Lee Johnston had escaped from Whispering Hills Psychiatric Hospital.

Zane's hands were shaking as he walked into the reception area where Peggy was bent over her word processor. "Dial 911. Ask for the police. Tell them that a patient who escaped from Whispering Hills threatened Kaylie once before and give them Kaylie's address—her apartment in the city as well as the house in Carmel." Uncapping his pen with his teeth, he scribbled out the information for her. "But first order the company helicopter to stand by," he commanded. "Tell Dave I want him to take me to Carmel and drop me off at the Buxton building."

"He's already waiting," Peggy said. "He was going to fly Hastings to—"

"Cancel that and have him wait for me."

"Will do." Peggy turned to the telephone and Zane raced out of the office. Heart thumping with fear, he took the stairs two at a time.

On the roof the helicopter was waiting, its gigantic blades churning in the night. Rain and wind lashed at Zane's face as he dashed across the wet concrete to the pad where Brad Hastings was climbing out of the passenger seat.

Covering his head with his briefcase Hastings yelled over the whir of the helicopter blades, "You just about missed us!"

"Emergency," Zane yelled back as he climbed into the copter and Dave dashed for cover. Glancing at the pilot, he said, "Carmel, on the double. Radio ahead for a company car—a fast one. And get me a backup."

"You got it," Dave replied, talking into his headset as Zane strapped himself in. The helicopter lifted off and Zane sent up a silent prayer. Fear tore at his guts as his worst nightmare played through his mind. He only hoped they weren't too late.

Kaylie grabbed her purse and squared her shoulders. She wasn't very good at eating humble pie, but Zane was worth it. This time, she decided, her pride wouldn't get in her way. Snatching a raincoat and umbrella from the hall closet, she headed through the kitchen and slung the strap of her purse over her shoulder.

She punched the answer button on her answering machine and locked the door behind her. In the garage, she heard the phone ring, but ignored the call. Even if the caller were Zane, she found the idea of surprising him in person appealing. If only she had a set of keys to his apartment, she'd turn the tables on him and wait for him in the dark...maybe in his bed with champagne?

She smiled to herself and reached for the button to open the garage door when she heard the sound—a small sound—like the scrape of leather on concrete.

Kaylie froze. Her skin crawled. Telling herself the noise was only her imagination, she strained to listen. Maybe she heard the scurry of a mouse or the neighbor's tabby cat. He was always hanging around when she stayed here. He could have been locked in the garage.

She punched the button but the door didn't open. Nothing happened. When she flicked on the light switch next to the opener, the garage remained dark.

Fear cut a swath into her heart, and she fumbled in her purse for her keys. She glanced nervously around the garage, to the shadowed corners. "Who's there?" she called, but heard nothing. "It's just your nerves," she told herself. Something moved in her peripheral vision.

Kaylie didn't wait. She shoved open the door to the house, letting the interior lights illuminate the darkened garage. Two steps inside a cold hand grabbed hold of her arm. Kaylie screamed.

Lee Johnston, his icy blue eyes blank, stared straight through her.

"Kaylie." His voice was rough and gritty. His flame-red hair was plastered to his head and the drip of rain ran down his neck and beneath the wet collar of his blue shirt.

Her knees went weak, but she pulled hard, intending to escape.

"Leave me alone," she screamed, but the words were only in her mind. Her throat was frozen. Light from the kitchen refracted off the knife in his hand.

Dizziness overwhelmed her. The premiere of *Obsession*. Her life flashed to a series of stills. Zane, oh, Zane, I'm so sorry, she thought.

"Kay-lee," her assailant mumbled and she tried vainly to wrench herself free. But he was strong and compact and determined. Thoughts ran through her mind. She needed a weapon. Tools in the garage. Knives in the kitchen. Anything!

"Kay-lee," he said again, his voice as chilling as the howl of a wolf. She backed up, stumbling over the edge of rakes and shovels. Lee kept up with her, his fingers biting into her arm, the knife's blade somewhere in the dark beside her.

"Let—let me go," she demanded, trying to stay calm, to hold at bay the panic that surged through her brain. Maybe she could talk him out of this! He'd never hurt anyone before—not really. But then, as he passed by the window, she saw the dark smudges on his shirt and knew the stains were blood. Not his, certainly. But whose?

Zane's? Her thoughts rambled crazily, and she thought for a blinding moment that Johnston might have sought his revenge on the man who had captured him years before. The only man she'd ever loved. *Oh, Zane. No, please, God, let him be alive.* Why hadn't she listened to him? Why?

Her knees threatened to buckle. If Zane were dead or lying hurt and wounded...

"No!" she wailed, throwing her body hard against Johnston. He tripped on a rake or shovel, and his fingers slackened. She leaped forward, and he lost his balance. The kitchen! If she could just get into the kitchen and run outside.

"Help!" she screamed, and scrambled past her car.

She rounded the trunk, moving slowly backward, listening to Johnston's movements in the dim light. Was he following her or trying to cut her off by rounding the front of the car? If only the garage door weren't locked! *Think, Kaylie, think!* There was an ax— Oh, God, where was it? Or a crowbar. Anything to protect herself. And the garage door opener—by the back door.

Heart pounding, she inched toward the door.

She heard voices—or was it her imagination? No, there were voices. Johnston heard them, too. He quit moving, though his breathing sounded close—between her and the kitchen. But where?

She stopped, listening, trying to focus. Moments passed. Tense, terrible moments.

Footsteps outside. "Kaylie! Kaylie!" Zane's voice rang through the house. "Oh, God, where are you?" He was alive! Kaylie's heart soared.

From a shadowy corner, Johnston lunged at her.

She screamed. "Zane! Don't come in here!" she cried. "He's got a knife—" But Zane came flying through the door, and in one quick motion, he threw himself into the darkness.

"Oh, please, no!" Kaylie cried as Zane propelled himself through the air and landed on Johnston and his raised knife. The blade flashed up, then swiftly down, landing with a thud in Zane's back before being torn out with a hideous sucking sound.

The two men struggled, and Johnston freed himself, struggling to his feet. Zane pulled himself upright, but swayed.

Kaylie thought she'd be sick. "No!" she screamed as Johnston raised his bloody knife again. She fell back against a shovel. Without thinking, she picked up the rusted tool and using all her strength, swung it, catching Johnston's knees. He dropped like a stone.

Zane sprang, quick as a cat. Blood oozed from the sleeve of his shirt. He rolled on top of the flailing man.

"Freeze!" A strong male voice yelled from the doorway, and Kaylie looked up to see a man in jeans and a sweater training a gun on Zane and Johnston.

"No!"

"Kay-lee, Kay-lee!" Johnston cried.

Kaylie shuddered.

"Back off!" the man in the doorway ordered, his face contorted in rage, his revolver aimed at Johnston's chest. "You okay?" he asked Zane.

"I thought you'd never get here."

"I radioed the police. Now, come on, let's get this lowlife out of here."

Sirens screamed outside. As Zane struggled to restrain Johnston, two policemen ran through the house and, pistols drawn, charged into the garage.

"Police! Everybody hold it!" the taller man said, his gun trained on Johnston and Zane.

"Call for an ambulance!" Kaylie cried, watching in horror as a scarlet stain spread across the back of Zane's shirt.

"Already done. Okay, someone called in about an escapee from Whispering Hills. What's going on here?"

Zane, his face white and drained, tried to explain, but Kaylie, frantic for his life, told the police that she'd answer all their questions once Zane was in the hospital. She wouldn't listen to the officers when they demanded answers. Instead she climbed into the back of the ambulance and held Zane's hand all the way to the hospital. He tried to smile, but failed, and his eyes closed wearily.

"You're okay," she said, her voice trembling as she assured herself more than him.

But he didn't respond, and she knew that he'd lost consciousness.

"Don't die, Zane," she whispered, clinging to his fingers as if she could will the life to remain in his body. She heard the whine of ambulance tires spinning against the rain-washed streets. She only wished she'd told him how much she loved him—how much he meant to her.

Lord, she'd been stupid; she knew now. Because of her stubbornness, Zane had nearly been killed. If only she'd listened to him, trusted him, relied upon him, *leaned* on him! If only she'd loved him enough to work with him to save their marriage. Oh, Lord, she'd been such a fool, she thought, tears tracking down her cheeks.

Now it was too late. Too late. Maybe much too late....

Chapter Thirteen

Kaylie didn't leave Zane's bedside. The doctors assured her that Zane was fine, that the wound was shallow. The blade of Johnston's knife had only penetrated Zane's shoulder muscle. Though he would be sore for a while, the team of experts at Bayside Hospital were convinced that Zane would be "good as new" in no time. Nonetheless, she camped out at the hospital that night.

"He's sedated. He won't wake up for hours," Dr. Ripley predicted. "You can't do anything for him now. Tomorrow, unless he takes a turn for the worse, I'll release him."

"I want to be here when he wakes up."

"I'll have the nurse call you." Ripley was a thin man in his early fifties with freckles splashed all over his face, neck and arms. His once-red hair was turning to gray, but he seemed as fit as most thirty-year-olds.

"I'd rather wait. It's important," Kaylie insisted.

The doctor slanted a brow. Motioning toward Zane, he said, "He might not be in the greatest mood when he wakes up."

"I don't care."

"Well, okay. Have it your way," the doctor finally agreed, instructing the nurse that Kaylie was to spend the night.

She spent the night in a chair, alternately dozing and waking with a start, her muscles cramping. The small room was never dark. Light from the parking lot street lamps filtered through the blinds, and illumination from the hall made the shapes in the room visible.

In her fitful hours of sleep, she relived, over and over again, the horrible moments in the garage. The knife. The blade plunging into Zane's shoulder. Blood pooling on the floor. Johnston, dead-blue eyes staring at her, laughing maniacally as she threw herself on Zane's unmoving body. Tears choked her throat. She couldn't lose him...she couldn't....

"Zane! No! Please, no!" She woke to find herself in the hospital room, Zane sleeping on the bed, the worst over.

Relief brought tears to her eyes.

Zane blinked twice, shifted and felt a brutal pain rip through his shoulder. He sucked in a swift breath. Shadowy images flitted through the mists in his mind—terrifying visions of the madman and his knife. Kaylie—where was she? His eyes blinked against an intense light.

"Zane?"

Kaylie's voice was like a balm to the pain. Thank God she was alive! Relief flooded through him. Those last frightening minutes in the inky garage, the maniac with his weapon...

Through the fog of his memory, Zane recalled leaping into the dark garage, flying at Johnston and struggling for the knife.

Now he focused with difficulty and discovered Kaylie standing on the other side of the bars of his bed, her hands white as she gripped the rails, her eyes clouded with worry. Her hair was tangled and mussed, her makeup long washed away, her clothes, the same as she'd been wearing the night before, wrinkled and smudged with blood—his blood. Her eyes were red-rimmed and cloudy green and her eyebrows pulled together with worry.

And she was gorgeous. He managed a smile. "You look like I feel."

Letting out her breath, she blinked against a sudden bout of tears. "So you're going to rejoin the living after all?"

"The jury's still out on that one," he grumbled, realizing he was in a hospital bed, bandaged and swathed, an IV dripping fluid into his wrist. Wincing, he attempted to sit up, but Kaylie's hands, cool and soft, restrained him.

"Slow down, cowboy," she said, and he noticed the tremor in her voice and saw the tracks of recent tears on her cheeks. "We've got all the time in the world."

"Do we?" he asked, his gaze locking with hers.

She sniffed loudly. "The rest of our lives."

"Why, Ms. Melville," he drawled, suddenly feeling no pain, "is this a proposal?"

She laughed, though her eyes were wet. Sniffing loudly, she brushed her tears aside with the back of her hand. "You bet it is. And I don't expect to end up a widow before I'm a bride, so you just take care of yourself."

"So now you're giving orders."

"And you're taking them," she announced firmly, though she swallowed hard. "After all, someone's got to protect you."

He laughed at that. "So what're you? My personal body-guard."

"No, Zane. Just your wife."

He reached up, and pain seared through his shoulder. Emotions clogged his throat. "You don't know how long I've waited to hear you say those words," he admitted, then with his free hand, playfully grabbed her. "I wish I had a tape recorder, because, no matter what, I'm holding you to it."

Her fingers linked through his. "I wouldn't have it any other way."

"Breakfast time." A nurse, pushing a rattling tray, shoved open the door. "But first I need to take your temperature and pulse and..."

Zane groaned, and the nurse winked at Kaylie. "Looks like he's out of the woods. Why don't you run down to the cafeteria and get yourself something to eat and a cup of coffee."

"Sounds like heaven," Kaylie admitted.

While the nurse tended to Zane, Kaylie made her way to the

ladies' room where she washed her face as best she could, repaired her makeup and ran a comb through her wild hair. Glancing in the mirror, she snorted. "Not exactly the glamorous talk-show hostess today, Melville."

For the first time, she thought about her job, and tucking her comb and brush into her purse, she walked toward the lobby. Spying a pay phone near the admitting area, she dredged up a quarter and dialed the station. The receptionist answered on the second ring.

"Hi, Becky, it's Kaylie."

"Oh! Kaylie, let me put you through. Jim's been trying to get hold of you."

"I'll bet," Kaylie remarked as the phone clicked several times and Jim Crowley finally answered.

"You made the front page," Jim announced. "And not of *The Insider* for once. You're in the *Times*."

"I'm not surprised," she drawled.

"You okay?"

Kaylie wondered. She was still shaken by the incident, no doubt about it. Her skin prickled at the horrific memory, and yet she felt better than she had in years. She loved Zane, and planned to be with him for the rest of her life. "I'm fine," she assured Jim.

A pause. "You sure?"

"Absolutely."

"It's pretty late. I don't suppose you'll be in." He sounded hopeful.

She laughed without much mirth. "Not today."

"That's okay. Alan already said he'd fill in, though he'd like to interview you about last night."

"No way."

"I told him that's what you'd say. Anyway, since it's Friday, I'm asking Chef Glenn to add a couple of appetizers to go with whatever today's concoction is."

"Hot and Spicy Chicken Linguine," Tracy said in the background.

Jim snorted. "Yeah, some Italian thing. I'll see you Monday."

She rang off and took the stairs to the cafeteria. There she ate alone, devouring a bagel and cream cheese and fresh fruit along with two cups of coffee. She felt more than one curious look cast in her direction and heard a few whispered comments.

"Kaylie Melville...yes, channel fifteen...a crazed mental patient went after her.... Yeah, maybe it was the same guy...the guy she was with is up on the second floor...no, not Bently... some other guy...you know those Hollywood types.... Her husband? *Ex*-husband, you mean...are you sure...? Well, what's she doing with him?

Ignoring the wagging tongues, Kaylie cleared her tray and picked up a newspaper near the lobby. Page one was splashed with the story. Pictures of her house in Carmel, photos of the retreating ambulance, and older shots of Zane and Johnston and her at the premiere of *Obsession* years before graced section two under local news. "Terrific," she muttered under her breath. "Just great."

Perusing the paper quickly, she decided Zane wasn't up to reading all about the "drama in Carmel" and stuffed the paper into the trash on her way back to his room.

The nurse had left. His breakfast, uneaten, had been pushed aside. Zane was propped up in bed, staring at the television, where a newscaster was reporting Johnston's escape and the attempt on Kaylie's life.

"Well, your name's on the tip of everyone's tongue today," he drawled.

"So's yours."

Zane rolled his eyes. "This is no good," he said. "The problem with all these reports is that it sensationalizes the crime. Who knows what nut is watching and thinking he'd like to get his name and picture on the television by imitating that maniac?" Scowling darkly, he scratched at the back of his hand. A bandage covered the spot where the IV needle had recently been attached to his skin.

"I think I'm safe," Kaylie replied. "Johnston's locked up."

"But how many more like him are out there?"

"It's the price of fame," she said, then nearly bit her tongue. Here it was. The same old argument. And she'd just inadvertently offered him a perfect opportunity to exploit his position. Still frowning, he clicked the remote control, and the lead-in music for *West Coast Morning* filled the room.

"Let's see what *your guys* say about it," Zane said, and Kaylie held her tongue, not wanting to let him know that Jim had already mentioned an interview to her.

Alan's face, gravely serious, was centered on the screen. "I'll be hosting the show alone today," he told the viewers, "because last night Kaylie Melville was viciously attacked by a knife-wielding assailant. The suspect is in custody, his alleged crime nearly identical to his assault on Kaylie seven years ago."

To Kaylie's horror, she watched old footage of the premiere of *Obsession*. Of course the cameramen had been there for quick peeks of the rich and famous. Those cameramen, who had been interested in showing who was dating whom and what dress Kaylie wore to the first showing, hadn't expected to capture a madman lunging at her on film. Nor had they intended for the terrifying drama to unfold in front of their lenses. But it had happened, and every heart-numbing second had been captured on film—from Kaylie's bloodless face, to Zane's heroic act that saved her life.

"Yes, history repeated itself last night at Kaylie Melville's beachside home in Carmel. Fortunately, once again her ex-husband, Zane Flannery, was on the scene to save her from a man who has been obsessed with her for years...."

Alan went on and on, recalling the details of last night's attack as well as bringing up the premier of *Obsession* again. He even publicly admitted that he and Kaylie were just friends, but very special friends, and he looked earnestly into the camera to wish her well.

"I think I'm gonna be sick." Zane clicked off the set.

"It's just his way," Kaylie said lamely, but she could hardly defend Alan. For, though he appeared concerned for her well-being, the entire segment reeked of publicity seeking and she couldn't help but think that all his references to *Obsession* were to drum up public interest in the old film in the hopes that the viewers and fans, as well as the studio heads, would demand a sequel.

"Well, for all his supposed friendship, he sure doesn't give a damn about exploiting you."

She couldn't argue with him and didn't. The less she thought about last night's attack, the better. She and Zane were together. Johnston was locked away. They were safe and in love. Nothing else mattered.

Zane was released just after noon, with strict orders to take care of himself and not strain the wound. "You've lost a lot of blood and you're carrying around fifteen stitches, so don't do anything foolish," Dr. Ripley told Zane as he signed the release forms.

To Zane's ultimate humiliation, Kaylie pushed him out of the hospital in a wheelchair and helped him into the passenger seat of his Jeep. Then she settled behind the steering wheel. The look she cast him should have tipped him off. Her green eyes danced with mischief as she headed east.

"Where're we going?"

"Can't you guess?"

He eyed her thoughtfully. "Don't tell me, you're kidnapping me to a certain mountain retreat...."

She laughed gaily. "I thought about it, but no, I've got something else in mind."

"What?"

"Lake Tahoe," she replied with an impish grin. "I know this great little place there. It's called the 'Chapel of No Return.'"

"No!"

"Scout's honor." She lifted one hand as if to pledge.

"So where's Franklin?"

"Your neighbor—Mrs. Howatch—called while you were sleeping and offered to watch him for the weekend." She grinned. "I hope she knows what she's getting into."

"Franklin likes her," Zane replied.

"Oh, it's just me he has problems with?" she teased.

"He'll get used to you. I did. Now, lead on, Ms. Melville," he suggested, settling back in his seat and staring at her as if he thought she might vanish and this entire fantasy give way to cruel reality.

Kaylie beamed. She felt as if she'd finally grown up enough to accept Zane as her husband. Yes, he'd been dominating and overzealous in his protection of her, but now she understood him better. She knew how frightened he must have been for her safety.

The few hours he'd been unconscious had been hell. She finally understood just what losing him would cost her. She didn't doubt that she loved him, always had loved him and always would. She didn't see that love as a curse any longer, but as a blessing. She wanted to spend the rest of her life with him, as his wife, as the mother of his children, as the lifelong partner with whom he would grow old.

And now, at twenty-seven, she felt secure and mature enough to handle him. No more temper tantrums—well, not too many. From here on in, they were partners.

She drove straight to Lakeside Chapel, and when Zane climbed out of the Jeep, stretched and grumbled that he wouldn't be married in anything less than the "Chapel of No Return," she offered to take him straight back to the city.

"I guess we'll just have to forget this whole marriage thing," she told him blithely.

At that he grabbed her roughly, spun her to him and growled in her ear, "Not on your life. I've waited too long for this."

She lifted her shoulders and rounded her eyes innocently. "Whatever you say, honey."

For that she was rewarded with a swat on the bottom. "Come on. No reason to keep the minister waiting."

Within thirty minutes they were married. The ceremony was simple. The preacher was a lively man who was pushing eighty, and his wife, a sparrow of a woman, served as pianist and witness. Another woman, heavyset and beaming, was the second witness, and at the end of the short ceremony, Kaylie and Zane were presented with a marriage certificate, a bouquet of roses, a brochure for Love Nest Cabins and a bottle of champagne.

"Not quite as elaborate as the first ceremony," Zane drawled, once they were back in the Jeep.

"But more lasting," Kaylie predicted.

"You think so?" His dark brow cocked insolently, but his gray eyes were flecked with humor.

"I'm sure!"

"So where to now?"

"Well, we could either go gambling...or..."

"Or what?"

"Or I could take you to the hotel and—" she lowered her voice suggestively and touched his thigh "—we could start the honeymoon."

He placed his warm palm over the top of her hand. "I'm definitely in favor of option two."

"Me, too." Her spirits soaring, she wheeled the Jeep into the parking lot of the hotel. Blue-green pines softened the lines of a rambling, three-storied lodge. With peaked dormers poking out of a sharply gabled roof and a covered porch that skirted the main floor, the rambling building rested on the shores of the vibrant blue lake.

"This is as close to 'heaven'—isn't that what you called your place in the mountains?—that I could find."

"I guess it'll just have to do," Zane drawled, as if he gave a damn about the hotel. All he wanted was Kaylie.

It took twenty minutes to register and have their bags carried to their third-floor suite. Impatiently Zane slapped a tip into the bellman's palm, then, when the young man left, locked the door behind him.

"Now, Mrs. Flannery, what was that you were saying about starting the honeymoon early?"

She laughed, the sound melodious as he wrapped his arms around her and lowered hungry lips to hers. Though his shoulder ached, he ignored the painful throb and got lost in the wonder of his wife.

Kissing her, holding her close, undressing her and feeling her clothes drop from her supple body, Zane felt a desperation that ripped through his soul.

Only hours before her life had been threatened by a knife-wielding madman intent on killing her.

The image was vivid and excruciating. What if he had lost her? What if Johnston's blade had found its mark? His heart nearly stopped at the thought, and he pulled her roughly against him, intent on washing away the horrid images in the smell and feel of her.

The nightmare was over. They could celebrate their lives and love.

Her body was warm and soft, yielding as he caressed her bare shoulder with the rough pad of his finger. She quivered at his touch, and her mouth opened easily at the gentle prod of his tongue. Her fingers were everywhere, as if she, too, felt the urgency of their union.

Life was so fleeting, so very precious, there was no time to waste. Her fingers pushed his shirt over his shoulders, and he flinched as she tugged on his sleeves and the wound in his upper back stung.

"Love me, Zane," she whispered, kissing the hairs on his chest, fanning the fire deep in his loins as her tongue touched his skin, rimming his nipples, lapping at his breastbone, tasting of him and causing wave after tormented wave of pure lust to wash through him.

With a groan he shifted his weight, shoving her slowly back against the down coverlet on the bed. He touched the outline of her bra with his fingers and mouth, kissing the soft curves of her breasts, kneading the white mounds until dark, petulant nipples peaked beneath the white lace. He teased those rosy buds with mouth and fingers as Kaylie writhed beneath him, arching anxiously, bucking her hips against his, silently begging for release.

Slow down, a voice in his mind protested. *Take your time.* But his body, and his desperation to love her, to prove that they had survived the terror of a madman's knife, wouldn't listen. His hands moved anxiously over her, tearing off her bra, stripping her of her underwear.

And she was just as desperate. Her hands worked at the waistband of his slacks, sliding them off his legs and kicking them aside as he mounted her.

With the first thrust, pain shot down his arm, ripping through him with a blinding agony that was matched only by the exquisite torture of her body moving in tandem with his. But he couldn't stop, and soon, as their tempo increased and their sweat-soaked bodies fused, he felt nothing but the sheer ecstasy of her body sliding against his.

"Kaylie, love," he cried, his voice as raw as a December night. He tried to hold back, resist, but the feel of her fingers digging into the muscles of his good shoulder and the deep-throated sound of her moans of pleasure brought him to quick and immediate release. He plunged into her with a primal cry that echoed through the room, and she shuddered against him, clawing and clinging, her face upturned in rapture, her low moan rippling through her body.

Collapsing against her, he held her tight, afraid that if he let go, he'd lose her. Rationally he knew that she was here, with him, and had pledged her life to him, but for so many years she'd been lost to him so that he clung to her as if to life itself. "I love you," he murmured into the sweat-darkened strands of her hair.

Propping up on one elbow, she gazed down on him with eyes that shifted from green to blue. "I thought the doctor said to take things easy," she teased.

"With you, nothing's easy."

Tilting her head back, she laughed, and the sound drifted to the rafters, high overhead. "I promise not to try to be impossible."

He slid her a knowing glance. "Don't make any rash statements."

"You're asking for it, Flannery."

His eyes sparked. "You bet I am." And with that, he grabbed her again, ignoring his doctor's instructions completely.

On Sunday morning Kaylie dragged herself out of bed, showered and dressed in clean jeans and a rose-colored sweater.

"What're you doing?" Zane asked, opening one sleepy eye and groaning as he watched her gather her hair into a ponytail and run a tube of lipstick over her lips.

"Duty calls," she replied, tilting her head to loop a gold earring through her earlobe. "I'm still a working woman, you know. I've got a million and one things to do before the show tomorrow.''

He grunted, and Kaylie sensed the first argument of their short marriage. ''You can call in and explain to Jim—''

''No.''

''But wouldn't you love to prolong the honeymoon?''

''Absolutely. But I can't. I've already missed more than my share of work lately.'' She caught his reflection in the oval mirror above an antique dresser. Draped across the sheets, wearing only his bandage and a day's growth of beard, he grinned that sexy grin that caused her heart to trip.

Still, she couldn't let him push her around and try to dominate her life. They had to start off on the right foot.

''You don't have to work, you know. I can take care of us.''

''It's my job, Zane. A job I happen to love. I'm not going to give it up.''

''Not ever?''

Turning, she said, ''Ever's a long time. But certainly not in the foreseeable future.''

''So how long do you *plan* to be hostess of *West Coast Morning?*''

''How about for as long as I want to? Or as long as the station wants me? You know, this job won't be indefinite. Whether the producer admits it or not, there is some age prejudice involved.'' She expected him to object, to give her reason upon reason why she shouldn't continue with her career, but he only lifted a shoulder.

''Whatever you want,'' he muttered.

She could have been knocked over with a feather. ''Wait a minute,'' she said. ''Whatever *I* want?''

''Umm. Long as you take care of yourself.''

''And you trust me?''

''I'm trying,'' he said, his smile fading. ''It's not easy.''

Surprised at his turnabout, she snagged a pair of his jeans from the floor of the cabin and tossed them at him. ''Come on, get dressed.''

''I could use a little help,'' he suggested, one brow lifting craftily.

"Could you?" She couldn't help but play along with his game.

"Well, I am an invalid."

She laughed out loud. "That'll be the day. You didn't seem like much of an invalid last night!"

To her surprise, he leaped off the bed and, catching her with his good arm, jerked her up against him. His lips came crashing down on hers with a savagery that stole her breath. "I lied about the invalid bit," he admitted, dragging her back to the bed and burying his face in the lush thickness of her hair.

"I know."

"I thought maybe I needed an excuse to get you back into bed."

"Never," she whispered against his lips. They tumbled onto the rumpled sheets together.

"You're married?" Alan's chin nearly dropped to his knees. "To Flannery?" Disbelief nearly choked him. "But you can't be.... He—he—"

"He's my husband," she replied. Polishing an apple with a paper towel in the station's cafeteria, she ignored the opened box of pastries and settled for a cup of coffee instead.

Alan tried desperately to recover. "Well, I read all about Johnston's escape," he said, "and I know that you must have been terrified. I mean, talk about nightmare déjà vu! But marriage? My God, Kaylie, what were you thinking?"

"That I loved him," she said, offering him a bright smile as she poured a thin stream of decaf coffee into her cup.

"You thought that once before."

"And I was right," she said, refusing to argue with him. She set the glass carafe onto the warming tray. "We—uh, just took a wrong turn." She took a sip from her cup and stared at him over the rim. "We won't make that mistake again."

Alan looked about to argue further, but snapped his mouth shut instead. Throwing his hands into the air, he shook his head. "Well, I guess there's nothing left but to congratulate you." To Kaylie's amazement, he hugged her. "Good luck, Kaylie.

You know I've only wanted what was best for you. I hope this time you're happy." She almost sloshed coffee all over him.

"I am," she assured him. "And thanks."

Margot was ecstatic. Kaylie and Zane arrived on her doorstep with a bottle of champagne and celebrated. "I'm so happy for you!" she said, tears streaming from her eyes. "I'm just sorry it took that awful Johnston to get you two together."

"At least that's behind us now," Kaylie said. "He won't be released for years—maybe ever."

"You hope," Zane replied, his expression guarded.

Kaylie wanted to ask him more, but Margot changed the subject and she forgot about the maniac for a while. After all, Lee Johnston was out of their lives forever!

The next two weeks sped past in a blur. Kaylie moved into Zane's apartment in the evenings after work, and Zane, still recuperating, divided his time between the office and home. They talked, laughed and made plans for the future, and slowly Franklin accepted her. At first the dog lay next to Zane, never leaving his side, but as the days passed and Kaylie became a permanent fixture in the apartment, Franklin relaxed, even following Kaylie after mealtimes.

Occasionally Zane and Kaylie argued, but Kaylie tried to keep her temper in check and Zane did a decent job of letting her maintain a certain level of independence.

All in all, the marriage seemed to work, though sometimes, if Kaylie's name or picture appeared in the tabloids, Zane would explode about "invasion of privacy, libel, and yellow journalism," and threaten to "sue the living hell out of those bastards," but once he was assured that Lee Johnston was locked up for a long time, Zane took everything in stride.

A model husband, she thought as she pulled into her parking space at the station one morning. Fog had blanketed the city, lingering in a chill mist that seeped into Kaylie's bones.

Unconsciously, she glanced over her shoulder, to see if the car that often stopped at the curb when she arrived at the station was in tow. But no silver Taurus emerged from the fog and she told herself to stop worrying; Johnston had been apprehended—no one else would follow her. Besides, she'd only spotted a car a couple of times. Once in a while a blue station wagon would occupy the same spot. Obviously the drivers were just another couple of early-morning commuters. Maybe they even carpooled together.

She locked her car and walked briskly into the studio where Tracy met her in the reception area. "Here are the updates for today's show and you're supposed to join an emergency meeting with Jim and Alan in Jim's office."

"Emergency?" Kaylie repeated. "What happened?"

"There's a problem with scheduling, I think. One of Friday's guests is backing out."

"And that calls for an 'emergency meeting'?"

"Go figure," Tracy said, rolling her eyes. "Alan is into high drama these days."

Well, that much was true, Kaylie thought as she tapped on the glass door of Jim's office and entered when he waved her in. Alan, already seated near Jim's desk, flashed her a smile.

"Problems?" Kaylie asked as Jim motioned her into the vacant chair next to Alan.

"Two cancellations on Friday's show," Jim explained, reaching into his drawer for a pack of cigarettes. "First the author who wrote the self-analysis book calls and explains that he can't make it for, quote, 'personal reasons' and would we be so kind as to reschedule him? Then we get a call from Jennifer Abbott's agent and Jennifer won't do the show."

"Why not?" Kaylie asked. Jennifer was one of the most controversial actresses on daytime television. Though always in the running for an Emmy, she was notorious for her contract disputes.

"Seems as if Jennifer is keeping mum until after the final round of her contract negotiations, whenever that may be. So for now we're out of luck."

"I thought Tracy had a list of local people who were willing to pinch-hit."

"We've been through it," Alan interjected. "And we've got a couple of 'maybes'..." He cast a quick glance in Jim Crowley's direction, and Kaylie had the distinct impression that they were holding back on her.

"So?" she prodded, uneasy.

Alan leaned forward, as if to confide in her. "So, I called Dr. Henshaw—you know, Johnston's psychiatrist—"

"I know who he is," she said tightly.

"And I asked him to appear."

"You did *what*?" She couldn't believe her ears. No way. *No damned way!*

"Well, face it, Kaylie. The public would like to know more about the man who attacked you. And since you're the cohostess, what better medium than our program to give the viewers a little insight into the complexity of the man?"

"And the police will allow this?" she asked, turning stricken eyes on Jim. "Won't it interfere with Johnston's trial? And what about patient confidentiality?"

Jim reached for a cigarette, then tossed the pack in the drawer and wadded up a stick of gum. "You don't understand. You wouldn't be asking him questions about Johnston...at least not directly. Actually, he'd be on the hot seat. We'd ask him to talk about an ordinary day at Whispering Hills, the makeup of the patients, that sort of thing, and then question him on Johnston's escape."

"I don't believe this," she replied, shocked. "I don't know why he'd agree."

Again the two men exchanged glances. Jim said, "Well, Henshaw does have something to gain from it all."

"What?"

"A little glory for himself," Alan explained. "He's been writing a book for years."

"What kind of a book?" Kaylie asked, dreading the answer.

Jim stepped in. "Apparently he's been working on psychological profiles of star stalkers for a few years. Must've started it before he got the job at Whispering Hills."

"Don't tell me," she said, "Lee Johnston is one of the cases in the book."

Alan grinned. "You got it. Anyway, the book is about done,

and suddenly a few publishers are interested. His agent is pushing for big bucks."

"And the publishers are interested because of Johnston's escape and all the press recently," Kaylie suggested.

"Bingo." Alan practically beamed. "Of course, after Johnston's trial, Henshaw can add a final chapter."

"Of course," Kaylie said dryly.

"How'd you find out about it?" she asked.

"I called." Alan's face turned crafty. "I figured there was a lot of public interest right now. I would have liked to have that orderly who was hurt in the escape, but the hospital won't allow it—nor will the police."

"But it's all right for Henshaw."

"As long as we zero in on the book and the escape. But we can't talk about the attack on you."

Kaylie, who had tried to keep as calm as possible during the whole discussion, shook her head. "I can't do this," she said, her stomach churning at the thought of reliving the horrible ordeal again. She looked over at Jim. "You can understand, can't you, why I can't do this? I was attacked—by a madman. And Zane could've been killed."

"Oh, Kaylie—" Alan interjected. "This isn't personal. It's just business."

She took a deep breath. Facing Johnston's psychiatrist, talking about the attack of seven years ago, reliving all the hellish details again. For what? To satisfy America's curiosity? To gain viewers? To sell Henshaw's book? To further Alan's career? To further hers?

It all seemed so petty. A headache erupted behind her eyes. She closed her lids and rubbed her temples. In her mind's eye she saw Johnston's knife thrust into Zane's back. She opened her eyes and shook her head. "I—I don't think I can separate personal from professional on this one."

"You got a better idea?" Jim asked, popping the gum into his mouth.

"A dozen of them," she said, her mind spinning to any other possibility. "There's the leader of the senior citizens' rights group, Molly McGintry. She's in town. Or Consuela Martinez, the woman who came into the country illegally, had her baby so that he could be an American citizen, then went public with the fact to fight our immigration laws. Or how about Charles Brickworth, the guy who's tearing down one of the most historic buildings in the Bay area?'' she asked, but she could have been talking to walls for all the good it did her.

By the time the meeting was over, Dr. Anthony Henshaw had agreed to be Friday's guest, and Kaylie, along with Alan, would get the grand privilege of interviewing him.

The thought turned her insides to jelly.

And she couldn't complain to Zane. What could he say except, ''I told you so''?

No, all she could do was find a way to get through the interview.

''Don't worry about it,'' Alan said, clapping her on the back as she reached for her purse. ''If we work things right, we could generate enough interest not only for a sequel to *Obsession,* but there might be enough of a story in Henshaw's book for a made-for-television movie or documentary.''

''Oh, Alan, forget it,'' she snapped, angry at the situation.

''Loosen up, Kaylie,'' he replied. ''You may not know it yet, but this is the best publicity we've ever had. And, face it, sure you were scared—hell, you went through a lot of pain and agony—but no one was really hurt, were they?''

''No one but Zane and an orderly at the hospital,'' she replied dryly, ''but maybe they can cut movie deals of their own.''

''There's no talking to you!'' Alan muttered, grabbing his briefcase and athletic bag and storming out of the building.

Kaylie hiked the strap of her purse over her shoulder. How was she going to break the news to Zane?

Chapter Fourteen

Zane kicked at his wastebasket, sending it rolling to the other side of his office. He'd wrestled with his conscience for weeks.

He strode down the hall. Wincing as his wound stretched, he rapped sharply on the door of Brad Hastings's office.

Brad was behind his desk. Tie askew, thin hair standing straight up from being repeatedly run through with his fingers, Hastings stared into the glowing screen of a computer terminal. He glimpsed Zane from the corner of his eye, typed a few quick commands and swiveled in his chair. "What can I do for you?"

"I think it's time to take Rafferty off the case."

"You sure?" Hastings had never before questioned Zane's judgment. But this was a difficult situation. "I thought you were still concerned for Kaylie's welfare."

"I am. But if she found out I was having her tailed, she'd hit the roof."

Hastings chanced a grin. "So who wears the pants in your family, eh?" He ribbed his boss, hazarding Zane's considerable wrath for a chance to needle him.

"Kaylie's big on independence."

"Whatever you say." Hastings shrugged and bit on his lower lip. "I could use Rafferty over on the McKay building."

"Trouble?"

"Looks that way. There's a glitch in the security system, probably a short or something and McKay wants to post a few extra guards. He's got some big client coming in with a truckload of jewels." Hastings consulted his screen again, and Zane looked over his shoulder, trying to show some interest in Frank McKay's import/export business. But all the while he talked with Hastings, he had the gnawing feeling that he was making a mistake—that Kaylie wasn't safe, that she needed his protection.

Paranoid, that's what he was, he decided.

Later, as he walked back to his office, he still wasn't convinced he'd made the right decision. But he had no choice. This was the way she wanted it, and he'd be damned if he was going to blow this marriage.

"Here are your messages, Mr. Flannery," Peggy said, waving the pink slips of paper as he started for his office.

"Oh, thanks."

"And your wife called."

His wife. It sounded so lasting. Grinning, Zane leaned across Peggy's desk. "I don't think I ever thanked you for getting through to the police so quickly. They were at the house in Carmel practically as soon as I was." Reading the messages, he started back to his office.

Peggy adjusted her headset. "I don't think you should thank me. By the time I got through, they'd already been called."

Zane stopped dead in his tracks, then turned on his heel. "They'd already been called?" he repeated slowly, his mind spinning ahead. "By whom? Someone at Whispering Falls?"

"I—I don't know," Peggy stammered. "I didn't think to ask. It took quite a while to connect with the right number in Carmel because I called the San Francisco Police Department first— you know, to check out her apartment here in the city. When I finally got through to the police in Carmel, I'm sure the dispatcher said something about already sending a unit over to her house. I—I guess I should have told you sooner, but everything turned out okay, and as soon as you were out of the hospital you took off to get married in Lake Tahoe...and..." She lifted her palms and blushed to the roots of her hair. Peggy prided herself on her work. "I didn't think it was that big of a deal."

From Peggy's reaction, Zane assumed the look on his face must be murderous. A hundred questions raced through his mind, but not one single answer filled the worrisome gaps. Who had called? How would that person know that Kaylie was in Carmel?

"Mr. Flannery...?" Peggy asked, apparently still shivering in her boots.

"Don't worry about it," he said, trying to keep his expression calm while inside he was tormented. He'd thought that having Lee Johnston readmitted to the hospital would solve the problem, but there were still some loose ends. It took all of his willpower not to march back to Hastings's office and order not only Rafferty, but six extra men to watch Kaylie every waking hour that Zane wasn't with her. "Call the police, get all the information you can.... Never mind, I think I'd better do it myself."

Back in his office, he shoved aside the desire to pour himself a stiff shot. He knew several detectives on the force, men he'd worked with at Gemini Security ages ago, before he'd started his own company. Now, because of his position as owner of a private detective/security firm, he shouldn't have to wade through a lot of red tape to get the information he wanted. He picked up the phone and rested his hips against the desk. "Come on, come on," he muttered as the call was finally routed to Detective Mike Saragossa.

"Hey, ol' buddy!" Mike drawled lazily from somewhere deep in the bowels of the SFPD. "'Bout time I heard from you. What can I do for ya?"

Kaylie's day had gone from bad to worse. After the meeting with Jim and Alan, she'd muffed the introduction of a newspaper reporter who was investigating crime within the city government, and Alan had rescued her. Then during an interview with a woman running for mayor, there was trouble with her microphone and, once again, Alan had to take over until the station break. The defective microphone was whisked away and a new one clipped quickly onto her lapel. Meanwhile, the candidate, Kathleen McKenney, was more than a little miffed at the inconvenience, and pointedly ignored Kaylie from that point on.

The last half of the show ran more smoothly, but by the end of the program, Kaylie couldn't wait to climb off her chair, wipe off her smile and relax. She headed straight to the cafeteria, drowned herself in a diet soda, then, after going over the problems with Jim, grabbed her notes for the next day and left the station. All she wanted to do was go straight home and curl up with a good book and spend the rest of the evening with her new husband.

But first, she thought as she climbed into her car and flicked on the ignition, she'd surprise Zane. Rather than wait for him at home, she'd catch him at work. She guided her car out of the lot and merged into traffic. Adjusting her rearview mirror, she spotted a car, not a silver Taurus, but a blue wagon, roll into traffic behind her. No big deal, she decided, but she'd spied that wagon before—on days when the Taurus hadn't been around the parking lot.

So what? Lots of people go to the same place every day. The driver was probably someone who works around here. She drove a couple of blocks, turned right twice, doubling back, and couldn't help but check the rearview mirror. Sure enough, about four cars behind, the wagon tailed her.

Fear jarred her. *Oh, Lord, not again!* She nearly rear-ended the car in front of her. *Stay cool, Kaylie. Get a grip on yourself!* But her heart slammed against her rib cage, and a cold sweat broke out over her skin. Her fingers clamped the wheel in a death grip.

At the next stoplight she slowed, checking the mirror every five seconds.

The light turned green, and she tromped on the gas, her concentration split between the road ahead and the mirror. The blue wagon followed three cars behind. Kaylie shifted down. Timing the next light, she sailed through a yellow and the wagon got hung up on a red.

Her hands were sweating, the steering wheel felt slick as she drove ten blocks out of her way before turning again and heading for Zane's office. She felt numb inside. No one would be following her. Johnston was locked up.

But Zane's words, spoken in an angry blurt at the last mention of Johnston in *The Insider*, came back to haunt her. "The more the press makes of this, the more likely some other wacko is going to try to duplicate the same sick crime. If not with you then with someone else—no one who's famous is safe!" He'd slapped the paper onto the table in front of her to make his point, and she'd pointedly picked it up with two fingers, rotated in her chair and dropped the entire paper into the trash.

"I didn't know you subscribed," she'd mocked, though part of his anger had been conveyed to her.

He'd scowled at her and motioned impatiently toward the trash. "Articles like that only cause trouble. Believe me, I know." And he did. One part of his business, especially in his office near Hollywood, had grown by leaps and bounds, patronized by stars who needed protection from overly zealous or crazed fans. Any one of those "fans" could potentially endanger the star's life or the lives of members of his or her family.

Kaylie shivered. Her heart knocking crazily, she drove into the parking lot, slid into an open space, then turned off the engine and, with a shuddering sigh, leaned her head against the steering wheel. "You're okay," she told herself, and slowly her pulse decelerated. Should she tell Zane about the cars—the Taurus and the wagon? Would he think she was imagining things, or worse yet, would it send him into the same paranoid need to protect her that had destroyed their marriage once before?

She wanted to be honest with him. Good marriages were based on honesty and yet, just this once, she might let the truth slip.

And what if you're followed again?

Oh, Lord, what a mess! She grabbed a handful of hair and tossed it over her shoulder. Climbing out of her Audi, she stood on slightly unsteady legs just as another car eased into the garage. Glancing over her shoulder, she gasped. Fear petrified her. The car cruising into the lot of Flannery Security was the same wagon that had followed her. The tail she'd thought she'd lost. Oh, God! How could he have known?

The blond man behind the wheel stared straight at her and she saw his face—young and hard, flat nose, cold eyes and straight hair—stare back at her. He opened the car door, and Kaylie didn't wait. Closer to the elevator, she sprinted across the cement and pounded on the button. The doors opened as the taste of fear settled in the back of her throat.

Zane! she thought desperately. She had to get to Zane! Inside the elevator she slapped the door panel. The doors swept shut, blocking out the blond man, and Kaylie sagged against the metal rail as the car moved upward with a lurch. Now, if only the man didn't run up the stairs faster than the elevator.... Again, fear tore at her.

"Zane, oh, God, Zane," she whispered, trying not to fall apart. When the doors opened, she half expected the man to be waiting, aiming a gun at her chest, but she found herself in the reception area of Flannery Security. She flew down the hall, past Peggy's desk and bolted into Zane's office.

"Kaylie?" He was standing at the windows, a dark expression on his face. She threw herself at him and clung to him, refusing to sob. "What the devil's going on?"

Trembling, she knew she was scaring him and wished she could calm down. "Call the police," she cried, "or send out your best man."

"Wh—"

"There's a man following me!" she cried, and Zane drew her closer to him, his muscles strong and hard.

"You're okay," he said, reaching behind him and pushing the button of the intercom, "Peggy, call Brad. Have him seal the building and send out a search team—an armed search team. There's a suspect somewhere in the building."

"The parking lot—" Kaylie clarified, glad for the feel of Zane's arms around her. Still holding her, Zane reached into the top drawer of his desk and pulled out his revolver.

"What's up?" Brad Hastings's voice boomed through the speaker.

"Someone followed Kaylie here. Check the exterior lot and the basement lot, all the staircases."

"You got it!" Hastings replied.

Zane checked his gun for ammunition.

Within seconds, the door to his office opened. "Is everything all right?" Peggy asked.

"Y-yes, fine," Kaylie stammered.

"Could I get you a cup of coffee?"

Kaylie shook her head, and Peggy, with a quick glance at Zane, stepped into the hallway and closed the door behind her.

"Oh, God, I didn't mean—I'm sorry."

Zane held her close and kissed her forehead. "Sorry for what?"

She had to tell him. She'd be foolish to keep information like this inside. Trying to calm down, she let him lead her to the couch.

Peggy knocked quietly, then left a tray of coffee for two on Zane's desk. When Kaylie tried to protest, the secretary held up a hand. "I know you said you didn't want anything, but frankly, you look like you could use a cup of coffee and a shot of bourbon." With those words of advice, she left the room again and locked the door behind her.

"Okay, so what happened?" Zane demanded, his lips a thin, dangerous line as he handed her one of the steaming cups.

Kaylie found strength in the warmth of the cup cradled between her palms. She hadn't known she felt cold, but now that the fear had subsided, she felt chilled to the bone. Haltingly, between sips, she found the words. "This isn't the first time," she admitted.

"What?" he nearly screamed. "What the hell do you mean 'isn't the first time'?"

"Just don't get mad...okay? I had this...feeling...for a few weeks now, but I told myself I was just overreacting to Johnston's attack. You know, seeing ghosts in every corner."

Zane became very still, every muscle in his body rigid and hard. "You should've told me."

"I know, but I didn't want to scare you."

"You just did."

"Maybe it was all in my mind," she said, then shook her head. "There are lots of Taurus cars on the road, and blue wagons are a dime a dozen."

Zane sucked a breath between his teeth. "You were followed here by a Taurus?" he asked, laying his gun on the table.

"No—it was the blue wagon." She explained about losing the car that had been chasing her only to run into it again in the parking garage.

She thought Zane would call additional men to seal off the garage, but instead he walked to the desk and punched the intercom. "Peggy, send Tim Rafferty in, if he's here."

A few seconds later a blond man of about twenty—the very man who had been behind the wheel of the blue station wagon—walked into Zane's office. Kaylie nearly screamed.

Zane dragged a hand through his hair. "Is this the guy?"

"Yes, but—" Cold realization started in the pit of her stomach and crawled up her spine.

"Tim works for me," Zane admitted, his face ashen. "Tim, this is my wife, Kaylie Melville. Kaylie…Tim."

"But—"

"I told him to follow you," Zane clarified.

"But why— Oh, God, no, don't tell me," she said, her heart dropping to her knees in disappointment. "You've already started it again, haven't you?" she whispered, her voice ragged.

"I had some of my men assigned to follow you for a few weeks—ever since I got the phone calls from Ted." He motioned for Tim to leave the room, and the blond slipped out, shutting the door behind him.

Kaylie was furious. Her heart pounded in her ears as she realized they were replaying the same mistakes all over again. Her voice so low she could barely hear her own words, she said, "How could you?"

"Because I love you, damn it. And I wasn't going to lose you again."

Her throat worked, but no words came. Strangled with disappointment, she stared at her hands.

"I told Brad just this morning to take all the men off the case."

"All the men? You mean there were more than one?"

"Six men rotated."

"Six? Tim must've missed the message."

"Don't make this any harder than it is, Kaylie," he said, returning the revolver to his desk drawer.

"Oh, Lord, Zane, you don't trust me at all, do you?"

He snorted. "I just don't trust the public."

Closing her eyes against the tears that threatened, she shook her head slowly from side to side. "I should have known you wouldn't change," she said, dying a little when she noticed the band of gold and diamonds on her left ring finger.

"I have changed."

"Not enough." Why had she been so foolish? A tear slid from the corner of her eye, and she dashed it away. "I—I wanted this to work."

"It will, Kaylie. We'll make it work."

"Will we?" She sniffed loudly, then squared her shoulders. She'd been played for a fool, a childish, simpleminded fool for the last time. "And how will you handle the fact that one of the next guests on *West Coast Morning* might be Dr. Anthony Henshaw?"

Zane's eyes narrowed. "Johnston's doctor? Is this some kind of morbid joke?"

"I wish," she said with a sigh. She rubbed her arms as if suddenly chilled and explained her conversation with Jim and Alan.

"And you agreed to this?" Zane charged.

"I didn't have any choice. The decision had already been made."

"But that's crazy," Zane said, pacing between the desk and the window. "It just promotes—" He clamped his mouth shut and, though still tense, leaned his hips against the windowsill. His eyes, when he stared at her, still burned, but his expression was soft. "You look like you've had a rough day. How about I take you home and cook you dinner?"

She rolled her eyes and struggled out of her chair. "You don't have to—"

"I want to," he said, trying to break the tension, though apprehension grappled with his forced calmness. What the hell was going on at *West Coast Morning?* Didn't they know that they were potentially setting up Kaylie as a target for the next publicity-hungry nut?

And what about "Ted"? Who was he?

Alan's name kept popping into his mind, but the voice on the tape didn't sound like Alan at all. And he didn't suspect Jim Crowley. So who? *Who?* Someone at the television station? One of Kaylie's friends? Or someone at the hospital who had invented a fictitious name?

They drove separately back to the apartment, and Franklin, the traitorous beast, padded after Kaylie when they walked inside.

Zane, true to his promise, poured them each a glass of wine, then began fixing dinner. But as he broiled steaks on the grill and steamed potatoes in the microwave, he thought about the upcoming show.

All his instincts told him the program was a big mistake. But his hands were tied. Kaylie had about come unglued when she'd found out he'd had men watching her, and, he supposed, glancing over his shoulder to the counter where she was chopping vegetables for a salad, he didn't blame her. He hadn't played fair.

And now he had to.

"Hey—watch out!" Kaylie cried. "Medium-rare, remember? I'm not into 'burned beyond recognition.'" She grabbed a long-handled fork from the drawer in the cooking island and flipped the steaks on the interior grill. Without asking, she dashed a shot of lemon pepper over the two T-bones.

"You're fouling up my recipe," he said with a good-natured gleam in his eye.

"Recipe?"

"I watch Chef Glenn on Friday mornings."

"Oh, give me a break," she said. "This is all well and good,

Zane, but you don't know a curry sauce from a fruit compote—''

He whirled, grabbed her and swept her off her feet. One of her shoes dropped to the floor. ''Watch it, lady,'' he growled in her ear, ''or I might have to take my spatula to you.''

''Promises, promises.'' She giggled as he carried her into the bedroom. ''Hey, wait. Zane,'' she cried, laughing. ''You can't—'' He tossed her onto the bed and, while standing over her, ripped off his shirt in one swift motion.

''But the steaks,'' she protested, forcing her eyes away from the wide expanse of his chest.

''I've decided 'burned beyond recognition' is the best way to serve T-bones.''

''But—''

He dropped onto the bed and covered her mouth with his. She was still laughing, but as his kiss deepened, her giggles gave way to moans. ''Zane, please,'' she whispered, still thinking of the steaks sizzling into charred bones.

The smoke detector started beeping loudly.

''Saved by the bell,'' she said with a giggle. For that remark, she was rewarded with a pillow in the face. Zane, muttering under his breath, jumped off the bed and hurried into the kitchen. In a state of dishabille, she followed, laughing when she saw the T-bones—small, black replicas of steak.

Zane turned off the grill and opened the windows to air out the kitchen. ''How about take-out Chinese, Mrs. Flannery?'' he asked, a slightly off-center smile curving his lips as he tossed the burned meat into the sink. The smoke slowly dissipated, and the smoke alarm quit bleating.

''Anything's fine with me.''

''But first we have some unfinished business,'' he said, thinking aloud, a menacing glint in his eye. He grabbed her again, and this time they weren't interrupted.

On Friday morning, Kaylie was nervous as a cat. She and Zane hadn't discussed the show again, and she'd finally forgiven him for having her followed. *It's going to take time,* she reminded herself. Zane was used to being in command, and slowly, with visible effort, he was allowing her to make her own decisions. Though, she suspected with a smile, it was killing him.

For the past few days there had been no silver Taurus, no blue wagon, no car or man following her. She couldn't help looking over her shoulder occasionally and checking her rearview mirror more often than usual, but she was convinced that Zane had kept to his word.

And she'd kept hers. She was more careful than she'd ever been and more in love.

She had great faith that this time, no matter what fate threw their way, she and Zane would make it. Together.

Zane couldn't get his mind off of today's program. He itched to go to the station, to watch Kaylie, to make sure that she was all right. Rationally, he knew that nothing would happen to her. Johnston's psychiatrist wasn't a madman; Henshaw couldn't hurt Kaylie.

But some other fruitcake could. He drove to work and dropped by Hastings's office. Brad, as usual, had been working for hours, though it was barely eight o'clock. He glanced up from his computer terminal when Zane walked in.

"Got a minute?" Zane asked.

"Sure. What's up?"

"This." Reaching into his jacket pocket, Zane withdrew the tape of his last conversation with Ted. "Did you find anyone who could have made this call?"

"Nope." Brad shook his head slowly. "But several of the guys here are convinced the voice is that of a woman."

"A woman." That didn't make things any easier. Zane stuffed the tape back into his pocket.

"You want us to keep working on it?"

"As long as you've got leads."

"Well, we're about dried-up. As for the tracer, most of the calls that we can't identify came in from booths—different booths located usually in the financial district."

"Well, that's something," Zane said, thinking aloud. "I don't suppose anyone we suspect lives or works there."

Hastings shook his head. "No one we've scared up so far."

"What about Alan Bently?"

"He'd be my guess as suspect number one," Hastings agreed. "He seems to have the most to gain by all this publicity. Want a printout on the guy?"

"Sure."

Hastings turned back to his computer, and his nimble fingers flew over the keys. A printer whirred to life, and soon a four-paged single-spaced report was lying in the tray. Brad handed the pages to Zane. "Here you go. Everything you always wanted to know about Alan Bently but were afraid to ask."

Zane's mouth stretched into a grin. "That's what I keep you around here for, Brad, that lousy sense of humor of yours."

"Nope, boss. You keep me 'cause I'm the best."

Zane laughed. "Well, that might be part of it," he agreed, sauntering down the hall. He grabbed a cup of coffee, settled into his desk chair and began perusing the report, line by revealing line. Most of the information, he'd read before. The names, the places, the people who were associated with Alan Bently.

"Maybe you're barking up the wrong tree," he told himself as he leaned back and propped his feet on the desk. He dialed the police department in Carmel, hoping someone there could tell him who the anonymous caller was. Someone had called the police, and if he guessed right, that someone had called long distance.

When the police couldn't help him, he dialed the phone company. He had a friend in administration who owed him a favor. Maybe he could finally get some answers—answers his own phone surveillance hadn't uncovered.

While waiting to be connected to his friend, he pushed a button on the remote control for the television and waited for Kaylie's show to begin.

Dr. Henshaw was the guest scheduled for the first segment of the show. Kaylie, more nervous than she'd been while interviewing the president's wife, flipped through her notes one last time.

"Fifteen minutes," Tracy called through the door, and Kaylie let out her breath. She straightened her skirt and made her way to the set, where she and Alan were introduced to Dr. Henshaw by the assistant producer.

A small man with a beard that rimmed his chin and no mustache, he seemed as anxious about the interview as she was.

"Ms. Melville," he said, clasping her hand and forcing a thin smile.

"Mrs. Flannery now," she replied, "but, please, just call me Kaylie."

Tracy cut in. "Okay, now look Kaylie or Alan in the eye when they talk to you. Forget about the cameras. When I give you this signal…"

Kaylie had heard the spiel a hundred times before.

"Places, everyone!" Jim said loudly, and people scurried. Tracy led Dr. Henshaw to his spot on the end of the couch, Alan perched in his usual chair and Kaylie sat in her usual chair.

"Quiet, please, and five…four…three…"

The lead-in music filtered through the speakers, and Kaylie forced herself to smile calmly, as if every day she interviewed the man who was her attacker's doctor.

"Good morning," Alan said, grinning confidently into the cameras, and the show was off.

Kaylie worked on automatic. They talked about the doctor's forthcoming book, which he'd sold just the day before to a major publisher, and they discussed psychosis in broad terms. Alan brought up Johnston's name, but only in regard to the premiere of *Obsession.* Not only were clips from the film shown, but also footage of the original attack. It took all of Kaylie's professional acting skills to appear calm and detached when inside, her heart was thumping and sweat was beading along her spine.

Just let me get through this, she prayed inwardly as she turned to Dr. Henshaw and asked him about security at the hospital. The doctor became slightly defensive, but soon the interview and the ordeal were over.

Later, after the final segment where Chef Glenn whipped up his favorite apple torte, Kaylie left the set on unsteady legs.

This has to be the worst, she thought, content to stay in her office for the rest of the day. She flipped on the radio, answered her mail and gathered some ideas for future shows. She wasn't going to be caught in a lurch again!

At three o'clock, Alan knocked on the door and stepped into her office. "Well," he said, smiling broadly. "Did you hear? The phones haven't stopped ringing. Today's show was a bona fide success! From the response, Jim thinks it may be in the top ten for the year."

Great. "It must've been the apple torte," Kaylie said, and Alan rolled his eyes.

"You should've seen the switchboard! Becky was going crazy out there. And that's not the best news."

"No?" Kaylie tried to sound interested, but her heart wasn't in it. Alan didn't seem to notice. "I've had a million calls but only two that really count. One from my agent, the other from Cameron James. He's agreed to direct again, and he's got a screenwriter lined up to work out a sequel to *Obsession!* Triumph Pictures is interested in producing, and one of the major studios—probably Zeus—is backing the film. It's only a matter of time!"

Kaylie didn't know what to say. Alan was flying so high, he was so exhilarated that she didn't want to burst his bubble by saying she wasn't interested. "What about *West Coast Morning?* she asked quietly.

"Oh, who knows! It would only be for a few months…Jim would understand."

"I don't know," Kaylie began.

"You don't know? *You don't know?* What's to know? This is the opportunity of a lifetime and *you don't know?* What is this? Are you already trying to squeeze a little more money—"

"Of course not."

"Then you're afraid, right? Afraid of failure? Or afraid of some loony taking after you again? Or is it something else?" he said, thinking aloud as he closed the distance to her desk. "Don't tell me, it's Flannery, isn't it? You're afraid of him— of what he'll say, aren't you?"

Kaylie's temper got the better of her tongue. "I don't think it's even worth discussing. I haven't heard anything concrete yet. No one's offered me a part and so, as far as I can see, it's a moot point."

Alan threw his hands into the air. "God, Kaylie! We are talking major motion picture here! And you're not even willing to pursue it? What's gotten into you?"

"Maybe she's just using her head." Zane was standing in the doorway, and his face was a mask of slow-burning fury. Something was wrong. Kaylie could read it in the set of his jaw. Slowly, he reached into his jacket pocket, withdrew a tape and flipped the tape onto Kaylie's desk. "How about explaining this?" he suggested to Alan.

"What—a tape? Music? Rap? What?" Alan shrugged and lifted his palms. "What's going on, Flannery?"

But Kaylie knew. On the tape was the voice of "Ted." The warning. But Alan? No way. Her gaze flew to Zane's, but he was concentrating on Alan.

"Nope. Just a conversation with a friend of mine. His name's Ted," Zane said, crossing his arms over his chest.

"Ted who?" Alan asked, sending Kaylie a glance that insinuated Zane was walking around with more than one screw loose.

"I don't know his last name. Maybe you can fill that part in."

"Me?"

Zane slipped the tape into the radio/cassette player on Kaylie's credenza.

"Zane, I don't think…" Kaylie began, but the tape started to play and the conversation between Zane and Ted filled the room.

Alan stared at the tape player as if he couldn't believe what he was hearing. Zane swung one leg over the corner of Kaylie's desk and leaned closer to the other man. "The voice on this tape is that of a woman—I don't know her real name—but I think you do."

"A woman? But—"

"It's disguised of course, but it's probably someone you know—maybe someone you date. And no, I'm not talking about Kaylie, because you've never dated her, but have led all the tabloids to believe it.''

''Are you out of your mind?''

''I don't think so.'' Zane let the words sink in, then once he was certain he had Alan's undivided attention, continued, ''I talked to the phone company, and it seems there are several long-distance phone calls on your bill. Calls to the Carmel Police Department on the night that Kaylie was attacked by Johnston and calls to reporters for *The Insider* and a couple of other tabloids. Unfortunately there aren't any calls from your phone to my agency when 'Ted' rang me up. But we have the general vicinity in which the calls were made. My guess is that one of your girlfriends made the call. My men are checking into that right now.''

''That's ridiculous,'' Alan said, but the lines around the corners of his mouth were tightening, and the glare he sent Zane was pure hatred.

Kaylie couldn't believe her ears. Not Alan. He couldn't, *wouldn't* put her life in danger!

''It only makes sense, Bently,'' Zane continued, rewinding the tape and playing it again, letting Ted's warning bounce off the corners of the room. Sweat dotted Alan's upper lip.

Zane motioned toward the recorder. ''You've been pushing for more publicity for the past year and a half. You've moved behind the scenes to make people aware of you—and my wife.''

''You're wrong, Flannery.''

''Am I?'' Zane clucked his tongue, and his foot swung slowly as he turned to Kaylie. ''You know why Henshaw agreed to come onto this program, don't you?''

''Because of his book,'' Kaylie said.

Zane nodded. ''And the movie rights tied into that book—rights dealing with Lee Johnston, rights to your story, our story and Alan's story.''

Alan's face drained of color. ''You're jumping to conclusions.''

''Am I?'' Zane demanded, his eyes narrowing on the shorter man. ''I don't think so. In fact, I've already had a conversation with the good doctor. He seems to remember placing a call on the night of Johnston's escape attempt, and not just a call to the police. He called you, Alan. So that you could milk this for all it was worth."

"That's ridiculous!"

"At first I thought Henshaw might have been in on Johnston's escape—helped him along a little. But he convinced me and—" he stared pointedly at his watch "—right now he's convincing the police that you and he only took advantage of a situation that had already occurred. So, when Johnston escaped, he called you and you eventually called the Carmel police. Why?"

"I didn't—"

"There are telephone records, Bently."

Kaylie's stomach lurched. Surely Alan wouldn't have done anything to hurt her—to put her life in danger.

Alan turned to Kaylie, and all of his bravado escaped in a defeated rush. He fell into a chair and buried his face in his hands. "I didn't mean to hurt anyone," he whispered, his voice muffled.

"Oh, Alan, no!" Kaylie cried, tears of anger building behind her eyes. "You couldn't have!"

"You got it backward," Alan admitted, his voice barely a whisper as he looked up, his eyes filled with regret. "That night—the night he escaped. Johnston called here, asking for Kaylie. I didn't know who he was...but by the tone of his voice I guessed. And later, Henshaw called with the news."

"Oh, God," Kaylie whispered.

"So you gave him her address in Carmel," Zane said, not letting up for a second.

"But I called the police—almost immediately! I—I..." The look he sent Kaylie was pathetic. "I just didn't know that he was already over halfway there, that he'd been hitchhiking and so...I called Henshaw back and told him I'd already taken care of everything and that Kaylie was all right and that I thought he and I should do some business together. I'd talked to him before—about a movie on Johnston's life and now, together, I thought we could put something together. Viewer interest would already be high," he said, as if the American public's wishes erased all of his mistakes.

"And that's why he agreed to appear on your show?" Zane persisted.

"Yes—to promote his book and to get people interested in Lee Johnston's story."

"You'd better call an attorney, Bently," Zane suggested, his voice filled with loathing. "A good one. You're up to your neck in this, and the police are bound to show up any minute. I gave them a full report." He reached across the desk and grabbed Kaylie's hand. "Let's get out of here."

She picked up her purse from habit, but her entire world seemed to be turned upside down. Alan? A man she'd worked with forever had used her, betrayed her, felt so little concern for her life? Lord, how had she been so blind?

"Kaylie," Alan said, his features set and grim. His voice broke. "I—I'm sorry. I never—"

"So am I," she managed to say as she let Zane guide her out of the television station. The police were already in the reception area, two squad cars parked outside, four officers charging through the connecting room.

News cameras, some from the station itself, others from rivals, whirred, and reporters were already gathering information for their nightly reports. Microphones were thrust at Kaylie, and cameras chased them as Zane and Kaylie, arms linked, dashed across the parking lot.

"Ms. Melville—can you give us some insight on the reports that Alan Bently was involved in Lee Johnston's escape?"

Kaylie refused to answer that one.

"How do you feel—"

Zane spun around. "No comment," he growled, glaring at the reporters.

"Mr. Flannery—you're Ms. Melville's husband and—"

"Right now I'm her bodyguard," he clarified, his face thrust within bare inches of the slim man who was wielding his microphone like some jousting lance. "And, if you don't want me to get physical, you'd better back off!"

With that, he turned, helped Kaylie into the Jeep and climbed behind the wheel. He roared off, leaving the cameras still whirring.

"My bodyguard?" Kaylie repeated, sagging against the seat and lolling her head back as she looked at her husband. "Oh, boy, I can hardly wait. 'Talk-show hostess demotes husband to bodyguard. Film at eleven.'"

"That little jerk deserved it," Zane insisted, cranking on the wheel hard to round a corner.

"I work with that 'little jerk.'"

"You have my sympathy."

"My *bodyguard?*" she asked again, chuckling at the ludicrous title.

"That's right. Your bodyguard, your husband, your lover, your spouse, your fantasy and hopefully the father of your unborn children!"

He touched her hand, and tears blurred her vision. Yes, Zane was all of the above, and much, much more. He was her life. "I should wring your neck," she whispered without much conviction.

"I think you can be more imaginative than that," he said, slanting her a sexy grin. "My body parts are willingly at your disposal...."

"You know what I mean," she replied, unable to smother a smile. "You're supposed to be letting me live my life."

"I just don't like to leave any loose ends dangling." Downshifting, he wheeled into the parking lot of their apartment building. "'Ted' was a loose end. The call to the police was a loose end. Those *Insider* lies about your relationship with Alan were loose ends!"

They rode up the elevator together, and Franklin, whining, greeted them. While Zane took the shepherd for a short walk, Kaylie dug through the pantry and found a bottle of champagne they'd never opened—the bottle from the chapel where they were married.

She should be furious with him, she supposed, but she wasn't. In fact, she liked the fact that he'd wrapped up all the loose ends. He hadn't stopped her from working, hadn't even objected when she'd mentioned that she might consider another movie. He was trying...and so was she.

She popped open the champagne and poured two glasses. Then, on a whim, she poured a little bit into a bowl. When Zane and Franklin returned, she set the bowl on the floor for the dog and handed Zane a glass.

"What's this?" he asked, but his gray eyes glinted.

"A celebration."

"Of what?"

"Kaylie Flannery's new independence." Without any more ado, Franklin began lapping from his bowl.

"This is sounding dangerous," he said, but he wrapped one arm around her waist, and she giggled, as they both sipped from their glasses.

"Well, I've become so independent, you see, that my husband's meddling in my life doesn't even bother me."

"I never meddle," Zane argued.

Franklin sneezed.

Kaylie laughed and, while balancing her glass, wrapped her arms around Zane's neck. "Don't ever stop caring, Zane Flannery," she said, her eyes crinkling at the corners.

"I never did," he vowed, and pressed champagne-laced kisses upon her waiting lips. "And I never will."

* * * * *

SPECIAL EDITION

Stories of love and life, these powerful novels are tales that you can identify with—romances with "something special" added in!

Fall in love with the stories of authors such as **Nora Roberts, Diana Palmer, Ginna Gray** and many more of your special favorites—as well as wonderful new voices!

Special Edition brings you entertainment for the heart!

SSE-GEN

Do you want…

Dangerously handsome heroes

Evocative, everlasting love stories

Sizzling and tantalizing sensuality

Incredibly sexy miniseries like **MAN OF THE MONTH**

Red-hot romance

Enticing entertainment that can't be beat!

You'll find all of this, and much *more* each and
every month in **SILHOUETTE DESIRE**. Don't miss these
unforgettable love stories by some of romance's hottest
authors. Silhouette Desire—where your fantasies will
always come true….

If you've got the time...
We've got the
INTIMATE MOMENTS

Passion. Suspense. Desire. Drama. Enter a world that's larger than life, where men and women overcome life's greatest odds for the ultimate prize: love. Nonstop excitement is closer than you think...in Silhouette Intimate Moments!

SIM-GEN

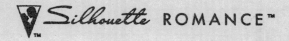
Silhouette ROMANCE™

What's a single dad to do when he needs a wife by next Thursday?

Who's a confirmed bachelor to call when he finds a baby on his doorstep?

How does a plain Jane in love with her gorgeous boss get him to notice her?

From classic love stories to romantic comedies to emotional heart tuggers, **Silhouette Romance** offers six irresistible novels every month by some of your favorite authors! Such as...beloved bestsellers **Diana Palmer, Annette Broadrick, Suzanne Carey, Elizabeth August** and **Marie Ferrarella**, to name just a few—and some sure to become favorites!

Fabulous Fathers...Bundles of Joy...Miniseries... Months of blushing brides and convenient weddings... Holiday celebrations... You'll find all this and much more in **Silhouette Romance**—always emotional, always enjoyable, always about love!